The *Laws* books are standalone thrillers featuring Denver homicide detective Bryson Coventry. Each book is completely independent of the others. They can be read in any order.

NIGHT LAWS
SHADOW LAWS
FATAL LAWS
DEADLY LAWS
BANGKOK LAWS
IMMORTAL LAWS (Next)
VOODOO LAWS (Upcoming)

What they're saying about Jim Michael Hansen's
BANGKOK LAWS

"Bangkok Laws is the 5th book in the highly regarded *Laws* series and the best to date. *** It's a white knuckle page-turner of a novel that keeps you glued to the page ... If this is the first book that you read in the series, you will not be disappointed. Hansen masterfully weaves the elements of suspense, sexual tension, retaliation and horror so well that you are unaware that a few hours have passed and you're done with the book. Bryson Coventry is one of the best characters in modern thriller/ detective fiction in the last five years."

—Adlo T. Calcagno (Mystery Dawg)
FUTURES MYSTERY ANTHOLOGY MAGAZINE, FMAM.biz

"[Y]ou will find a storyline that is probably more real-to-life than you care to imagine, strong believable characters, both hideous and lovable, and a knock-out conclusion, that trust me, you definitely will never see coming. Another top-of-the-line winner for Mr. Hansen and one you do not want to miss."

—Shirley Johnson, Senior Reviewer, MIDWEST BOOK REVIEW
MidwestBookReview.com

"If you're planning to travel to Bangkok to sample some of the sleazy and forbidden entertainments found there, beware that it doesn't cost more than you are willing to pay. *** Highly recommended as a tale you will have to finish once you begin to read. Talented author Jim Michael Hansen has woven a fascinating plot ... to satisfy even the pickiest thriller fan. Action aplenty with false trails and red herrings to draw the reader into dead ends and keep us trying to outguess the villains who do what they do sooo well. A book guaranteed to hold your attention and provide you with reading satisfaction. Enjoy. I sure did."

—Anne K. Edwards, NEW MYSTERY READER MAGAZINE
NewMysteryReader.com

"Avid readers have their favorite authors and [Jim Michael Hansen] has become one of mine. *** The best part of Hansen's writing is that I get dropped into the depths of the story within two or three pages. As with most of the series, I started and finished this book in one sitting. I whole-heartedly recommend *Bangkok Laws*. It is great, whether or not a person has read the other *Laws* books."

—Kathy Martin, IN THE LIBRARY REVIEWS
InTheLibraryReviews.net

"Bryson Coventry, head of Denver's homicide unit and serial womanizer, has survived four previous outings but this one may be his undoing, as he becomes involved in the collateral damage of a global killer. *** Coventry and his cast of cohorts continue to evolve with each outing. Rough as the Rockies, but also refreshing. Can't wait for the next in the series."

—Jack Quick, BOOKBITCH REVIEWS
Bookbitch.com

"From the seedy sex dens of Bangkok to the crystal clear skies of Denver, Jim Michael Hansen takes you on a voyage into a very dark world of sexual slavery, and ultimately, cold-blooded murder. *** Jim Michael Hansen has a unique ability to tempt the reader with a trail of crumbs that ultimately sucks you into the spellbinding vortex he has created in *Bangkok Laws*. You will turn the pages so fast your fingers will bleed."

—Jeff Foster, ARMCHAIR INTERVIEWS
ArmchairInterviews.com

"Jim Michael Hansen is about to unleash another electrifying *Laws* book that will keep you, the reader, turning page after spine-chilling page to see what lies around the next curve. So get ready to follow Coventry through a never-ending roller coaster ride . . ."

—Wanda Maynard, SIMEGEN REVIEWS
Simegen.com

"[T]he action hooks the reader from the start. *** This is [Jim Michael Hansen's] fifth novel and he is still *wowing* his readers."

—Tracy Farnsworth, ROUNDTABLE REVIEWS
RoundtableReviews.com

ALSO BY JIM MICHAEL HANSEN
AVAILABLE NOW

NIGHT LAWS
Trade Paperback—ISBN 10: 0976924307
ISBN 13: 9780976924302

Denver homicide detective Bryson Coventry is on the hunt for a vicious killer who has warned attorney Kelly Parks, Esq., that she is on his murder list. Something from the beautiful young lawyer's past has come back to haunt her, something involving the dark secrets of Denver's largest law firm. With the elusive killer ever one step away, Kelly Parks frantically searches for answers, not only to save her life but also to find out whether she unwittingly participated in a murder herself.

"*Night Laws* is a terrifying, gripping cross between James Patterson and John Grisham ... Hansen has created a truly killer debut."

—J.A. KONRATH, author of *Whiskey Sour, Bloody Mary* and *Rusty Nail,* JAKonrath.com

SHADOW LAWS
Trade Paperback—ISBN 9780976924340
Unabridged CD Audio Book—ISBN 9780976924395

Denver homicide detective Bryson Coventry, and beautiful young attorney Taylor Sutton, are separately hunting vicious killers but for very different reasons. As the two dangerous chases inadvertently intersect, both of the hunters get pulled deeper and deeper into an edgy world of shifting truths where there is more at stake than either could have imagined, nothing is as it seems, and time is running out.

"As engaging as the debut *Night Laws*, this exciting blend of police procedural and legal thriller recalls the early works of Scott Turow and Lisa Scottoline."

—LIBRARY JOURNAL

FATAL LAWS
Trade Paperback—ISBN 9780976924364

When several women are found buried in shallow graves near one another, each murdered in a brutally different way, Denver homicide detective Bryson Coventry finds himself pulled into the edgy world of Tianca Holland—a woman involved enough to be a prime suspect, vulnerable enough to be the next victim, and beautiful enough to be more than just a distraction.

"[Jim Michael Hansen] builds suspense effectively, and his hero is both likeable and multidimensional. A too-little-known hard-boiled series that deserves attention."

—BOOKLIST

DEADLY LAWS
Trade Paperback—ISBN 9780976924333

Third-year law student Kayla Beck receives a chilling telephone call. A stranger has chosen her to be the rescuer of a woman he has abducted. Kayla can either attempt to rescue the victim and possibly save her life or she can ignore the call and never be bothered again. If she disregards the call, however, no one else will get a similar opportunity. The woman will die. What happens next catapults both Kayla and Denver homicide detective Bryson Coventry into a deadly world where the FBI has been hunting unsuccessfully for years; a world of unknown boundaries and dangers; a world where, in the end, the only hope of getting out is to go all the way in.

"*Deadly Laws* successfully pairs an intriguing premise and solid suspense."

—BOOKLIST

A "clever and engrossing mystery tale involving gorgeous women, lustful men and scintillating suspense."

—FOREWORD MAGAZINE

BANGKOK LAWS
Trade Paperback—ISBN 9780976924319

As Denver homicide detective Bryson Coventry finds himself entangled in the collateral damage of a killer who uses the entire world as his playground, newly-licensed attorney Paige Alexander lands her very first case—a case that could possibly destroy the most powerful law firm in the world; a case involving a deadly, high-stakes international conspiracy of terrible proportions; a case that started in Bangkok but will not end there.

"Another top-of-the-line winner for Mr. Hansen and one you do not want to miss."

—MIDWEST BOOK REVIEW

IMMORTAL LAWS
Trade Paperback—ISBN 9780976924357

While Denver homicide detective Bryson Coventry investigates the savage murder of a young woman who is found with a wooden stake through her heart, blues singer Heather Vaughn learns that she and the dead woman are both bloodline descendents of men who were reputed to be vampires. When the evidence suggests that obsessed hunters are roaming the world and eradicating vampire descendents, both Heather Vaughn and Bryson Coventry find themselves swept into a modern-day thriller born of ancient and deadly obsessions.

"Guaranteed to keep you reading, this is one of the best thrillers I've read yet."

—NEW MYSTERY READER MAGAZINE

VOODOO LAWS
Trade Paperback—ISBN 9780976924371

As homicide detective Bryson Coventry's frantic search for a missing woman pulls him deeper and deeper into a world of voodooism and death curses, Denver attorney Mackenzie Lee lands a terrifying case. Her client, Erin Asher, was stalked by a man while clubbing downtown Saturday night. That man, still at large, is the primary suspect in one of Coventry's murder cases that occurred across town at the same time. The client is, in effect, the suspect's alibi. But giving him that alibi, and getting him off one murder, may very well enable him to commit a different one—hers. Mackenzie Lee investigates on her client's behalf, only to find that they are both in the deadly throes of a force more sinister than either of them could have imagined.

BANGKOK
LAWS

A Bryson Coventry Thriller

JIM MICHAEL HANSEN

Dark Sky Publishing, Inc.
Golden, CO 80401

Dark Sky Publishing, Inc.
Golden, CO 80401
DarkSkyPublishing.com

ISBN 978-0-9769243-1-9

Library of Congress Control Number: 2007900449

Cover photography / Getty Images

10 9 8 7 6 5 4 3 2 1

Made in the USA

DEDICATED TO
EILEEN

Acknowledgements

The author gratefully thanks and acknowledges the generosity, encouragement, support and contributions of the following fantastic people—Tonia Allen, Paul Anik, Baron R. Birtcher, Rebecca Blackmer, Kathy Boswell, Mark Bouton, Aldo T. Calcagno, Tony M. Cheatham, Angie Cimarolli, L.B. Cobb, James A. Cox, Lisa D'Angelo, Linnea Dodson, Dawn Dowdle, Anne K. Edwards, Geraldine Evans, Tracy Farnsworth, Carol Fieger, Denise Fleischer, Jeff Foster, Eric L. Harry, Carolyn G. Hart, Joan Hall Hovey, Shirley Priscella Johnson, Harriet Klausner, J.A. Konrath, Andrei V. Lefebvre, Sarah Lovett, Karen L. MacLeod, Kathy Martin, Wanda Maynard, Cheryl McCann, Russel D. McLean, Evan McNamara, Stephanie Padilla, John David Phillips, Sally Powers, Lt. Jon Priest, Jack Quick, Patricia A. Rasey, Ann Ripley, Kenneth Sheridan, Dawn Sieh, Shelley Singer, Andrea Sisco, Bob Speer, Mark Terry, Nancy Tesler, Safiya Tremayne and Laurraine Tutihasi; and

My many friends at libraries and bookstores across the country; and

The many wonderful people I have had the pleasure to meet at my author events; and, most importantly,

My readers.

Chapter One

Day One—June 11
Monday Morning

ALAN EWING SAT IN THE COCKPIT of the Grob Aerospace SP jet, cruising on autopilot at 30,000 feet through a pre-dawn sky, checking the instruments only when necessary. He could still smell Bangkok in his clothes and taste it in his mouth. In another ten minutes he'd begin the descent into Denver International Airport.

Such a pity.

He'd turn around in a heartbeat if he could.

His cargo sat in the back—four guys from International Gems—drunk and slapping each other on the back for their magnificent ability to buy three suitcases full of precious gems and minerals for hardly any money. In another few minutes, when the aircraft started to lose altitude, they would no doubt swear each other to secrecy one more time, to be sure their innocent little wifey-poos didn't find out about their three or four trips to the Soi Cowboy blowjob bars.

BJ bars.

Amateur stuff.

It was almost a sacrilege to waste good Bangkok time on soft-core stuff that was available right here in the States. But if they wanted to be too stupid or too scared to taste the real gratifications of the city, then that was their problem. Ewing wasn't going to tell them what they were missing. Not to mention that they wouldn't have the guts in any event to go where the deep pleasures were.

IN FACT, IF THE TRUTH BE TOLD, Ewing himself had been apprehensive the first time—no, not *apprehensive*, downright scared. A skuzzy looking man about five feet tall showed up at Ewing's hotel room after dark, counted the $1,000 in cash that Ewing handed him, then grinned and slipped back into the Bangkok night. All night long Ewing worried that he had been ripped off. But, true to plan, a driver showed up at his hotel the following morning. Once they got on the road, Ewing had to put a hood over his head and lay down in the seat, so he'd never be able to tell anyone where the location was.

Then they drove for a long time.

Maybe to somewhere far outside Bangkok.

Maybe in a big circle to somewhere not so far.

When they finally stopped, Ewing had to keep the hood on while the driver grabbed his arm, pulled him out of the vehicle, and made him walk. That was the worst two minutes of the whole thing. He pictured a sinister shape sneaking up behind and pointing a gun at the back of his head while the driver stepped aside to keep from getting splattered with blood and brains.

But that didn't happen.

Instead, they entered a door and, after it closed, the driver pulled Ewing's hood off. They were in a stone corridor with a musty smell.

The passageway led to a large windowless space.

An older man and a younger one were seated at a table. Both looked like they could kill Ewing right then and there, all in a day's work. The younger one smiled, extended his hand and said in English that his name was Kovit.

Then he clapped.

Two seconds later a door opened and three men led twenty women into the room.

Each one was blindfolded.

And naked.

Kovit clapped again.

The women turned in a circle to the right.

He clapped again and they turned in a circle to the left.

Then he looked at Ewing.

"Nice?"

Ewing swallowed and nodded.

"Yeah."

"You can have one, two, or whatever you want."

Ewing chose a petite Asian woman in her late teens or early twenties at a cost of $1,000, meaning a second $1,000, for four hours. The rules were simple. He would have a fully equipped dungeon to himself where he could do anything he wanted to the woman, except disfigure or kill her. If he left any marks that wouldn't clear up within three days, he would be charged extra, depending on the severity of the injuries.

That was Ewing's first trip to the place.

More than two years ago.

He ended up being charged an additional $500.00.

Which was more than fair, considering.

Jim Michael Hansen

THE LANDING AT DIA couldn't have come any sooner. In another ten minutes Ewing would have fallen asleep at the controls. His watch said 6:42 a.m.

The hanger was empty except for the guards.

The parking lot was quiet.

The four passengers tipped him $500 for getting them home alive, and then disappeared. Ewing threw his suitcases in the back of the 4Runner and headed south on Pena Boulevard, then west on I-70, with the cruise control set at three over the limit. He let his mind replay the sins of the last three days while he rubbed his cock. The bed would feel good. He couldn't wait to get naked, spread out on top of the sheets and play with his dick until it exploded.

Then he'd sleep for twelve hours straight.

HE LIVED IN A FRENCH TUDOR east of Colorado Boulevard in an upscale neighborhood with tree-lined boulevards, befitting a skilled jet pilot. He parked in the garage and decided he wasn't in the mood to mess with the suitcases right now, so he left them in the vehicle and shuffled his tired feet into the house.

He stopped in the kitchen long enough to take a long swallow of cold Gatorade. Damn good stuff. Then he headed to the master bathroom and took a piss while he brushed his teeth.

He stripped naked and briefly contemplated taking a shower before he decided he was too tired. His 32-year-old body reflected in a full-length mirror.

Toned and taut, thanks to 24-Hour Fitness.

Watching himself, he played with his cock until it got hard.

16

He had to admit, he had a pretty nice dick.

Eight inches long.

Thick.

Perfectly straight.

Rock hard.

Capable of shooting a load three feet.

He turned off the lights and headed for the bed.

His cock pointed the way, like a divining rod.

IT WAS THEN THAT HE HEARD SOMETHING. He turned his head just in time to see the blurred shape of a person.

Then pain came.

White hot.

Excruciating.

His spine stopped working and the feeling in his legs disappeared.

As soon as he hit the carpet the person stabbed him again.

And again.

And again.

Ewing counted the stabs for as long as his brain let him and realized that in two more seconds he would be dead.

One second later everything went black.

Chapter Two

Day One—June 11
Monday Afternoon

PAIGE ALEXANDER TRIPPED over her own 25-year-old feet and dropped an armload of dishes piled three high. They hit the tile floor and made that unmistakable earth-shattering sound that meant stupidity-in-action.

Every face in Sam's Eatery immediately turned.

One or two had compassion.

Most just wanted to see the train wreck before it was too late.

She immediately stooped down and began to pick up the pieces, as if she could undo the whole thing if she just moved fast enough. As soon as she bent down everyone lost interest and went back to their precious little conversations.

No one came over to help.

Her face had minimal makeup.

Because makeup cost money.

She wore frayed jeans, a T-shirt and two-year-old tennis shoes. Her hair was thick and straight and looked like a model's when she let it. Right now it was braided into an uneventful ponytail. She wanted to reach into her back pocket and finger the piece of paper. It was a tattered copy of her admission to the bar of the State of Colorado, dated three months ago. She needed to run her fingers over it for a few seconds to remind herself that she was a duly licensed attorney, and that this job wouldn't last forever. But she couldn't, because both her hands were busy frantically picking up glass.

She shouldn't even be here.

She should be in a fancy office somewhere practicing law.

BUT SHE HAD LEARNED A FEW THINGS about the Denver legal market over the last three months. She learned that there aren't many jobs available for entry-level attorneys to start with, no matter who you were, and that there weren't *any* jobs for a student who only ranked at the 50 percent mark of their class.

She could have ranked higher.

Say, for example, if she hadn't been forced to maintain a full-time job to keep food in her mouth and a bus pass in her pocket. But law firms didn't care about excuses. All they wanted to know is if she was in the top 10 percent, on Law Review or Moot Court, and had any publications under her belt.

So here she was, technically licensed as a lawyer but with no office.

Or clients.

Or co-workers.

Or library.

Or secretary.

Or fax machine.

Or malpractice insurance.

Or clothes.

Or experience.

What she did have was a floor full of broken plates and an idiot manager who didn't even have the decency to come over to help.

She found a spoon in her hand and bent it in half.

SUDDENLY SOMEONE WAS DOWN IN THE MESS with her. She glanced over, expecting to see Amy. Instead she found a woman who looked to be in her mid-twenties, incredibly beautiful—in fact, so striking that Paige couldn't take her eyes away.

"Be careful," the woman said. "Some of these pieces are sharp."

Before Paige could respond, something pricked her finger.

And blood came.

Not a lot.

In fact, hardly any.

But enough that she shook her head at the irony. "I'm not even supposed to be here," she said.

"Why? Where are you supposed to be?"

"Practicing law somewhere."

"You're a lawyer?"

"That's what my license says," Paige said.

The woman looked hesitant, as if deciding something. Then she pushed her long blond hair out of her face and said, "Would you mind if I asked you a couple of questions later? Maybe after you get off work or something?"

"You mean legal questions?"

"Right."

Paige smiled.

"Sure, I don't care. Just don't ask me anything tricky."

The woman grinned and then grew serious. "Have you ever been to Bangkok?"

"No, why?"

"Just curious," the woman said.

"Have you?" Paige asked.

"Yes."

Chapter Three

Day One—June 11
Monday Night

———————

BRYSON COVENTRY, the 34-year-old head of Denver's homicide unit, kept one eye in the rearview mirror of his Tundra as he turned onto Colfax Avenue. The headlights behind him made the same turn, just as they had the prior two times.

"Please Please Me"—one of the Fab Four's best—came from the radio.

As much as he hated to do it, he muted the song. Then he called Detective Shalifa Netherwood at home and said, "I need you to make a few calls and get something done for me."

"Who is this?"

"Not funny," he said.

"It's nine o'clock at night," she said.

He didn't know that but said, "I know."

"Don't you ever just knock off?"

"I'm getting ready to," he said. "But I have a situation. Someone's following me and I want to know who it is."

Two minutes later an unmarked patrol car tailgated the vehicle behind Coventry, followed for thirty seconds, and then dropped off. Three minutes later Coventry's cell phone rang and Shalifa's voice came through.

"The car has California plates. It's registered to someone named Ja'Von Deveraux," she said. "According to her license, she's twenty-seven. She looks like a model."

"A model, huh?"

"Maybe she wants to tell you about little Bryson," Shalifa said.

He chuckled.

"Hopefully the kid looks like his mother," she added.

HE WOVE OVER TO THE EDGIER section of Denver, south of downtown, near the bondage paraphernalia shops and the massage parlors, and parked the Tundra in front of a dim-lit tavern called the Lighthouse. A couple of grade-C hookers sat at the bar and checked him out as he walked in.

One of them looked at the other and said, "Cop."

They turned away.

He leaned in next to them and said, "Evening, ladies," then handed his business card to each one of them. "You call me if you ever need me, day or night."

They laughed.

"I'm serious," he said. Then he ordered a Bud Light and a glass of cold white wine. He carried them to a red-vinyl booth near the back, where the lights hardly reached, and slipped in. He was nearly done with his beer when the woman finally walked in.

Coventry waited until she spotted him.

And then he waved her over.

The look on her face said it all.

Busted.

Coventry held up the glass of wine, indicating it was for her. She stopped, as if deciding whether to bolt out the door, but then walked towards him.

Coventry liked her before she even got to the booth.

She had long blond hair, perfectly straight, slightly wind-tossed. Even though she wore a loose long-sleeve shirt tucked into khaki pants, her movement denoted a strong body. She wore no makeup and looked all the sexier for it. There was something about her eyes that wouldn't let him look away.

He swallowed.

Damn.

He already wanted her.

And not just for sex.

For everything.

This had happened before.

He recognized the feeling, which was sort of like being strapped into a roller coaster and starting to climb that first endless hill.

"You're Ja'Von Deveraux," he said.

She accepted the glass of wine, took a sip and sat down next to him, on the same side of the booth, dangerously close—almost touching.

"I assume that you saw me following you," she said.

"I did."

"I thought that was an unmarked car behind me back on Colfax," she said.

"It was."

She took another sip of wine. "I need to be more careful," she said. "I didn't realize I was getting so sloppy."

Coventry raised an eyebrow.

"Be more careful doing what?"

She said nothing and instead studied his eyes. "One's blue and one's green," she said.

Coventry nodded. "One of my many flaws."

SUDDENLY HIS CELL PHONE RANG. Barb Winters, the proud owner of new breast implants and a few new male callers, said, "We got another one. Some guy named Alan Ewing. Word is he got stabbed a bunch of times in the back. In his own bedroom, no less."

"Who found him?"

"The girlfriend."

"She did it," Coventry said. "Just have someone arrest her and then call me in the morning."

Winters laughed.

"I'm serious," he said. "Stabbing is an act of passion. He cheated on her, she found out about it and stabbed the life out of him. Case closed."

Winters grunted. "Whatever, Mr. Crystal Ball Man," she said. "Anyway, Shalifa's on call and is headed over there. She wanted me to let you know about it in case you wanted to stop over and bring her some coffee."

Ja'Von took Coventry's hand and put it on her leg, just above her knee. He moved it around, not much, just a few inches or so, to get a feel for her muscles.

Nice.

Very nice.

He sensed that he could move it all the way up if he wanted.

Instead of doing that he swallowed and said to Winters, "Give me the address."

SHALIFA NETHERWOOD COULD HANDLE the crime scene just fine all by herself, that wasn't the issue. The issue was that he already wanted this new woman for more than just sex and was concerned that jumping into bed with her might spoil things.

"I have to run," he said.

"Where to?"

"A homicide," he said. "You know I'm a detective, right?"

She nodded.

He almost asked, *How?*

But didn't feel like getting into it right this minute.

Then she looked as if she just came up with a great idea. "Let me go with you."

"I can't. It's off limits."

"I'll wait in your truck."

He pondered it.

"I might be an hour or two," he warned.

She put her hand on his, which was still on her leg. "I don't care. I'll take a catnap or go for a walk or something. Then we can go to your place afterwards."

He raked his thick brown hair back with his fingers. It immediately fell back down over his forehead.

"I don't even know who you are," he said.

She brought her mouth close to his.

So close that the warmth of her breath filled his senses.

"That's why we need to go to your place," she said. "So you can find out."

Chapter Four

Day One—June 11
Monday Evening

———————

DYLAN JOOP RACED HIS AUDI through the twisty mountain canyon west of Denver, amazed that no cars had popped up in front of him yet to kill the fun. Outside the car to the left, Clear Creek tumbled in the opposite direction, spilling white water over boulders and rocks. Inside the car, to his right, sat a manila envelope that had been hand delivered this afternoon. Inside that envelope were several pictures of Madison Blake, a petite raven-haired beauty.

The target.

The instructions came by telephone an hour after the envelope arrived. "Just take her for now and keep her somewhere safe. We're not sure yet if she's going to die or not, so don't let her see your face or give her a way to find you. Don't kill her until and unless we give the orders."

Fine.

Whatever.

He passed the second tunnel, pulled into a dirt turnoff and killed the engine. There were no other cars around. He swapped his tennis shoes for climbing shoes and hiked fifty yards north to the face of a rock cliff that looked as if it went straight up—a Class 5.11, at least. He stretched his six-feet-three-inch body until he was good and limber and then began to climb.

Without gear.

Or protection.

He had only soloed this particular climb once before.

And it hadn't been pretty.

He'd gotten into a jam about twenty-five feet up, in a position where he couldn't go up or down, wedged in an off-width crack. He stayed there for as long as he could—ten minutes or more—and finally resigned himself to the fact that it was time to jump.

Unfortunately there were no good landing spots.

Only rocks.

He picked the place least likely to kill him, let go and kicked off at the same time, twisting on the way down and then shielding his head with his arms and hands just before impact.

The plan worked.

He broke a leg but lived.

That was four years ago.

When he was twenty-nine.

THIS TIME HE WOULDN'T MAKE THE SAME MISTAKE. Plus he was in better shape now—down to 208 pounds of totally ripped muscle. Before, he had pretty good abs, a six-pack.

Now he had an eight-pack.

And whereas before he could only do forty-five pull-ups, now he could do fifty.

Still, the mountain worried him.

He stayed to the right, avoiding the troublesome area, even though the face was steeper there. He wished he had gotten here an hour earlier. The twilight was actually starting to slip into darkness. The rock was getting colder and starting to suck his warmth. In another thirty minutes or so it would be downright dangerous. The climb would take at least that long, even with no glitches.

He got to the place he made it to before, but this time was ten feet to the right.

He kept climbing.

Five feet higher.

Now thirty feet above the ground.

With lots of exposure.

Then something bad happened.

The wall actually extended outward, past vertical, plus there was no way to go either to the right or the left. He remembered seeing a chimney somewhere in the area, but couldn't remember exactly where. He would either have to downclimb, which was always dangerous, or do a dynamic move—jump up and catch an overhang with his hands, dangle, and just hope there was somewhere to go up once he got there.

He jumped.

And caught the edge.

The abrasion of the rock immediately assaulted his fingers.

He hung there for a second until he got a solid bomber-hold. Then he pulled up with his arms to where he could see above.

Damn it!

There was nowhere to go.

The rock above him was totally vertical for a good ten feet with no crevices or cracks to grab.

He hung there for five minutes.

Then looked below and picked the least insane spot to land.
He let out a war cry at the top of his lungs and pushed off.

Chapter Five

Day Two—June 12
Tuesday Morning

———————

PAIGE ALEXANDER WOKE EARLY on Tuesday morning and decided that her apartment was too small. In fact, her whole life was too small. She got the coffee going and then fired up her laptop and logged on to the Colorado Bar Association website to see if any new job openings had been posted in the last twelve hours.

None had.

Well, that wasn't exactly true.

One had.

Vinson & Botts was looking for an associate to add to its intellectual property department. May as well apply to be the president of the whole freaking universe, she thought.

She ate a nonfat yogurt, snapped the plastic spoon in half before throwing it away, put on a baseball cap and pulled her hair through the back. Then she carried her 20-speed Trek bicycle down the apartment stairway to ground level. Fifteen minutes later she arrived at the 24-Hour Fitness on Alameda where she worked the weights for a half hour and then hit the elliptical trainer until her T-shirt was soaked.

She wasn't big.

Five-three.

A hundred and five pounds.

Some people might say she was too small but she liked her size. It fit her personality. Plus she was in good shape and her body moved easily. She could get up and sit back down a hundred times a day and never even notice. If she needed a paper clip, and it was on the other side of the room, she'd just go over and get it.

No problem.

She liked her proportions too.

Her chest would never turn heads. Her thighs, ass and stomach, on the other hand, were just about perfect. When guys felt her up, that's where they spent their time. In the bedroom, men liked to have her on top because she was so light and such a good wiggler.

Not that she'd wiggled in over four months.

She was the cute librarian when she pulled back her hair. When her hair came down, she was a lot more than cute. And when she let her stomach muscles show, heads turned.

She showered at the club and then peddled the Trek over to the Starbucks on Alameda. When she arrived, the woman—Ja'Von Deveraux—was already waiting for her.

YESTERDAY, WHILE PICKING PLATES OFF THE FLOOR, Paige got a good enough look at Ja'Von to tell that she was incredibly attractive. Now she realized that the woman was even more beautiful than she initially realized.

She was five-eight or nine.

With a strong body and long blond hair.

A California lifeguard meets movie star look.

Most of the men in the place had half an eye on her.

They drank two cups of coffee, chatting about everything and nothing, before Ja'Von got to the point of the meeting.

"Okay, so here's the deal," Ja'Von said. "I'm a private investigator with a small office on Market Street, in San Francisco. About two months ago, in early April, I got a strange phone call. The caller said he was with a law firm, but didn't want to disclose the name of it because the firm wanted to hire me for a highly confidential matter, so confidential that they didn't even want the name of the firm in my files. It turned out that the firm wanted to get some dirt on a man named Bob Copeland."

"Why?"

"Good question," Ja'Von said. "The same one I asked, as a matter of fact. But the man wouldn't say. Anyway, the firm had information that Copeland was going to be traveling to Bangkok. They suspected that he was going there to have sex with lady-boys. You know what a lady-boy is, right?"

No.

Paige didn't.

"Well, they're basically young Asian men who look and act exactly like girls, except that they have a cock," Ja'Von said.

"Oh."

"Most of them are actually quite beautiful," she added. "Anyway, the firm wanted me to follow Copeland to Bangkok and confirm that he was screwing lady-boys. I was also supposed to get as much documentation as I could."

"Meaning photographs?"

"Exactly," Ja'Von said. "Preferably of Copeland and a lady-boy mingling or drinking together, but if not that, at least pictures of him walking in and out of bars that had reputations for lady-boys. I was supposed to take a digital camera. Then, if I got pictures, I was supposed to download them to my laptop and email them to myself. That way I could download them once I got back in the States and would still have them even if my camera and laptop got lost or stolen."

"Clever," Paige said.

"Routine, actually," Ja'Von said. "Anyway, I struck a deal with the law firm. They agreed to pay me a total of $20,000—win, loose or draw—plus all my expenses. Half was to be paid up front and the other half was to be paid on completion. Ten thousand dollars in cash arrived at my office by courier the next day. With that money I bought a roundtrip plane ticket to Bangkok and took off."

She paused.

And her lower lip trembled for a second.

"What happened next is a long story," she said. "A long ugly story."

Chapter Six

A WARM MORNING LIGHT crept into Coventry's bedroom and washed it with a golden patina. Ja'Von Deveraux lay on top of the covers sound asleep. Coventry got out of bed as unobtrusively as he could, looked at the woman's incredible naked body for a few seconds, and decided he was the luckiest man on the face of the earth. He showered downstairs so as to not wake her, left a note on the kitchen table, and then ate a bowl of cereal in the Tundra as he drove east on the 6th Avenue freeway to headquarters.

He flicked the radio stations and got mostly jock-talk until he got to 105, the oldies station, just as "Black Velvet" started playing. He left it there and concentrated on trying to not get blinded by the sun as it lifted off the horizon directly ahead of him.

As usual, he was the first person to arrive at work.

He kick-started the coffee machine and put his cup under the flow as soon as it started, filling the cup only halfway and then adding hot water.

It was too strong.

Almost downright nasty.

But better than waiting.

Alan Ewing was starting to turn into a mystery. After talking to the girlfriend last night, a woman by the name of Barbara Smith, Coventry didn't think she did it.

From what he had learned so far, Ewing was the pilot of a jet jointly owned by six companies. He had just returned from Bangkok and apparently got stabbed in the back before he even got his suitcases out of his car.

The girlfriend would have known when he was coming back.

She also had a key.

But so far she didn't seem to have a motive.

And seemed to be telling the truth about not having a clue why Ewing got killed or who did it.

Nothing had been taken from the man's house.

So rule out robbery.

SHALIFA NETHERWOOD SHOWED UP AT 7:30, gave Coventry a weird look, and headed to the coffee pot without saying anything. Then she plopped down in the seat in front of his desk and took a noisy slurp from a disposable cup. She wore a white blouse that looked extra crisp against her African American skin. Coventry stole her out of vice more than a year ago. Although she was technically still the newbie of the homicide unit, she had already cut her teeth on Denver's worst.

David Hallenbeck.

Nathan Wickersham.

Jack Degan.

Lance Lundeen.

Trent Tibadeau.

Dalton Wrey.

"Someone said they saw a woman sitting in your truck last night, while we were processing the scene," she said.

He shrugged.

"That's true."

"A black woman?"

"No, white."

She frowned. "They're always white, Coventry. When are you going to get a black one?"

"I've had black women," he said.

"And?"

"And, they were all nice. I got no complaints. This particular one just happens to be white."

"How many black women have you had, all told?"

"I don't know."

"More than five?"

"I don't know, I don't keep count."

She rolled her eyes.

"All men keep count, Coventry. So more than five—or what?"

He chuckled.

"Yeah, more than five."

"More than ten?" she asked.

"I don't know. About ten, maybe. Why?"

"Nothing. I just want to be sure you're not missing out on the best thing in life."

"So you're taking care of me, is that what it comes down to?"

She nodded. "Someone has to. Tell me about whitey. Is she just another bed-buddy or are we all going to have to put up with you going gaga again?"

COVENTRY TOLD HER THE STORY. The woman—Ja'Von Deveraux—was a private investigator from San Francisco. She was in the process of relocating her practice to Denver and happened to see Coventry on the news a couple of weeks ago. She liked him, did some investigation and decided that he was a solid guy—someone worth meeting.

So she tailed him last night, hoping he would end up somewhere public—a restaurant or something—where she could accidentally bump into him and make his acquaintance.

They ended up meeting.

And hit it off.

End of story.

"That's your story?" Shalifa asked.

"Yeah. Why?"

She laughed.

"Don't get me wrong, Bryson, you're not half bad looking," she said. "But do you really believe that a woman's going to see you on the news and get so lightheaded that she has to hunt you down?"

He cocked his head.

"You think she's lying?"

"Damn straight she's lying," Shalifa said. "The only question is—why? My guess is this. She's going to want to tap you in connection with her P.I. work. First she'll sleep with you. Then, a month or two from now, you'll get a phone call. *Bryson, could you do me a little favor, and run some prints for me? What do you know about a guy named Joe Blow?*"

She laughed.

"What?" he questioned.

"No, here's the phone call you're going to get," she said. *"Bryson, I happened to be in someone's house, just snooping around a little, nothing serious. Anyway, there was a big misunderstanding and I just happened to get arrested. Would you have time to come down here and straighten things out for me?"*

Coventry knew he was supposed to laugh.

But didn't.

"Do you really think she's using me?"

She got serious.

"You're a stud, Bryson," she said. "If we didn't work together, I'd take a run at you myself. But this is too much of a coincidence. Maybe I can see it better because I'm a woman and can read women better than you. Normal women don't see guys on TV and then hunt them down. Something fishy is going on. My advice to you is to watch your back."

He chewed on the words.

"And above everything else," she added, "don't let the little guy get involved. And especially don't let him call the shots."

"The *little guy?*"

"The little guy, Mr. Happy, Bob, whatever it is that you call him," she said.

He laughed.

"I'm serious, Bryson," she said. "I know you've been looking for someone to be in your life and I know you've had some bad luck. I just don't want to see you have even more bad luck."

Coventry stood up, walked over to the coffee pot and refilled. Then he turned and said over his shoulder, "She's incredibly hot. Did I mention that?"

"Did you hear a word that I just said?"

"I'm sorry," he said. "Have you been talking?"

She gave him a sideways look. "Don't blame me when it all goes south. I did what I could."

He chuckled.

"What?" she asked.

"So is what you said true?"

"What do you mean?"

"You said that if we didn't work together, you'd take a run at me yourself."

"I never said any such thing."

"Oh, okay," he said. "Too bad, though, because I would have said, *Ditto*."

Chapter Seven

Day Two—June 12
Tuesday Morning

—————————

LOWER DOWNTOWN—LODO—IS AN UPSCALE HOTSPOT at the northern edge of Denver given to trendy bars, restaurants and shops, all anchored by Coors Field. Dylan Joop's LoDo loft sat smack dab in the heart of the matter. He stepped onto his balcony with a cup of hot coffee in hand and looked down.

The city buzzed.

Vibrant.

Alive.

Joop was too, but barely.

The fall off the face of the cliff last evening knocked him out—for a long time, actually. He remembered waking up to a pitch-black world, half frozen, not having a clue where he was, before finally making his way back to the Audi and discovering that it was almost midnight.

His entire body ached.

Even now.

Every single part of it.

But nothing was broken, that he could tell.

One thing he knew for sure.

He'd go back there a third time.

And get it right.

No stupid-ass mountain was going to beat him.

Period.

End of sentence.

MADISON BLAKE—THE TARGET—TURNED OUT to be a 22-year-old single female with a string of low-paying jobs in her wake, currently employed as a Molly Maid.

Why she had been chosen as a target was beyond Joop's comprehension. The best he could figure, she must have seen something she shouldn't have. Maybe she snooped around a little too much while cleaning someone's house.

He didn't know.

He didn't care.

To him, she was nothing more than a pile of money.

HE FOLLOWED HER FOR A COUPLE OF HOURS in the morning, to get a feel for her, and then pointed the front end of the Audi west. He gassed up in downtown Morrison at the base of the foothills, then wound up Highway 74 into the mountains—through a river canyon that wasn't quite as nice as Clear Creek but was still pretty damn spectacular.

He passed Idledale, kept going under a clear Colorado sky, then turned onto a gravel road, kicking up a dust trail as he disappeared into thick Ponderosa pines.

A hundred yards down the road he stopped the vehicle in front of a chain-link gate with a warning sign: *Private Property. No*

Trespassing. A second sign said *No Hunting.* And a third said *Keep Out.* All of the signs were marked with shotgun blast, just to make a point.

He got out.

Unlocked the gate.

Drove the Audi through.

Relocked it.

And then continued down the road for a half mile, into the heart of his 1,000-acre property, where he parked in front of three old boxcars, coupled together, sitting on a short stretch of track that dead-ended at either end of the cars.

They had been there when he purchased the property.

He had always been curious how they got there, but never curious enough to research it.

Pine scent perfumed the air.

He inhaled deeply and marveled, once again, at how deathly quiet the place was. Not a sound came from anywhere.

No traffic.

No music.

Nothing.

Except the occasional flap of a bird's wing or a marmot's rustle in the brush.

THE BOXCARS HAD BEEN EMPTY when he purchased the property. He linked them together with a wooden deck, converted the middle one into a kitchen and sitting area, and modified the right one into a bedroom and bathroom.

The left car was empty.

A quick inspection of the cars showed that no one had tried to intrude since he had last been there two weeks ago.

Good.

He jogged.

Then shot the 45-pound compound bow for a half hour.

As he came up with the perfect plan to take Madison Blake.

Chapter Eight

Day Two—June 12
Tuesday Morning

PAIGE ALEXANDER DIDN'T EXACTLY KNOW what ugly story Ja'Von Deveraux was about to lay on her, but did know that Starbucks wasn't the place for it. So they stepped outside and walked down Alameda next to heavy traffic.

Ja'Von turned her face to the sky and let the sun fall on it.

Then seemed to brighten.

"This is better," she said. "Anyway, I arrived in Bangkok in the afternoon and studied maps, got my bearings, checked my equipment, that kind of thing. Bob Copeland landed just before nightfall, spent an hour in his hotel room, and then headed over to a place called Soi Cowboy, located in a sleazy sex district filled with blowjob bars, gender-benders and STDs. I got some pictures of him going into one of the bars and then waited outside. Half an hour later he still hadn't come out. So I went in, took a seat at the end of the bar and ordered a beer. I was the only white woman in the place. I couldn't see Copeland anywhere and figured he'd gone into one of the back rooms to get his cock sucked. Then I started getting seriously sleepy. The next thing I knew, I woke up naked, with a splitting headache, in a stone cell."

Paige pictured it.

And dreaded hearing the rest of the story.

"So someone spiked your drink," she said.

Ja'Von nodded.

"I was turned into a sex slave," she said, "a bondage sex slave to be precise. Men would pay to take us to one of the dungeons. They were allowed to do anything to us that their sick little minds could think up. Most of them liked to put us into tight, inescapable rope bondage, and then screw us in the mouth. They'd keep our teeth open with metal spreaders so we couldn't bite. That's an average day. But lots of days were worse. A lot worse. One of the dungeons was set up for water bondage. I literally peed down my leg every time they carried me in there."

"I can't even imagine," Paige said.

"I'LL TELL YOU MORE ABOUT ALL THAT LATER," Ja'Von said. "Anyway, I was there for about a month when something happened. One of the customers bought me for a snuff."

"A snuff?"

"Right," Ja'Von said. "A snuff is where they torture you, usually for days on end, and then kill you for the grand finale. The place didn't allow snuffs on the premises. So if a customer wanted to do a snuff, he had to buy the woman outright and then take her somewhere offsite. I was at the point where I had already been paid for, stuffed into the trunk of a car and was being transported. We ended up veering off the road and tumbling down an embankment. The driver died in the crash. I was

in the trunk for two full days and nights before someone spotted the wreck."

"My god," Paige said.

"Now let me tell you where you fit into all of this," she said.

PAIGE COULDN'T IMAGINE in her wildest scenarios how she
could possibly fit into this.

Then Ja'Von told her.

"I've had a lot of time to think about what happened,"
Ja'Von said. "I've done a lot of research. I'll be the first to admit
that drinks get spiked in Bangkok and bad things end up happening, to both men and women. But my mind keeps going
back to that first night when I followed Copeland into the bar. I
remember the bartender's eyes falling on me almost immediately. At the time, I thought it was because I was a white
woman, a blond one no less, and stood out. But now I think it
was because he was expecting me."

"What do you mean?"

"I think he knew I would be coming in," Ja'Von said.

"How would he possibly know that?"

"Here's my theory," Ja'Von said. "Bob Copeland wasn't a
real target at all. He was a rabbit. Someone set me up to follow
him to Bangkok for the sole purpose of abducting me into slavery."

Paige heard the words.

And understood them.

But found the concept so bizarre that she really couldn't
fathom it.

"Come again," she said.

"All right," Ja'Von said. "Let me break it down. I'm not trying to be conceited, but I'm an attractive woman."

"Agreed."

"I'd be worth a lot of money in the kind of place where I eventually ended up," Ja'Von said. "Now, suppose someone targets me—and I have no idea if it was someone from Bangkok or someone from here in the States. But assume the fact, that I've been targeted. Now the question is, how do they get me to Bangkok? It would be too complicated to abduct me here in the States and then try to smuggle me into Thailand. Too many things could go wrong. But what if I traveled there of my own accord? Do you see where I'm going with this?"

Paige nodded.

She did.

"So they set up Bob Copeland as a pretend mark for me to follow," Ja'Von said. "I fall for it and head to Bangkok. Now they have me in the country and all they have to do is get me to the place where they're going to abduct me. And that's easy, because Copeland leads me right to them. I get abducted and Copeland walks out the back door with his ten grand or whatever it is that they paid him to be part of the charade."

PAIGE COCKED HER HEAD.

"It's a theory," she said. "But what makes you think that's what happened as opposed to just some random misfortune once you got there?"

Ja'Von grunted.

"Lots of little things," she said. "First, when I got back to the States, I found out that someone had rifled through both my apartment and my office. Several of my files were gone, including the Bob Copeland file. My computers were all stolen too. So

I found it strange that I suddenly didn't have any evidence at all of the Bob Copeland assignment."

"That is strange," Paige said.

"You bet it is," Ja'Von said. "Here's something else that's strange. I tried to track Copeland down to see if I could shake him up into admitting he had been part of a conspiracy. It turns out that he totally disappeared without a trace."

"He did?"

"He did," Ja'Von said. "There's one more important fact. I got in touch with my phone company and talked them into getting some information for me. It turns out that all the calls to me, from the person who said he was representing a law firm, came from a payphone in the lobby of a building here in Denver. A law firm by the name of Vinson & Botts has its offices in that building."

Vinson & Botts.

"That's the biggest firm in Denver," Paige said.

Ja'Von nodded.

"The world, actually."

"Huh?"

"I've done a lot of research on them," Ja'Von said. "They have offices all over the world. Three are here in the United States—namely New York, Denver and San Francisco. But they also have offices in London, Paris, Prague, Tokyo and Hong Kong to name a few. Here's the important thing—their website says they'll be opening a Bangkok office within the next year, which means they're over there now putting it together."

"Bangkok, huh?"

"Right."

"Interesting."

"Isn't it?" Ja'Von pushed hair out of her face. "There are

other law firms in that building, lots of them in fact. But Vinson & Botts is the only one that has any kind of connection to Bangkok, at least that I can find."

Paige picked up a twig and snapped it.

Ja'Von let it steal her attention for a moment and then refocused. "Anyway," she said, "this whole discussion started when I asked you if I could ask you a question, and you said yes. So here's my question. Are you ready?"

Paige nodded.

"If my theory is correct, and someone from Vinson & Botts hired me to go Bangkok so I would be abducted into sexual slavery, would I have a lawsuit against the law firm?"

"I can't imagine how you wouldn't," Paige said.

"Okay then," Ja'Von said. "Do you want to be my lawyer?"

Chapter Nine

Day Two—June 12
Tuesday Morning

BRYSON COVENTRY SPENT THE MORNING alone at Alan Ewing's house, going through the victim's phone bills, daily calendar, drawers, and whatever else he could find—looking for the name of someone who hated the man enough to stab him in the back seven times. It turned out that Ewing had a pretty nice sound system, so Coventry brought one of his Beatles CDs from the Tundra and let it spin while he worked.

He found nothing out of the ordinary.

Which surprised him.

Usually hate that strong leaves a lot of footprints.

Dinosaur-sized.

Maybe they were here but Coventry couldn't see them because half his brain cells were focused on Ja'Von Deveraux. Women had always come easy to him. In fact, according to the FBI profiler Dr. Leanne Sanders, that was Coventry's downfall and the main reason he was still single at thirty-four. So it didn't require a quantum leap in logic to believe that Ja'Von actually did see him on TV and decided to find a way to meet him.

On the other hand, Coventry had to agree with Shalifa.

It would be unusual.

Especially for someone as exotic as Ja'Von.

One thing he did know for sure. He needed to see her again, as soon as possible, and get an answer. If their foundation wasn't solid, then he needed to know that before he got too wrapped up in her to care.

Damn.

Nothing was ever easy.

And who was he trying to kid?

He was already wrapped up in her too much to care.

"Love Me Do" came from crystal-clear speakers.

Coventry cranked up the volume and plopped down on Ewing's couch, wondering if there was anything else he should do before he left. The song was so simple, so obvious, that it didn't seem as if anyone had written it. It seemed more like one of those songs that were always there somewhere in the universe and then just finally got spotted by someone who happened to be in the right place at the right time.

Like John Denver's "Country Roads."

Or the Beach Boys' "Don't Worry Baby."

Even "Born to Run," to some extent.

Ja'Von Deveraux.

Who was she?

WHEN COVENTRY GOT BACK TO HEADQUARTERS, he bypassed the elevators in the parking garage and walked straight up to the sixth floor to see if Paul Kubiak had any luck processing Alan Ewing's computer.

Before he pushed through the door, he realized that his left hand was empty. So he walked down to homicide on the third

floor, got a cup of coffee, and then got out of there before anyone could corner him.

He headed back up the stairs, sipping on the way.

Luckily, Kubiak hadn't gone to lunch early. The man
scratched his big old truck-driver's gut and said, "The rumor is
that you have some hot woman hunting you down."

Coventry made a sour face.

"This place is worse than a sewing circle," he said.

"Same thing happened to me once," Kubiak said.

Coventry cocked his head.

"Oh?"

"Only it was because I ran over her cat."

Coventry grunted.

"Don't do that," he said. "You'll use up all nine of their lives
at once."

Kubiak grinned, took a bite out of a doughnut, and told
Coventry that the computer had already been unlocked and
given to Shalifa. Two minutes later, in homicide, Shalifa said she
spent the morning going through Alan Ewing's computer files.
She also tapped into the victim's email history. There was no
evidence that the victim's relationship with his girlfriend was
strained. Quite the opposite, if anything. Nor was there anything
to point to another woman on the side.

"The only thing weird that I found," Shalifa said, "was a lot
of bondage pictures downloaded onto his hard drive."

"Really?"

Shalifa nodded.

"The guy was a big-time sicko," Shalifa said.

"Well that's interesting."

"Isn't it?"

A HALF HOUR LATER, Coventry finally got through to Ja'Von on her cell phone and arranged to meet her at Wong's on Court Street for a late lunch. She wore white cotton shorts and an aqua sleeveless blouse. Seeing her for the first time by the light of day, the blueness of her eyes took on a whole new dimension.

He swallowed.

She slipped into the booth next to him and whispered in his ear, "I'm still shaking."

He grinned.

"Good," he said. "Then my evil plan worked."

"Worked isn't even the word," she said. "I'm already addicted." She put her hand on his leg. "So when do I get my next fix?"

The waitress suddenly showed up.

They ordered.

Then Coventry jumped headfirst into the subject, the dreaded subject, on his mind. "One of my partners, a detective by the name of Shalifa Netherwood, found out about you and asked me a bunch of questions this morning," he said. "When I explained what happened, she said that you were up to something. She said you were probably snuggling up to be able to tap me for information to help your P.I. practice."

Ja'Von tilted her head.

"And what did you say?" she asked.

"Well, I basically told her she was wrong."

"And yet you're bringing the subject up," Ja'Von said. "Which means you have your doubts. I'm disappointed. I thought we had a connection."

"We do. It's just that Shalifa has this sixth sense about people, especially women."

"Well she's wrong," Ja'Von said. "Are you sleeping with her?"

Coventry chuckled.

"No."

"Have you ever slept with her?"

"No."

"Have you ever wanted to sleep with her?"

He shrugged.

"She's my partner," he said. "I can't have those kinds of thoughts."

Ja'Von took a sip of tea and said, "Here's some stuff you'll find out about me as time goes on. First, my P.I. practice is totally confidential, which means I'm not even going to tell you what I'm doing, much less ask you for help. Second, I will never, ever, either directly or indirectly, ask you for help or a favor in any way, shape or form. That's not the way I operate. But most importantly, I would never put you in a compromising position. That wouldn't be right of me. Or fair to you. I've never had any intention of anything like that happening and it never is going to happen, plain and simple." She looked into his eyes. "Any questions?"

He nodded.

"Just one."

"Go ahead."

"Are you still addicted, or did I blow it?"

She squeezed his hand.

"I could use a fix right now, to tell you the truth."

Chapter Ten

Day Two—June 12
Tuesday Night

DYLAN JOOP HUGGED THE PITCH-BLACK SHAPE of a thirty-foot Ponderosa pine in the backyard of a house, waiting for his little black-haired target—Madison Blake—to show up. A sliver of moon floated in the east but didn't throw enough light to expose him.

Still, to be extra cautious, he wore a ski mask.

The woman should show up any time now.

He fingered the black hood in the left pocket of his sweatshirt. Once he got his knife to her throat, and tied the hood over her head, she'd calm down considerably.

The plan was a pretty good one.

Joop drove around until he found a house for sale that looked like no one was living there. From a payphone he called Madison Blake and said she was recommended by the people on Birch Street, where Joop had followed her this morning in her Molly Maid car. He said he was a real estate agent by the name of Jim Hansen who needed a house dusted and vacuumed in preparation of a big showing tomorrow morning.

"If I pay you direct, can you go over tonight?"

They talked money.

So much money that she said, "Okay, but don't tell anyone."

"There's a lockbox on the front door but someone took the key," Joop said. "What you need to do is go around to the back. We leave the sliding glass door unlocked."

"Okay."

"We'll have some wallpapering going on until about nine," he said. "But you can show up any time after that."

"Like, 9:30?"

"That'll work," Joop said. "I'll leave the money in an envelope on the top cabinet to the right of the kitchen sink."

"Okay."

"Thanks. I really appreciate it. And please do a good job. This is really important."

That was this afternoon.

Joop lit his watch.

9:28 p.m.

Suddenly headlights flickered up the street.

Game time.

A VEHICLE PULLED INTO THE DRIVEWAY, the engine stopped and the headlights went off. A car door opened and then shut. Then a trunk opened and shut. Thirty seconds later a dark shape came around the rear corner of the house. As best as Joop could tell, the woman carried a vacuum cleaner in one hand and an oversized bag in the other.

No doubt filled with paper towels and cleaning products.

Joop left his hiding spot at exactly the right time.

And approached with coffin-quiet steps.

She didn't have a clue.

Even as he closed the last five feet.

He brought his left hand from behind and clamped her mouth shut while he brought the knife to her throat with his other hand. "Don't make a sound!" he warned.

She froze.

He held her tight.

Immobile.

Until his gut told him that she had decided to not do anything stupid. Then he put the hood over her head. "I'm not going to hurt you," he said. "This is so you don't see my face. That way I'll be able to release you again. Do you understand?"

"Yes."

"Good," he said. "You're doing just fine. All this will be over in a minute. Put your hands behind your back."

She did.

And he pulled out the rope.

"All you have to do is cooperate and nothing bad will happen."

Before he got her tied, a voice cut the night.

A woman's voice.

Rounding the back corner of the house.

"You're not going to believe what that jerk brother of mine just told me."

Then Madison Blake screamed.

Joop pushed her to the ground.

Then ran towards the other woman.

Fast.

With the knife in hand.

She turned and ran.

But not fast enough.

No.

Not by a long shot.

He reached for her hair.

Got it.

Then yanked as hard as he could.

So hard that her body stopped moving forward and actually lifted off the ground as her head snapped back.

Chapter Eleven

Day Two—June 12
Tuesday Afternoon

ALTHOUGH PAIGE TOLD JA'VON that she'd be her attorney, the cold reality of the undertaking made her hands tremble all day Tuesday as she paraded around in her waitress apron and delivered food to people who hardly noticed that she existed.

She probably couldn't get a job with Vinson & Botts as a secretary, much less a lawyer. So how was she supposed to cross swords with even one V&B attorney, much less an army of them? They'd cut her to ribbons before she took ten steps towards the courthouse.

She needed to back out.

And called Ja'Von during a break to tell her.

The woman didn't answer.

But a half hour later she did. "I've been giving this a lot of thought," Paige said. "You need to get a real lawyer. There's no way I can—"

"Stop," Ja'Von said.

"But—"

"Ah, ah, ah," Ja'Von said. "I know where you're headed and

I'm not interested in hearing it, so save your breath. You're my lawyer, so get used to it."

"You'd be better off with someone experienced," Paige said. "You really would. I hate to loose my first client, but that's the cold hard truth. Hell, I don't even have a fax machine. But that's not the point. The point is that I don't have the experience or the depth to go after a target as big as V&B. It would be like a mosquito trying to eat an elephant."

Ja'Von laughed and said, "Maybe we don't need to eat it. Maybe we just need to give it a good bite and infect it with a disease."

"I'm serious," Paige said. "They'll put up a scorched-earth defense."

"What's that?"

"That's where they bury you in paper, file one motion after another, don't produce documents unless ordered by the court, pull witnesses out of thin air, and basically scorch the earth for anything and everything that could possibly help them win. They could throw two or three million dollars in billable hours at the case and never even blink."

A pause on the other end.

"Speaking of money," Ja'Von said. "I don't have any. Did I mention that before? The little that I do have is already ear-marked to keep food in my stomach and gas in my car. So I won't be able to pay you anything. You'll have to take the case on a contingency fee basis."

WHEN PAIGE GOT OFF WORK MID-AFTERNOON, instead of peddling the Trek to the bus stop on Colfax Avenue as usual, she headed into the heart of Denver's bustling financial district and found a place to lock the bike at the bottom of the Cash Register Building at the corner of Lincoln and 17th Street—a tall office building with a top shaped like an old cash register.

She stepped into a fancy marble elevator wearing her jeans, T-shirt and tennis shoes, and pushed the button for floor thirty-four, the lowest of the four floors that housed Vinson & Botts.

On the way up she noticed a large ketchup stain on her shirt.

Damn.

It looked like blood.

The elevator dumped her into a common area.

To the right was a wall of glass.

She looked for a restroom, found none, then swallowed and pushed through fancy doors into a space that could very easily have been a wing from the Louvre. She knew nothing about art but even her untrained eye registered the fifteen or twenty oil paintings as important and rare.

The place oozed money.

And power.

The receptionist—a conservatively dressed woman—sat at a contemporary glass desk that resembled a futuristic command center. She wore a hands-free telephone and directed incoming calls to their destinations on a nonstop basis. She momentarily fixed her eyes on Paige's ketchup stain but kept all expressions off her face. Behind her, in a glass-walled conference room with a commanding view of the Rocky Mountains, twelve or fifteen attorneys sat in high-back leather chairs at a cherry wood table, concentrating on a professionally dressed woman giving a Power Point presentation.

Two attorneys walked into the area, talking intently, and disappeared down a hall at the opposite end.

Neither of them looked at Paige.

So this is what the elephant looks like.

It was even bigger than she thought.

She turned and walked out.

It wasn't until she got in the elevator that she noticed her hands trembling.

SHE GOT BACK TO HER APARTMENT AFTER FIVE and peddled past her worn-out, broken-down Chevy—a vehicle that hadn't run in six months because a new transmission still hadn't fallen out of the sky and landed in it. It still served a purpose, though, as a storage unit. She kept her winter clothes in the trunk and all of her old law books in the back seat.

There was no need to worry about anyone taking the radio.

They did that long ago.

She ate a Lean Pocket off a paper plate as she paced back and forth.

Damages weren't the issue.

If there was liability—emphasis on the *if*—the damages were huge. Paige couldn't even begin to guess what a jury might award to redress a woman who had been held in sexual slavery for over a month. It would probably be a pile of money that could be seen from outer space.

So the issue wasn't damages.

The issue was liability.

How could Paige possibly prove that the most prim and proper law firm in Denver—correction, in the world—was engaged in a conspiracy to enslave a woman? The concept seemed so bizarre. What jury would possibly believe that without a pile of proof?

A pile that could also be seen from outer space, to be exact.

Chapter Twelve

Day Three—June 13
Wednesday Morning

BRYSON COVENTRY LIVED ON A DEAD-END STREET nestled
in the side of Green Mountain where the houses looked down
on Denver, fifteen miles to the east. His house was a green split-
level, third from the end, backing to the mountain. The
neighborhood had no flowers because flowers were deer candy.
Foxes, rabbits and rattlesnakes roamed the mountain. At night,
the coyotes barked, and every once in a while the skunks stank.
Traffic noise couldn't reach this far.

Coventry had drapes in his bedroom but never closed them.

He needed the room to lighten when the sun came up, just
to be absolutely sure he didn't waste a minute of the day. He
liked the night but loved the day.

Nothing got him more stressed than waking up late.

This morning he woke an hour before sunrise because that's
the only time he could carve out of his life to jog. But his body
wouldn't let him get out of bed right away, so he turned onto
his back.

Ja'Von lay next to him.

Breathing deep and steady.

Listening to her, right then and there, he realized something.

She needed to move in with him.

Today.

So he could repeat this moment tomorrow.

And the next day.

And the next.

He must have shifted his weight because Ja'Von moaned and said, "Are you awake?"

"No."

She chuckled.

And climbed on top of him.

Then wiggled until he got hard.

"Something's wrong," he said. "My life doesn't work like this."

"It does now," she said.

HE HADN'T BEEN AT HEADQUARTERS for more than fifteen minutes, not even long enough to inhale the first pot of coffee, when dispatch called and said, "Got some more job security for you."

Coventry fired up a second pot of coffee, filled a thermos, and then headed to the crime scene, which turned out to be a vacant house on the south edge of Denver.

A house for sale.

A white Molly Maid car sat in the driveway. Three uniforms were in the process of stringing tape around the perimeter of the property.

Coventry recognized one of the officers.

Adam Woods.

A triangular bodybuilder with a taste for steroids.

One more guy who had traded his hair for muscles.

"I'll be damned, the big guns," Woods said when he spotted Coventry.

"Still pumping, I see."

"You got to do what you can," he said.

According to Woods, the neighbor looked out the kitchen window this morning, saw a body and called the police. "She came over when we got here," Woods said. "Other than seeing the body this morning, she doesn't know anything."

"She didn't hear anything or see anything?"

"Nada."

"Does she know when the Molly Maid car showed up?"

Woods frowned.

"I don't know. I didn't ask her that."

A black-and-white magpie landed on the roof of Coventry's truck. He walked over and shooed it off.

Bird droppings ruin paint.

Then he headed to the backyard to view the body.

A white female in her early twenties lay on the ground with her head twisted radically to the side, indicating a severely broken neck. Coventry kneeled down for a closer look.

The woman had an energetic face, even in death.

She struck him as someone who sang hip-hop with the window open as she drove.

Someone far too young to die.

He said, "I promise."

Then stood up.

Surprised at his words.

He hadn't made a promise in over a year.

"About time," he said to himself.

HE WALKED UP TO THE TUNDRA, not wanting to mess up the scene until it had been fully photographed and processed, only to discover the magpie back on his roof. "Go on, get out of here." When the bird flew off, Coventry opened the door and stood on the floorboard to be sure the paint was okay.

Damn it.

A large liquid splat sat smack dab where it shouldn't.

He grabbed a Kleenex out of his pocket and wiped it off, trying to not get any on his hands, just as Shalifa Netherwood pulled up and walked over.

"My universe is back to working the way it's supposed to," he said.

"Huh?"

"Never mind," he said. "It's an inside joke."

"What are you going to do with that Kleenex?"

Good question.

He threw it into the bed of the truck.

"It's going to blow out of there," Shalifa said. "That's litter-ing."

He knew that.

"Well, what do you propose I do with it?"

"Set it inside, on the floor mat," she said. "Then throw it away when you get home." Coventry knew she wouldn't give him any peace until he complied.

So he did.

"Happy?"

She nodded.

"Where's the body?"

OVER THE NEXT FEW HOURS THEY DISCOVERED a truck-load of useful information. First, the victim, a 21-year-old named Samantha Rickenbacker, was a stocker for the Home Depot in Golden, and didn't work for Molly Maids like they first thought.

But her roommate—Madison Blake—did, and in fact was assigned to the car in the driveway. Blake's purse was found under the driver's seat. The house didn't belong to a Molly Maid client. So if Madison Blake had been at the scene and came to clean—which seemed obvious given the vacuum cleaner and bag of products in the backyard—she was moonlighting.

The two women rented an apartment together in Arvada.

No one answered the door when Coventry knocked.

Not the first time, at ten.

Or the second, at eleven.

Or the third, at noon, when he arrived with a search warrant.

"So where's Madison Blake?" Shalifa asked.

"That's the question," Coventry said. "She's either involved in this up to her ass, or she's another victim. My money's on the latter."

"Why the latter?"

"Because if she was involved, she wouldn't have left the car behind, much less her purse," he said.

Shalifa nodded.

"So she's another victim," she said.

"That's my guess," Coventry said. "The bigger question is whether she's a live victim or a dead one." He paused and added, "I made a promise to the dead woman."

Shalifa was shocked.

"I didn't know you did that anymore," she said.

"Neither did I," he said.

"So how does this other woman, Madison Blake, fit into the promise?" Shalifa asked.

"It extends to her, by default."

She cocked her head.

"That means you're going to work my ass to the bone."

"Both of our asses," he said. "I have one too, remember."

She laughed.

"You call that an ass?" she said. "That's not an ass. That's just a place where an ass is supposed to be."

Chapter Thirteen

Day Three—June 13
Wednesday Morning

DYLAN JOOP SLEPT WITH THE DOORS of the boxcar open last night so he'd be able to hear an approaching car in the unlikely event that someone had tracked him. But no sounds cut through the black Rocky Mountain air other than the occasional howling of coyotes. He woke early morning to a rummaging noise in the corner. A black squirrel saw Joop throw the covers off, froze for a heartbeat, and scampered out the door. Joop stepped outside, took a long heaven-sent piss on a lodgepole pine, and then pounded on Madison Blake's boxcar.

"Everything okay in there?" he shouted.

Silence.

"Answer me!"

More silence, then, "I have to use the bathroom."

"In a minute," he said.

Unfortunately for Madison Blake, she managed to pull the hood off and run a good distance last night while Joop found himself busy snapping the other woman's neck. He didn't catch her until she made it around the corner of the house to the street.

Under a streetlight, to be precise.

And pulled his ski mask off in the fight.

Which gave her a good look at his face.

Meaning that release was no longer an option.

She would have to die at the end. Too bad, but she'd brought it on herself. He got the coffee pot going, showered, grabbed the .357 SIG, and then opened the heavy door of his captive's boxcar. She cowered in the corner, wearing the same look on her face as the black squirrel.

Joop grinned at the similarity.

"Get out here," he said.

She obeyed.

Now, by the light of day and up close, Joop realized how small and frail the woman was. She couldn't be taller than five-one, and probably weighed in at ninety or ninety-five. What she lacked in size she more than made up for with her eyes, big brown eyes that took up half her face, peeking out timidly from behind pitch-black hair.

Her lower lip quivered.

Very nice.

She wouldn't try to escape.

He could already tell.

He turned his back while she used the facilities, then chained her left ankle to an eyebolt in the middle boxcar and fed her cereal and coffee.

She said nothing.

And instead studied his every move.

Suddenly his cell phone rang.

He swallowed.

Dreading what was about to come.

And stepped outside to talk in private.

IT TURNED OUT HE WAS RIGHT.

The voice on the other end said, "You had some collateral damage last night, a woman by the name of Samantha Rickenbacker."

Joop kicked the dirt.

"This isn't an exact science," he said. "Sometimes things happen."

"We hire you to have things not happen," the voice said. "If we wanted things to happen, there are a hundred different people we could call."

"I have Madison Blake," Joop said. "That's what you wanted and that's what you got."

"We can't afford slop," the voice said. "That causes huge problems on our end."

Joop already knew that.

And decided not to mention the other complication, namely that Madison Blake saw his face.

HE CLOSED THE PHONE AND STOOD THERE, not knowing if the call was meant as a slap on the wrist or something a lot more serious. On the one hand, he had already established himself with years of loyal service and perfectly executed operations. On the other hand, he had broken Rule No. 1, set in stone on day one and emphasized many times thereafter.

No collateral damage.

Ever.

Understood?

Yes.

We hope so.

Also, Joop had let the woman see his face, which meant that she had to die. He didn't know if this was the beginning of the end. But one thing he did know—his job wasn't one that you got fired from and then retired to some warm place with white sand and women in bikinis bringing you little drinks with umbrellas. The end of the relationship most likely meant the end of his life.

Or at least they'd try.

Who would they send?

Probably one of Joop's counterparts. Unfortunately, he had no idea who they were. He knew there was at least one more like him, and maybe two, operating in Europe; and probably at least one more right here in the States.

But he had no idea if they were male or female.

Tall or short.

Young or old.

He needed to keep his guard up.

As if he was being hunted by the best in the world.

Starting immediately.

He also needed insurance.

Something that he could hold up and say, *Take a good look. If you kill me, this will come back to bite you in the ass.*

HE WALKED BACK TO THE BOXCAR and found Madison Blake sitting at the table exactly as he left her. Seeing her gave him an idea.

"Who wants you dead?" he asked.

Her lower lip trembled.

"What do you mean?"

"You pose a threat to somebody. Who is it?"

She looked genuinely puzzled.

"I don't know."

"Think!"

He must have had a fury in his voice because she cowered as if expecting him to strike her.

"Nobody," she said. "I'm just a maid."

"Do you sniff around when people aren't home?"

"No."

"Do you take things?"

"No."

"No?"

"No."

"Then why are you here?"

Her face trembled and then she broke into tears.

He could care less.

They meant nothing.

He grabbed her by the hair, pulled her head back and stuck the barrel of the SIG in her mouth.

"I said, why are you here?"

When she tried to mumble something, he pulled the steel out.

"I don't know," she said. "I didn't do anything wrong. All I want to do is go home. Please don't hurt me. I'm pregnant."

Chapter Fourteen

Day Three—June 13
Wednesday Morning

AT THREE IN THE MORNING, Paige crawled out of bed, fired up her computer and typed a letter, addressed to the Managing Partner of Vinson & Botts:

> The undersigned represents Ja'Von Deveraux. Ms. Deveraux was retained by Vinson & Botts (V&B) to perform services in connection with the surveillance of Robert Copeland. V&B agreed to pay Ms. Deveraux $20,000 plus expenses, whether her surveillance was successful or not. In reliance upon this agreement, Ms. Deveraux traveled to Bangkok, Thailand, and incurred expenses of $7,238. The total owed to Ms. Deveraux is $27,238, less $10,000 (paid to date), leaving a balance due and owing of $17,238. Ms. Deveraux requests payment of this outstanding balance forthwith.
>
> Very truly yours,
> Paige Alexander, Esq.
> Attorney-At-Law.

Then she went back to sleep.

AT TEN IN THE MORNING—WEARING KHAKI PANTS, a white blouse and black leather pumps—Paige pushed through the glass doors of Vinson & Botts and walked straight to the receptionist with her client, Ja'Von Deveraux, at her side.

"Who's the managing partner of the firm?" she asked.

The receptionist studied her, wondering whether to answer, and apparently saw no downside because she said, "Thomas Fog."

Paige set an envelope on the fancy glass station.

"We have a letter for Mr. Fog," she said.

The receptionist looked at it, explained that she would be sure Mr. Fog received it, and asked if there was anything else.

"We'd like it delivered now if we could," Paige said. "We're just going to wait for a reply."

"You're going to wait?"

"Right."

Then she and Ja'Von took seats on a couch at the far end of the reception area.

Paige swallowed and looked at Ja'Von.

"First blood," she said.

Ja'Von nodded.

Earlier this morning, over coffee at Starbucks, Paige had explained her strategy. The first thing they needed to do was to get V&B to admit that it had hired Ja'Von. Asking for money due and owing was the best way to get that admission.

An hour later the receptionist walked over.

"Mr. Fog has been in meetings all morning," she said. "He asked me to tell you that he'll look at the letter this afternoon and call you tomorrow."

Paige shook her head.

"Tomorrow's too late," she said. "Tomorrow we file a lawsuit as soon as the court opens. If that's what Mr. Fog wants, we're happy to leave now."

The receptionist frowned.

"Hold on a minute," she said. "Let me see how he wants to handle this."

Twenty minutes later, Paige and Ja'Von were escorted into a small conference room.

They waited there for over an hour.

Then a 40-ish pleasant-looking man wearing an expensive suit walked in and closed the door behind him. He had deep blue eyes, the kind that look at someone and understand them immediately. The kind that can tell if someone is lying or not.

Trial-lawyer eyes.

HE HAD THE HARRIED AIR OF SOMEONE trying to squeeze twenty hours of work into an eight-hour day. He shook both their hands and said, "I'm Thomas Fog and I'm very sorry to have kept you waiting. Please accept my apologies. I've read your letter, Ms. Alexander, and have had my assistant try to verify that the firm hired Ms. Deveraux."

He frowned.

"So far, we're not having any luck." Then to Ja'Von, "Who was it exactly that you spoke to?"

Ja'Von looked at Paige.

Not wanting to answer without permission.

And Paige nodded.

"The person wouldn't say," Ja'Von said.

"You have no name?"

"No."

"Did this person say they were from Vinson & Botts?"

Paige nodded her head.

"No," Ja'Von said. "He said the matter was confidential. So confidential that he didn't even want the name of the law firm in my files."

Fog cocked his head.

"So what makes you think this man was with V&B?"

"I was able to get my phone records," she said. "The calls came from a phone registered in the lobby of this building. For some reason he always gave me the impression he was with a big firm. Plus this firm is in the process of opening a Bangkok office. It's the only firm in the building that has a tie to Bangkok."

Fog looked at her hard.

Then at Paige.

"Ms. Alexander," he said, "your letter states that $10,000 has already been paid."

"That's correct," Paige said.

"Do you have a copy of a check or wire transfer or anything else to show that the payment came from V&B?"

Ja'Von jumped in.

"The payment was made in cash," she said. "It was made in that manner as part of the firm's plan to keep its involvement confidential."

Fog stood up.

Looked out the window.

And then back at them.

With a puzzled look on his face.

"You're not giving me much to go on," he said. "If the firm owes you money, Ms. Deveraux, we'll definitely pay you every penny. I trust that you can see my dilemma though." He smiled. "I'll tell you what, let me get the word out to the other attorneys regarding this matter and see if anyone knows anything about it. How's that? Fair enough? If someone steps up and says they hired you, case closed. We'll get a check to you in full right away, with our apologies." He looked at Paige. "Plus any associated attorney fees."

Paige stood up.

Ja'Von joined her.

"How much time are you looking at?" Paige asked.

He shrugged.

"I think a week should be adequate," he said.

Paige put her hands on the table and leaned across.

"We'll be back at ten o'clock tomorrow morning," she said. "You can either give us a check at that time, or I'll be marching straight down to Denver District Court to file a complaint."

Fog looked as if he was about to say something harsh.

Instead he said, "I'll see what I can find out by then."

Paige turned and walked out of the room.

Trying to catch her breath.

And not pass out.

DOWN AT STREET LEVEL, Ja'Von asked, "Why the rush?"

"The more time we give them," Paige said, "the more time they have to come up with some brilliant plan. Our best chance is to get them running and hope they stumble over their own feet."

"You think they will?"

"Run, yes, stumble, no," Paige said. "How'd I do? Did I look like a real attorney? I was so nervous that I felt like passing out.

I had a picture of you having to drag me out by my arms, cave-man style."

Ja'Von hugged her around the shoulders.

"You *are* a real attorney, honey," she said. "I knew it the first time I saw you. Vinson & Botts is about to learn it, too. And then, sooner or later, at some point down the road, you'll know it yourself." She chuckled and added, "I couldn't believe it when you leaned across the table and stared him down. Where did that come from?"

Paige laughed.

"I don't know," she said. "It just happened."

Ja'Von pointed her face to the sun and spun around.

"I'm starved," she said. "Let's go to the Hard Rock Café, my treat. I want to tell you about this man I met."

Chapter Fifteen

Day Three—June 13
Wednesday Afternoon

THE SEARCH OF THE ARVADA APARTMENT shared by the victim, Samantha Rickenbacker, and the missing woman, Madison Blake, turned up nothing to suggest that either woman had any enemies of significance or that either had done anything to warrant being a murder target. No drugs were found. According to their bank statements and bills, they weren't rich but lived within their means.

Coventry found a store-bought pregnancy kit in the bathroom cabinet, waved it at Shalifa, then opened the box and found it only half full.

Then he looked down at the trashcan.

And frowned.

It was full.

He dumped the contents in the bathtub but found no used samplers.

"I love going through trash for nothing," he said. "Be sure we get a pregnancy test on the victim."

"Why?" Shalifa asked.

"Because if she's pregnant then I'm really going to be bent out of shape," he said. "And if she's not, that means Madison Blake may be."

"In which case you're going to be bent," Shalifa said.

Coventry nodded.

"Right."

"So either way, you're going to be bent."

He raked his hair back with his fingers and said, "Right, but I want to know why."

FROM THE APARTMENT, they took Wadsworth south to the 6th Avenue freeway, headed west and turned left at the Colfax Avenue interchange just as Jimmy Buffet's "Why Don't We Get Drunk?" came on the radio.

Coventry turned it up.

Home Depot appeared almost immediately on their left. When he drove past it, Shalifa looked at him weird and said, "You just passed it, cowboy."

"Two things," he said. "First, you can never stop the car when a Jimmy Buffet song is playing. Second, I smell coffee up the road."

Shalifa rolled her eyes.

"Jimmy Buffet? You need to get some rap music in this truck, Coventry. Something that makes you want to stand up and shake your ass."

"I don't have an ass, remember?"

Five minutes later, with a thermos full of 7-Eleven coffee in hand, Coventry doubled back to the Home Depot parking lot and killed the engine.

They cut through the garden department.

Coventry picked a lily on the way and handed it to Shalifa.

"What am I supposed to do with this?"

He didn't know.

Inside, they got directed to Samantha Rickenbacker's immediate supervisor, a man named Ben Adams who owned a head full of really bad hair-plugs and a mouth full of yellow teeth. He wore a stained asparagus-green T-shirt that looked like it hadn't come off in twenty years.

Adams and his co-workers portrayed Samantha as a friendly, conscientious worker who always reported on time and wore a smile. She never showed up drunk or high or unreasonably stressed or distracted. From what they knew, she didn't party all that much and definitely wasn't into the club scene. She didn't have a boyfriend at the moment, or in recent months, that anyone was aware of.

Walking back to the truck Coventry said, "She's just your basic, really nice young lady."

"I didn't know they made those anymore."

When Coventry fired up the truck, Shalifa flicked the radio stations until she got a hip-hop song.

"Finally," she said. "Real music."

Coventry grunted.

"There's a Beach Boys song playing in there somewhere, and you're wasting it."

BACK AT THE CRIME SCENE, Coventry wrote down what he had forgotten before, namely the name and number of the realtor on the sign in the front yard. As they walked towards the back of the house, he called the man.

Jim Hansen.

He wasn't in, so Coventry left a message.

Suddenly a woman emerged from around the corner of the house and joined them in the backyard. She appeared to be about fifty, an ex-cheerleader type, with bottle-blond hair and a few more pounds than she had in high school. She carried a book called *Deadly Laws*.

"Are you the police?" she asked.

Coventry nodded.

"We are."

"I'm Becky Moon," she said. "I live across the street. When I got home I found a note on my door to call some officer named Adam Woods. When I saw you over here, I thought I'd just come over and talk in person."

Shalifa said, "That'll work," and pulled out a pen and spiral notebook.

Then interviewed the woman.

Who had an interesting observation.

"Yesterday, there was a car parked in front of this house," she said. "About two o'clock. I just took it to be someone who was looking at the house."

"What kind of car?"

"Foreign," she said. "My brother works for Ford so we always buy American. I have this habit, whenever I see a car, of seeing if it's American. The car I saw here yesterday wasn't."

"Do you know what kind it was?" Shalifa asked.

The woman shook her head.

"I don't know anything about foreign cars and don't want to," she said. Then she turned to Coventry. "I see you drive a Toyota."

"It's made in the U.S.," Coventry said.

"It is?"

He nodded.

"Indiana or Illinois, I can't remember which," he said.

"I didn't know that."

Coventry raked his hair back with his fingers. It immediately flopped back down over his forehead.

"Would you recognize the car, if we showed you pictures?" he asked.

"No."

"What color was it?"

"Something medium."

"Medium?"

"Right," she said. "It wasn't anything real light colored, like white or silver. And it wasn't anything too dark either."

"Red?"

"It could have been."

"Blue?"

"It could have been."

"Brown?"

"Same thing," she said. "It wasn't white and it wasn't black. Sorry, that's about the best I can do."

"Did you see the person driving it?"

"No," she said. "I didn't see any people, only the car."

COVENTRY'S PHONE RANG. It turned out to be the realtor, Jim Hansen, returning Coventry's call. He hadn't heard about the murder and when Coventry told him he said, "Perfect. Now no one will buy that stupid place."

"Why not?"

"Ghosts," Hansen said. "People won't buy a house if there's been a suicide or a murder."

"That's not rational," Coventry said.

"It doesn't matter."

In addition to the ghost information, Hansen had a few other interesting tidbits. The owners had already moved to California more than two months ago. Hansen hadn't shown the house in more than two weeks. He did not, repeat not, call Molly Maids and request a cleaning. Why would he? Nor would the owners have had a reason to do so.

"You sound familiar," Coventry said. "Do I know you?"

"I don't think so."

"That's weird," Coventry said. "For some reason I have the feeling I know you."

ON THE DRIVE BACK TO HEADQUARTERS, Shalifa reset all the radio buttons in the Tundra to hip-hop stations.

"At first I thought that this whole thing may have just been a spur-of-the-moment sexual attack," Coventry said. "Now I'm pretty sure we're dealing with a premeditated plan. And I think the intended victim was Madison Blake and not Samantha Rickenbacker."

Shalifa looked at him.

"Why do you say that?"

"Here's my theory," he said. "The guy already knew that Madison Blake worked for Molly Maids. Her apartment complex is too congested for a killing or abduction. So he wanted to lure her somewhere quiet and dark. He scoped out this house during the day, looked in the windows and saw the rooms empty, and knew that no one would be around at night. Then he called Madison Blake and arranged for her to show up here after hours to make a little extra spending money. He didn't want to break into the house, because that would be one more layer of complication, which meant that he couldn't open the front door for her. So he told her to come around to the back. When she did, he was waiting for her and attacked. What he didn't foresee is that her roommate would be with her."

Shalifa nodded.

"That all fits," she said. "If you're right, then the car in front of the house yesterday definitely belongs to our guy."

"Yes it does."

"It also means that someone went to an awful lot of trouble."

"Yes it does again."

"Why?"

"That's what we need to concentrate on," Coventry said. "Motive."

Shalifa smiled.

"That and the other thing," she said.

Coventry cocked his head.

"What other thing?"

"Her phone records," Shalifa said. "The man was here scouting out the house at two in the afternoon. Samantha Rickenbacker got killed between nine and ten. That means that somewhere between two and nine, someone called Madison Blake and talked her into coming here."

Coventry beamed.

Then felt his face sag.

"What?" Shalifa asked.

"This guy's smart," Coventry said. "He would have called from a public payphone, and one where there's no surveillance cameras. We need to run it down, obviously, but that's what we're going to find out."

Jim Michael Hansen

"Which brings us back to motive," Shalifa said.

Coventry nodded.

"Something was definitely going on in Madison Blake's plain-vanilla life that wasn't so plain-vanilla," he said. "We need to figure out what it was."

Chapter Sixteen

Day Three—June 13
Wednesday Afternoon

————————————

DYLAN JOOP PARKED THE AUDI AT THE TURNOFF near the base of the cliff, the same one he fell off Monday evening, and laced his climbing shoes while his heart raced. A cloudless blue Colorado sky floated above. The June temperature was absolutely perfect, 82 and counting. This time, unlike the prior two times, he pulled out a pair of Bushnell auto-focus binoculars and studied the formation.

He found a path.

A path that stunk.

But one that just might be feasible, with a bit of luck.

He stretched, took a deep breath and said, *Let's see what you got.* Then he started up, staying to the left, concentrating on nothing other than being a perfect climbing machine.

He made it to the twenty-five foot mark.

Then the thirty.

And kept going.

At thirty-five feet he had passed too many spots that wouldn't be kind to anyone stupid enough to downclimb. The only

89

way off the face was up.

At fifty feet he was getting close to the top and found a nice place to wedge himself and get his breath. Suddenly his cell phone rang. The sound shocked him because he didn't know he'd left it in his pocket.

He pulled it out and answered.

"We have a situation," the voice said. "Something we need you to hop on right away."

"I thought I was too sloppy for your taste," Joop said.

A pause on the other end.

"Are you in or not?"

"We never talked about my retirement," Joop said.

"Meaning what?"

"Meaning that when I'm done, for whatever reason, I become a liability instead of an asset. You'd be better off if I didn't exist at that point," he said.

A black-and-white magpie flew by.

"Do you speak French?" the voice asked.

He didn't.

"Why?"

"You have a counterpart in France who retired five years ago," the voice said. "I'm going to have him contact you so you can see he's still alive."

Joop considered it.

He'd need to be sure it wasn't a charade, but felt confident that he'd be able to tell.

"You do that," he said.

"Expect the call," the voice said. "In the meantime, like I said, we have a situation."

Chapter Seventeen

Day Three—June 13
Wednesday Night

—————————

IT WAS ALMOST DARK when Paige's shift at Sam's Eatery ended, not a minute too soon. The manager's philosophy today seemed to be that the beatings would continue until morale improved. Paige peddled the Trek over to the Colfax bus stop and sat on the bench next to a young Hispanic woman who didn't answer her cell phone even though it rang every thirty seconds. Paige sensed a boyfriend on the other end, one who just got dumped.

Probably a cheater.

Paige looked at the woman and said, "Screw him."

"Exactly."

When the RTD bus finally showed up, Paige put the Trek in the bike rack, flashed her pass to the driver and took a seat near the front. The vehicle shuddered and shook with protest as it pulled into traffic and the pungent smell of diesel intensified.

She was anxious to get home.

To work the Internet.

And find out what she could on Vinson & Botts.

Plus Bob Copeland.

She got off at the Union/Simms stop, which still left her a two-mile peddle to her Lakewood apartment. Twilight had given way to darkness, causing the streetlights to kick on ten minutes ago.

She flicked the switch for the Trek's rear light.

Nothing happened.

She jiggled it.

Still nothing.

The batteries must be dead.

SIMMS WAS A FAIRLY MAJOR LAKEWOOD ROAD, two lanes in each direction, and well lit. She hugged the edge, like always, and kept a good lookout for idiots armed with cars as she got the bike going as fast as she could. Unfortunately, she seemed out-numbered tonight.

Then, damn!

Headlights were right behind her.

Coming fast.

She sensed an impact. Some primitive survival gene from a deep part of her brain made her immediately jerk the handlebars to the right.

The front tire hit the curb.

And sent her flying over the side of the bike.

A white-hot pain immediately exploded from her kneecap.

And her forearm scraped against something jagged.

She focused on the car as soon as she stopped tumbling. There was no good reason for it to come so close. It was the only one heading this direction. There were no vehicles in the lane next to it. Either the driver completely didn't see her or didn't give a rat's ass.

"Idiot!" she shouted.

The vehicle suddenly decelerated at a dangerous rate, squealed around the corner, and disappeared down a side street.

Her forearm, raw and bloody, began to throb with pain. She brushed dirt and gravel out of the wound and knew that it would need a serious cleaning once she got home.

Her kneecap felt like someone had taken a hammer to it.

It didn't want to bend.

But it had been banged plenty of times in the past and she recognized it as a temporary injury in spite of the pain.

The front tire of the bike was flat.

Home was a mile down the road.

She started to walk it home, limping, keeping her right leg stiff at the knee.

When she got to the side street, the vehicle was thirty yards down, sitting there with the lights on, almost as if it was waiting for her. She hurried across the street and kept going as fast as she could.

When she looked behind her, the vehicle was at the corner.

It paused.

As if watching her.

Then it squealed to the left and disappeared in the opposite direction.

WHEN SHE GOT BACK TO HER APARTMENT, she called Ja'Von Deveraux and said, "Remember when I said *first blood* this morning?"

Ja'Von remembered.

"Well now we have *second blood.*"

Then she told Ja'Von the story.

"It could have just been some drunk," Ja'Von said. "Hell, I almost get run over three times a day."

"Maybe," Paige said, "but watch your back tonight. If they're after me then they're probably after you too."

"Nothing strange has happened at my end," Ja'Von said. "Are we still on for tomorrow?"

Paige studied her forearm in the mirror and said, "You better believe it."

Then she sat down at the computer and drafted a Complaint.

Ja'Von Deveraux v. Vinson & Botts, Denver District Court, Denver, Colorado.

Third blood.

Chapter Eighteen

Day Three—June 13
Wednesday Evening

———————

AN HOUR AFTER ALL THE SANE PEOPLE in the office had gone home, Bryson Coventry's stomach growled and his concentration waned. He twisted a pencil and, for a second, considered shoring himself up with another cup of coffee. But when he held his hand out to see how bad the caffeine shook his fingers, he figured he'd probably had enough. So instead he called Ja'Von and asked where she was.

The answer surprised him.

"In your kitchen."

"My kitchen?"

"Cooking you dinner," she said.

When he walked in the front door twenty minutes later, rap music came from the radio and a mouth-watering garlic aroma wove through the air. Ja'Von was in the kitchen, singing.

Barefoot.

She wore thin, flimsy white shorts that did little to hide an incredibly taut ass.

"Spaghetti," she said.

He shook his head and looked at her strangely.

"What?" she asked.

"You know the words to this song?"

She did.

"I've never even heard it and you know the words to it," he said. "How did you get such bad taste in music?"

She stuck her tongue out.

"This dinner comes with a price," she warned.

"What kind of price?"

"After we eat, you have to take me somewhere to do something that I've never done before."

"Like what?"

"I don't know," she said. "That's for you to decide. Take me on a new adventure. Expand my universe. It doesn't have to be anything big or mind-blowing, just something I've never done before. I'm putty in your hands."

He came up behind her, reached around and put his hands on her stomach.

"You don't feel like putty," he said.

"Try some of the other places," she said.

AFTER GETTING A GUT FULL of the best spaghetti and garlic bread in the universe, Coventry made Ja'Von sit on the couch and promise not to watch as he carried mysterious stuff from the lower level and threw it in the back of the Tundra.

Plus two bottles of wine.

Then they took C-470 east, exited at Wadsworth, and pulled into the parking lot of the Chatfield Marina shortly before dark. They carried sleeping bags and overnight items to a 30-foot Hunter sailboat moored at the end of E-Dock.

The boat rocked as Coventry stepped on board and held his hand out to steady Ja'Von. "This isn't mine," he said. "It belongs to a friend."

Ja'Von was impressed.

"I need a friend like that," she said.

Coventry fired up the inboard diesel but left the sails wrapped. Then they motored over to the no-wake zone at the south end of the lake. He dropped the anchor in 15 feet of water and let out 150 feet of rope. A sunset began to form over the Rocky Mountains, no more than a mile or two to their west. Not a wisp of wind disturbed the air and the water didn't show a single ripple.

Ja'Von had never anchored out in a boat overnight.

So Coventry's debt to her for dinner was officially satisfied.

The lake was pretty much theirs and theirs alone.

The fishermen were either over by the dam or heading to the loading ramps.

They nestled into the cushions and watched the sunset, sipping white wine from plastic glasses. Coventry told her about the Madison Blake case and his frustration of not being able to find someone with a motive.

"My guess is this," Ja'Von said. "She either snooped around while she was cleaning someone's house and ended up seeing something she shouldn't have, or else she just flat out took something."

Coventry had already thought of that.

And told her.

"We got the names of the owners of all the houses that she had cleaned for the last year," he said. "None of them filed a police report or complained to Molly Maids regarding anything stolen or missing. As for her seeing something she shouldn't, I

97

can't think of a good way to ferret that out."

Ja'Von tried to think of a way.

And couldn't.

"Unless she was blackmailing someone," he added. "But we haven't found any tangible evidence to suggest that."

"No big deposits into her bank account, no new cars, nothing like that?" Ja'Von asked.

"Nada," he said.

"Was she out shopping for anything expensive?"

"Same thing," he said. "Not that we know of."

"Weird."

"She might be pregnant," he added. "If she is, maybe some rich married guy is responsible and doesn't want the wife to find out, much less pay child support. But again, that's just a theory. We have no evidence."

He studied the sunset as the last of the color disappeared.

Then Ja'Von said, "I have another thought."

Suddenly his cell phone rang.

IT TURNED OUT TO BE DR. LEANNE SANDERS, the FBI profiler from Quantico, Virginia. He pulled up an image of a classy woman, about fifty, with shapely step-master legs. The kind of legs on the covers of noir crime books, the kind of legs men kill for.

"I'm heading to Denver," she said. "I thought it only fair to warn you."

"Why? What's going on?"

She exhaled.

"It's a long story and I'll fill you in when I get there," she said. "In a nutshell, INTERPOL has their sights on a Frenchman named Jean-Paul Boudiette. He's headed to Denver and so am I."

HE HUNG UP, looked at Ja'Von and said, "Sorry for the interruption. You were telling me that you had another thought."

She nodded.

"Two thoughts, actually," she said.

"Shoot."

"Your whole premise about Madison Blake may be wrong," she said. "You're looking for someone with a motive to harm her."

"Exactly."

"Well, maybe she isn't the target at all," Ja'Von said. "Maybe she's just a pawn to get someone else to do something."

"What do you mean? That she's being held for ransom or something?"

"Right, something like that. She's not the end, she's the means to the end."

Coventry was impressed.

Very impressed.

And said so.

"Then you're really going to like my second thought," Ja'Von said.

"Which is what?"

"Which is this." She stood up, pulled her T-shirt over her head, unfastened her bra and tossed it behind her. The tiny bit of light that was left from the sunset landed on her breasts and stomach and arms with a warm golden patina.

She ran her hands through her hair.

Coventry swallowed.

He had never seen such a perfect body.

Well, that wasn't true.

He had.

But he had never wanted a woman so badly.

That *was* true.

She took a long sip of wine—no, not a sip, a drink—and then set the cup to the side and straddled him. Her weight felt so incredibly perfect.

So very right.

And when she brought her mouth to his, and held her lips an inch away, so teasingly, her essence filled the universe.

There was nothing else.

Only her.

Chapter Nineteen

Day Four—June 14
Thursday Morning

THURSDAY MORNING, WITH THE EXHILERANCE of yesterday's successful climb still flowing through his veins, Joop let Madison Blake use the facilities, fed her, gave her a sedative and waited until it took effect. Then he carried her into the boxcar, chained her left ankle to the inside just for good measure, locked the door from the outside, and pointed the Audi out of the mountains towards the Denver skyline.

He bought a cup of leaded at Starbucks and sipped it on the way back to his LoDo loft.

The Rocky Mountain News reported a short article about the death of Samantha Rickenbacker and the disappearance of Madison Blake on Tuesday night.

Photographs of both women were provided.

He hadn't gotten a very good look at the surprise woman—Samantha Rickenbacker—on the night in question.

Her picture was pretty nice.

Too bad.

The coffee pot gurgled with the unmistakable sound of the

101

last drops of water falling into the pot. He filled a cup and then fired up the Gateway to work the Internet.

Looking for anything that would disclose the identity of his European counterpart—the person most likely to be sent to kill him if the decision was made to take him out.

Mid-morning his phone rang.

A FRENCHMAN NAMED VARDON ST. GERMAINE said, "I was asked to contact you. The word is you're nervous about what happens when the relationship ends."

The man spoke good English.

With an accent but not much.

Joop paced.

He hadn't expected an actual call.

"Go on," he said.

"I retired five years ago," St. Germaine said. "They went their way and I went mine. It was as if neither of us ever existed. That's all there is to it."

Joop walked out onto the terrace.

Down below people moved like ants.

"How do I know you're legitimate?" he asked. "How do I know you're who you say you are?"

St. Germaine laughed.

"You don't," he said. "And you above all people know that I'd never tell you anything that would associate me, or them, with an event."

"Would you trust you, if you were me?" Joop asked.

The man didn't hesitate.

"I don't trust easily," he said. "And neither do you. So the point is moot. I will say this, though. I was told since day one to never, ever have or create any documentary proof or evidence of what I've done. I assume you've been told the same."

Joop had.

And admitted it.

"They take that obligation very seriously," the Frenchman said. "When I first retired, I had the same concerns as you, namely that they would be much better off if I was dead. Quietly dead. That's the big concern in your mind right now, if I understand the situation correctly."

True.

It was.

"At first," St. Germaine said, "I thought about setting something down in writing, you know, dates, names, events, stuff like that—an insurance policy, in effect. You know, make the kind of document that would create a lot of collateral damage if someone decided to take me out and the police found it after the fact, say in my safe deposit box or mailed anonymously to the police by one of my relatives or friends. But I resisted the urge, and in hindsight that was the best decision I ever made."

"So stick with the rules, is what you're telling me," Joop said.

"Exactly," St. Germaine said. "Stick with the rules."

Joop chuckled.

"What?"

"That's exactly what they would want me to do if they were going to take me out," Joop said.

"That's true," St. Germaine said. "Ironic, isn't it? The best way to stay alive is to make yourself fully vulnerable and then sit back and hope you made the right decision. The question is— do you have that kind of trust?"

"No," Joop said.

St. Germaine laughed.

"Neither did I, but I did it anyway."

His voice trailed off, as if the conversation was concluded.

"Tell me one thing," Joop said. "Who replaced you?"

The Frenchman hesitated.

Clearly deciding.

Then he said, "That goes against the rules. I'd be putting myself in jeopardy."

"Only if they found out," Joop said. "You trusted them. Now trust me. I'm giving you my word that no one will ever know you told me. I'll never mention the man's name to any-one."

St. Germaine exhaled.

"He goes by several names. I have only heard one of them—Jean-Paul Boudiette."

"Can you describe him?"

"No," St. Germaine said. "I've never seen him. I've only heard his name, and that was just once, more than four years ago." He paused and then added, "I hope that I don't later learn that I misplaced my trust in you."

"You won't," Joop assured him.

"We are a special breed, you and I," the Frenchman said. "Stay true to the cause and everything will work out the way it should."

"At least it did for you," Joop said.

"Oui."

AN HOUR LATER HIS PHONE RANG AGAIN. This time it was his contact who said, "Did you get a phone call?"

He did.

"And?"

"And I feel better," Joop said.

Only half true.

But the right words to say.

"Good. The important thing right now is to stay focused on Madison Blake. This other subject won't even be relevant for another ten or twenty years."

"Fine."

"Don't take that as a license to have any more collateral damage though," the voice said.

"I understand."

"We all make mistakes," the voice said. "But we need to keep them to an absolute minimum."

"I understand."

"Actually," the voice said, "don't ever repeat this because I'll deny it. But so far, you've done an incredible job. In fact, I think it's time to raise your compensation. By the way, we're probably going to have a decision as to what to do with the woman soon, maybe as early as this afternoon. If we decide she needs to die, we're not going to want her body found—ever. So start giving that some thought."

Chapter Twenty

Day Four—June 14
Thursday Morning

THURSDAY MORNING, a few minutes before ten, Paige Alexander muscled her bicycle through the heavy doors at the bottom of the Cash Register Building in the heart of Denver's financial district, and walked through the fancy lobby towards the elevator banks. She wore the same clothes as yesterday, except this time she also wore a backpack. Inside it was a Complaint.

A security guard trotted over and intercepted her.

"Sorry, no bicycles are allowed in the building."

She looked at him as if everything was okay.

"This is evidence in a case," she said. "It's going up to Vinson & Botts."

The man hesitated and then said, "Okay."

Ja'Von was waiting for her by the elevator banks with a puzzled look. "What's with the bike?" she asked.

"It's symbolic," Paige said.

"Symbolic, how?"

"A show of defiance."

Ja'Von cocked her head. "It shows my lawyer rides a bicycle," she said. "If we're trying to scare the pants off them, I'm not sure that's the best way to do it."

Paige grinned.

"It's my way of saying I know they were behind the incident last night," she said.

"But you don't know that," Ja'Von said.

"Not a hundred percent," Paige admitted. "But I will after I see their reaction."

UNFORTUNATELY, HOWEVER, THOMAS FOG didn't react at all when he walked into the conference room carrying a large manila envelope in his hand, even though the bike leaned against the wall and grabbed his attention for a heartbeat.

He wore a blue silk tie and summer-weight suit.

"Thank you for coming," he said. "Your time is valuable, so let me get right to the point. We've researched the issue as best we could in the time you've given us. We can't find any evidence that anyone from the firm hired Ms. Deveraux."

Paige frowned.

But Fog smiled.

"Nevertheless," he added, "Ms. Deveraux appears, to my mind at least, to honestly believe that this firm hired her. We're prepared to give her the benefit of the doubt in the name of resolving this matter quickly and fully so we can all go on to more important things."

He pulled a check out of the envelope.

Twenty thousand dollars.

Payable to the order of Ja'Von Deveraux.

"We added a couple of thousand to cover any associated attorney fees," he said. Paige handed the check to Ja'Von for her inspection. "So, I think that concludes our business."

Paige cocked her head.

Something was wrong.

But she couldn't put her finger on it.

Then Fog pulled a stapled set of papers out of the envelope. About four pages.

He slid the document across the table to Ja'Von as he looked at Paige and said, "We'll need Ms. Deveraux to sign a release, of course, just so all the paperwork is in order."

Ja'Von pulled a pen out of her purse and started flipping to the last page.

"Hold on," Paige said. Then to Fog, "You don't mind if we read this first, I assume."

He looked at his watch. "Of course not. Why don't we do this? You read it and talk to your client about it while I duck back to my office and return a few phone calls. Then we'll wrap things up."

Fine.

WHEN FOG STEPPED OUT, Paige whispered in Ja'Von's ear, "This room could be bugged a thousand different ways. Let's go down to the lobby so we can talk in private."

They left the bike against the wall.

And the check on the table.

Then headed down to the lobby, bought coffee and took a table in the indoor courtyard under a large green umbrella. After Paige read the release she tossed it on the table, took a swallow of coffee, and smiled.

"I thought so."

"What do you mean?"

"This release isn't something that just acknowledges that you've received payment in full for P.I. services rendered," Paige said. "It's a thousand times broader than that."

"What do you mean?"

"What I mean is, it's a full release of any and all claims that you might possibly have against the law firm, known or unknown, for whatever reason, from the beginning of time until present." She studied Ja'Von's face and added, "What that means is, if you really do have a claim for conspiracy, this release would bar you from bringing it."

"So what are you saying? That they know we're thinking about other claims and are trying to cut them off at the knees by buying us out on the contract claim?"

Paige nodded.

"That's exactly what I'm saying," she said.

"Well, we can't have that," Ja'Von said.

Paige shook her head.

"No we can't, can we?"

Chapter Twenty-One

Day Four—June 14
Thursday Morning

THE WIND KICKED UP DURING THE NIGHT, churning the lake into a sloppy chop. Ja'Von slept through it but Bryson Coventry was already half awake, worrying about Madison Blake, and ended up climbing topside several times to be sure the anchor was holding.

Each time the 25# CQR was still cemented to the bottom.

The boat had swung south but wasn't drifting.

He dressed before dawn, pulled the anchor and motored into the marina through the dark, managing to dock the vessel without scraping the hull in spite of the wind. Then they drove home. He showered, slapped Ja'Von on the ass and headed for the door. Ja'Von grabbed him by the arm, pulled him back inside and wrestled him to the floor.

"I want rug burns," she said.

Coventry rolled her over, pinned her down and kissed her.

"Tonight," he said. "I'm already late."

"Now."

"Tonight," he repeated. "Be warned."

HE ATE SOGGY CEREAL IN THE TUNDRA as he drove to headquarters.

Traffic was thin.

Most of the maniac drivers were still asleep.

Not all of them, but most.

Coffee.

Lots of coffee.

That's what he needed.

And not later.

Now.

Right this minute.

He got to work before anyone else, as usual, and fired up the coffee machine. Waiting, he noticed that his shirt was buttoned crooked and decided that right now, before coffee, he didn't care. As soon as the stream started falling, he put his cup under it but only filled it halfway, and cut the rest with hot water and cream.

Ah, delicious.

It immediately flowed into his veins and started to make the world right. The FBI profiler, Leanne Sanders, Ph.D., walked into the room fifteen minutes later, looked at the pot and said, "That last cup's mine."

She wore an expensive summer dress-suit.

A diamond the size of a small planet weighted her left hand.

The hem of her skirt fell five inches above her knees.

Not too high to be improper.

But high enough to accentuate the shapeliest pair of legs to walk the planet. Coventry scooped her up in his right arm and swung her around.

She stood back.

Looked at him.

And made a weird face.

Then she undid his buttons and re-buttoned them properly.

"Good thing I'm here to take care of you," she said, patting his chest.

"You have no idea."

She looked at him again, as if sensing something hidden but not being able to put her finger on it. Then she said, "God, I don't believe it. You're in lust again. I can see it on your face."

He grinned.

"Something like that," he said.

HE TOLD HER ABOUT THE MADISON BLAKE CASE as he made another pot of coffee, hoping she'd shed light on the matter. She listened patiently and asked, "Any chance she has rich relatives or a rich boyfriend? Maybe they got a ransom demand we're not aware of."

Coventry grunted.

"Nothing like that," he said. "The whole thing just baffles me. It's too weird to be a garden-variety abduction. Someone went to too much trouble. There's something sinister going on that I just can't get my arms around."

She gave him a sympathetic look.

Then checked her watch.

"Have to run," she said. "My target lands at DIA in two hours."

"Tell me about him," Coventry said. "What's his name again?"

"Jean-Paul Boudiette."

"Right, him," he said. "What's INTERPOL want with him?"

She stood up, kissed him on the cheek, headed for the door and said over her shoulder, "Suspicion of murder. I'll call you later."

Coventry watched her as she walked.

Just before she got to the door, Shalifa Netherwood entered the room, hugged Leanne and said, "Did you know that the guy behind you is staring at your ass?"

Leanne looked at Coventry.

Then back at Shalifa.

"I thought I felt something," she said.

Shalifa chuckled. "Hell, even I felt it, and he wasn't even looking at me."

AFTER DR. SANDERS LEFT, Shalifa poured a cup of coffee and plopped down in one of the two worn-out leather chairs in front of Coventry's equally worn-out desk. "I've been checking up on Ja'Von Deveraux," she said.

Coventry winced.

"Don't do that," he said.

She ignored him.

"She's legit," Shalifa said. "She really is a duly licensed California P.I. The only thing out of the ordinary that I noted is that she made a police report a couple of months ago. It seems that both her house and her office were broken into. Her computers disappeared and so did a lot of her files. Maybe that has something to do with why she's relocating to Denver."

Coventry frowned.

He didn't care.

"You really have to stop telling me this stuff," he said. "I don't want to know things about people unless they want me to."

She shrugged.

And pulled an envelope out of her purse.

"I have the police reports if you want to see them," she said.

He shook his head.

"Shred them," he said.

"Really?"

"Now," he said.

She walked over to the shredder and stuffed the envelope in.

"Happy?"

"No," he said. "I'll be happy when we find Madison Blake." The oversized industrial clock on the wall, the one with the twitchy second hand, drew his eye for a heartbeat. "She's our primary focus today," he said. "We need to get real brilliant, real fast."

Chapter Twenty-Two

Day Four—June 14
Thursday Afternoon

AT THE BOXCARS, DYLAN JOOP SHOT THE BOW until his arm screamed from repeatedly pulling back the 45-pound string. A bright blue Colorado sky floated above and the pines charged the air with a wonderful, sticky-sweet aroma that only exists in the mountains. The sunshine, as always, went straight to his brain and brightened everything.

Last night he convinced himself that his back was marked.

That he was a dead-man walking.

Now, in the daylight, he wasn't so sure.

He hoped not.

He had worked long and hard to get his life to a perfect state.

The call he was waiting for came mid-afternoon. "Is the woman awake?"

"She is."

"Did you prepare her?"

"Of course."

"Okay. Let's do it."

"Fine. Hold on."

JOOP POUNDED ON THE BOXCAR WITH A CLOSED FIST, unlocked the Master padlock, rolled the heavy door open far enough to enter, and waved an eight-inch serrated knife at his captive—Madison Blake—as he climbed in. She cowered in the corner and peered out with frightened eyes from behind greasy black hair.

"Time to talk," Joop told her. "Remember, don't say a word until I give the go-ahead. Are we clear on that?"

"Yes."

"What?"

"Yes."

"I hope so," he said. "Otherwise there's going to be some serious drama."

She swallowed.

"Are you still there?" Joop questioned into the phone.

"Yeah," the voice said. "Go ahead and put the phone up to her ear. I'm going to patch our caller in. Once I do, don't say anything. I don't want him to hear your voice." Joop sat down next to the woman, got his ear next to hers and put the phone between them.

"Be good," he said.

A MAN'S VOICE CAME THROUGH, one that Joop had never heard before. "Who am I speaking to?" the man asked.

Joop's captive looked at him.

Seeking permission to answer.

Joop nodded.

116

"This is Madison Blake," she said.

"Are you the same Madison Blake who works for Molly Maids?"

Joop nodded consent.

"Yes."

"Are you okay?"

"Yes."

"What is your social security number?"

Joop nodded.

"750-293-8286," she said. "No, wait, 750-923-8286."

"Where do you live?"

She told him.

"What color are your curtains?"

"Blue."

"You have a window facing the back parking lot, correct?"

"Yes."

"There's a sticker on that window. What's it say?"

"I don't remember a sticker," she said.

"Think."

She did and then remembered.

"It says, *Warning—Guarded by Attack Ferrets.* It's not ours. The previous renters put it there."

The line went dead.

JOOP SMILED, PATTED THE WOMAN on her head and said, "You did good. Did you recognize the person talking to you?"

"No."

"You don't have any idea who he was?"

"No. Who was he?"

Joop shrugged.

"I don't know," he said.

She looked hesitant, as if she wanted to ask him something but was afraid.

"What is it?" Joop asked.

"Can I come outside for a while? I don't like being alone in here in the dark. I won't do anything wrong, I promise."

Joop stood up and shook his head.

"No," he said.

Then he hopped out, closed the door and relocked it, picturing the darkness closing in on the woman.

FIVE MINUTES LATER HIS CELL PHONE RANG.

"That went well," the voice said. "I was afraid that she'd shout something out."

"I had a knife by her face," Joop said.

"Good move. I'll be in touch. Remember, we're not going to want her body found if we decide to kill her."

Joop nodded.

"I already have a place," he said.

Chapter Twenty-Three

Day Four—June 14
Thursday Evening

THE WIND KICKED UP AFTER SUPPER and then the rain came. Paige Alexander and her client, Ja'Von Deveraux, wound through the side streets of Lakewood with the windshield wipers on full blast until they became confident that no one followed. They ended up in a dim hole-in-the-wall bar on Union, sipping bad wine and nibbling pretzels, in the booth near the restrooms.

Ja'Von's treat.

Outside the weather pounded on the building.

Soft country-western music played, barely audible above the storm, just enough to dampen the air.

Paige kept her back to the seat.

And one eye on the door.

"The big question we have at this point is—how do we proceed?" Paige said. "I have to admit, when you first told me your theory, I didn't think we'd actually find anything to support it. I mean, face it, most law firms aren't in the slave trade business."

Ja'Von cocked her head.

119

"Most law firms aren't international in scope," she said. "They don't have the connections."

"True, but still—"

"Having been there, I can tell you one thing," Ja'Von said. "It's very lucrative. There's a real demand for tall, blond women like me in that part of the world. Lots of men are looking for a different flavor and are willing to pay insane money to get it. There's a lot of sick little perverts out there with deep wallets."

Paige nodded.

"How sick exactly? Give me an example."

Ja'Von retreated in thought. A deep-seated seriousness washed over her face. Then she told a story so vivid and detailed that Paige felt as if she was right there.

JA'VON WOKE UP NERVOUS, primarily because they hadn't booked a single session for her yesterday, and in fact let her spend most of the day getting sun and stretching her legs outside in the courtyard. That wasn't because she hadn't been demanded.

She had.

No doubt about that.

No, it was because they wanted her well rested and in good shape for today.

Meaning something brutal.

For an important client.

One who would reach deep in his pocket.

And would expect an equal amount in return.

They didn't come for her until mid-morning, after she had paced back and forth in her cell for hours. They took her to a dungeon she hadn't seen before—bigger than the others and stocked with more devices.

No doubt reserved for special clients.

Unlike the prior times, they didn't fasten her down any-where. Five minutes after they left, an Asian man entered, about fifty years old, with thinning black hair and a stern look.

He was short.

Incredibly short.

No more than five-one or two.

And thin.

Her first thought was that she could take him in a fair fight. Her second thought was that she better not try. Something in his eyes was wrong, off, diseased almost.

"I have purchased you for the whole day," he said. The words didn't surprise her as much as the fact that he spoke English, very good English in fact. "You will do everything I say without protest. Things are going to be bad for you. But if you resist me in any way, or if you show me even the slightest disrespect, things will be a hundred times worse. Do you understand what I just said?"

She nodded.

"Say it!" he said.

Her lower lip trembled.

"I understand," she said.

He bound her in a standing spread-eagle position, stretched tight and gagged, with her feet poised on large air-filled balls. He felt every nook and corner of her body, twisting her nipples and playing with her, until her leg muscles lost control and her feet slipped off the balls.

And she fell into a hanging position.

Supported only by her wrists and ankles.

She swung and wiggled as much as she could in protest.

Hoping against hope that the little freak had at least some measure of decency left in his soul.

Instead of letting her down, however, he walked over to the wall and lifted a small, sharp whip off a hook.

"I think we're warmed up now," he said. "Let's begin."

PAIGE WAVED HER HAND, not able to listen to any more.

"Enough," she said.

Lightning suddenly exploded, so close that Paige lifted up. When she realized that the building hadn't been directly hit, she chuckled nervously and took a long swallow of wine.

Then she looked at Ja'Von.

"We know V&B is dirty," she said. "But we still don't have any tangible proof."

"What about the check they offered?"

Paige shook her head.

"That was tendered in connection with what the law calls a settlement discussion," she said. "That means that nothing that happened in the meeting, including the fact that they offered payment, can be used as evidence at trial. It's excluded from admission under Rule 408."

"Well that sucks," Ja'Von said.

Paige nodded.

Very true.

But she said, "The law works that way to encourage settlement discussions. If a party's offer could be used as evidence against them, then no one would ever make an offer, meaning no cases would ever settle, meaning five times as many cases would end up going to trial."

"So what do we do?"

Paige drained the rest of her wine.

Then got the bartender's attention.

And held up two fingers.

He poured two new glasses, carried them over and set them on the table. Ja'Von handed him a ten and told him to keep the change. He grinned as if he had just won the lottery and said thanks in a voice that meant it.

Paige twisted the new glass.

"I've been thinking about what you said," she said. "The thing that impresses me about the whole operation is that they have to get the woman—in this case, you—to voluntarily travel to Bangkok. Like you said, it would be too messy to try to abduct someone here in the States and then try to sneak them halfway across the world. Commercial airlines would be out of the question, meaning they'd either need private planes or some sort of water travel. Either way, there would be a thousand things that could go wrong."

"Right," Ja'Von said.

"That's the key," Paige said. "They need to get the woman to go to Bangkok of her own volition. But that's only half the battle. Once she's there, they need her to go to the abduction site—in your case, a bar. Being a P.I., you were the perfect type of target."

Ja'Von nodded.

"Notice I said *type* of target," Paige said.

Ja'Von wrinkled her forehead and said, "Meaning what?"

"Meaning that other female investigators would be equally susceptible to the same charade," she said. "Have you done any research to determine if other female P.I.s went to Bangkok and ended up missing?"

Ja'Von shook her head.

123

Then clinked Paige's glass.

"You're brilliant," she said.

THEY TALKED FOR ANOTHER HALF HOUR. "By the way," Ja'Von said at one point, "the man I'm seeing—Bryson Coventry—doesn't know anything about any of this."

"He doesn't?"

"No. I'm too afraid to tell him."

Paige tilted her head.

"What do you mean?"

"I'm afraid he'll see me as tarnished," Ja'Von said. "I'm going to tell him, eventually. But I need to get a more solid foundation with him first."

"Does he know about me?" Paige asked.

"No. If I tell him I have a lawyer he's going to want to know what for."

"Understood."

WHEN THEY FINALLY GOT UP TO LEAVE, the storm still hadn't let up. "This is like San Francisco on steroids," Ja'Von said. Of course, neither of them had an umbrella. They took a deep breath, ducked out the door and ran for Ja'Von's car, splashing through puddles.

Something about the vehicle was wrong.

It looked too low to the ground.

Then they figured it out.

All four tires were slashed.

Ja'Von slapped her hand on the hood.

"Damn it!"

Paige swallowed, pushed rain out of her eyes and said, "This is another warning shot. But how the hell did they know we were here? I'm positive we weren't followed."

Ja'Von said, "They're sneaky little bastards. That's for sure."

Chapter Twenty-Four

Day Four—June 14
Thursday Night

BRYSON COVENTRY SPENT THE DAY tracking down and interviewing anyone and everyone in the world who knew Madison Blake—friends, relatives, co-workers, you name it. In the end, no one had the vaguest idea why anyone would want to abduct or harm her.

No one had heard from her.

No one knew where she could possibly be.

He drove to her apartment, searched through every square inch, again found nothing and then slumped down on the couch.

He cleared his mind.

And waited for something—*anything*—to fall out of the sky and land on him.

Nothing did.

"Damn it! Give me something!"

Silence.

Only silence.

Inescapable silence where there should be the ordinary, everyday sounds of two young women going about their ordinary, everyday lives.

Anxiety washed over him.

A dark anxiety.

He tried to shake it.

But couldn't.

Time kept passing and each minute that disappeared into oblivion meant one less to find the woman before it was too late.

Assuming it wasn't already too late.

Thunder crackled outside, pulling him to the window for a look. Charcoal clouds rolled in with a furious pace from the mountains. Mean, nasty clouds, on a mission. In another ten minutes the sky would drop with a vengeance.

He called Ja'Von.

No answer.

His stomach growled.

Suddenly starved.

He looked at his watch—8:12 p.m. No wonder he was so hungry. He rummaged through the refrigerator, found the makings for a sandwich, but then decided that he better not. He slumped down on the couch and closed his eyes, just to rest them for a second.

He was sound asleep when his cell phone rang.

He fumbled for it.

Light no longer came through the windows.

The room was dark.

Night had come.

THE VOICE OF LEANNE SANDERS CAME THROUGH. "Do

you have paper and pencil with you?" she asked. Coventry heard rain in the background and could tell that she was in the meat of the storm, not inside a vehicle. He pictured her walking down a dark street.

He stood up, groggy, and headed to the kitchen.

"Yeah, where are you?" he asked.

"Following my target."

"That French guy?"

"Right. He's on foot and paying a lot of attention to a house over here in the east side of the city. My gut tells me he's ten minutes away from making a hit. Write this address down," she said, giving it to him.

Coventry grabbed a pencil and scribbled the digits on the countertop.

"Can you find out who lives there and call me back?"

Coventry paced.

"You need backup," he said.

"No!"

"But—"

"Can you get me that name or not?"

He kicked the chair.

"Give me two minutes," he said.

"Damn it!"

"What?"

Then the phone went dead.

"Leanne?"

No answer.

"Leanne!"

COVENTRY RAN DOWN TO THE TUNDRA, squealed to the 6th

Avenue freeway and headed east with the windshield wipers on full blast. Just as he brought the vehicle up to speed he realized that he remembered the street name but not the number.

Suddenly a vehicle in the adjacent lane shifted.

A Hummer.

Coventry felt the impact somewhere in the side bed of the truck and fought to keep from spinning out.

Then he put his foot to the floor.

Chapter Twenty-Five

Day Four—June 14
Thursday Night

DYLAN JOOP DROVE DOWN THE TWISTY MOUNTAIN road towards Denver, through a dark night, smack dab in the middle of a terrible storm, with the windshield wipers swinging back and forth as fast as they could and still not able to keep the slop off. Duran Duran's "Rio" came from the radio, loud, the way it was supposed to be. He sang when the chorus came up, barely able to hear his own voice. It reminded him of his days as a lead guitarist in a so-so rock band back in eleventh grade.

Eternities ago.

Before his first kill, even.

The carefree days.

But the poor days, too.

The trailer-trash days.

Would he go back if he had a chance?

Good question.

Then he decided, no.

No way.

Screw poverty.

Poverty is overrated.

WHEN THE LIGHTS OF CIVILIZATION APPEARED, Joop headed straight to his favorite strip club, off Santa Fe in southern Denver. The women there weren't necessarily the hottest in the world but they were the loosest.

And the private-dance area was the darkest.

He had five hundred dollars in his pocket and didn't care if he spent every last penny.

Tonight he was going to chill out.

Tomorrow would be different.

Tomorrow he would kill Madison Blake. He'd give her a choice—a bullet to the back of the head, a knife to the heart, or she could do it herself in private with a razorblade. He didn't care and had no interest in having her suffer.

The cover charge was $5.00.

He paid with a hundred-dollar bill and put $10.00 in the tip jar, which got him a hug from a cute brunette and a hand down his pants for about five seconds.

The women inside must have smelled the money.

Two of them latched on and were already rubbing their tits on him before he even got to the bar. But then again, maybe it wasn't the money. He was, after all, an attractive man.

Make that an attractive man with an incredible physique.

A physique good enough to get up that stupid rock in Clear Creek Canyon.

Even if it did take him three tries.

He didn't care how drunk he got tonight.

He'd take a cab when the time came.

He owned the night.

He already knew where he'd bury Madison Blake tomorrow.
So all he had to do at this point was sit back and chill.

HE CLOSED THE CLUB FIVE HOURS LATER with seven beers in his gut, and ended up going home with a stripper named Phoenix.

With a real name that started with a B.

Brenda.

Or Barbara

Or Bernadette.

Something like that.

A gorgeous long-legged thing who loved to clamp his head between her vice-like thighs and get tongued. Midway through that licking, when he had the woman worked up into a solid sweat, his cell phone rang.

"Don't answer," she said.

He ignored it at first, then pulled it out and looked at his watch.

2:38 a.m.

What the hell?

"Hello?"

A voice came though.

A familiar one.

"We had a situation develop earlier this evening."

"What kind of situation?" Joop asked.

"Something serious," the voice said.

Chapter Twenty-Six

Day Four—June 14
Thursday Night

PAIGE DIDN'T HAVE A LOT OF STUFF but did have a not-too-ancient Gateway laptop that got her on the Internet whenever she wanted. Tonight, as the storm raged outside, she and Ja'Von hit the search engines—looking for another female P.I. who had been lured to Bangkok and disappeared.

Someone they could cross-reference to.

And maybe find a common denominator.

So far, an hour into it, they had nothing.

Nada.

Zippo.

The bar-buzz wore off more than a half hour ago. Now, getting nowhere fast, the exuberance waned too. Ja'Von was in the bathroom with the door closed when her cell phone rang.

"Will you get that?" she shouted.

Paige did.

"Ja'Von's receptionist," she said.

"Ja'Von's receptionist?"

"Yes."

"Where's Ja'Von?"

"She's in a meeting with John."

"John?"

"Right," Paige said. "But she'll be out in a minute. Who should I say is calling?"

"Hannah."

Paige held the phone away from her mouth and shouted, "It's Hannah."

"Hannah?"

"Right."

"Tell her I'll be right there."

"Did you hear that?" Paige asked.

Hannah had.

Paige went back to working the Internet, but listened with a half-ear as Ja'Von talked. It seemed to be about nothing. Afterwards, Ja'Von said, "Hannah does some work for me now and then. She wants to know if I've made up my mind yet whether to relocate to Denver."

Paige cocked her head.

"Well, have you?"

Ja'Von nodded.

"I don't have a choice," she said. "That man I told you about—Bryson Coventry—has one blue eye and one green one. Did I mention that before?"

No.

She hadn't.

"And they're both for me." A worried expression washed over her face and she added, "Of course, he doesn't know yet that I had a hundred different cocks shoot cum on my face in Bangkok."

Paige winced at the visual and said, "If he has any real sub-

134

stance, it shouldn't matter."

Ja'Von grunted.

"*Shouldn't* is a big word, sweetie; a universe-sized word."

A HALF HOUR LATER they found an interesting article from the Miami Herald. A P.I. by the name of Rebecca Vampire disappeared in May of last year while "out of the country."

"Vampire?" Paige asked.

"Right, Vampire."

"You're kidding."

"No, it says it right here, Rebecca Vampire."

A photo accompanied the article.

"She sure doesn't look like one, though," Ja'Von added.

The woman was hot.

And blond.

"Do you recognize her?" Paige asked.

"No."

Chapter Twenty-Seven

Day Four—June 14
Thursday Night

WHEN 6TH AVENUE ENDED as a freeway and turned into a street as it entered metro Denver, a street with intersections, Bryson Coventry did his best not to T-bone anyone as he busted through red lights. He made it all the way to Colorado Boulevard and by some miracle actually caught a green light and continued east. The windshield wipers swept back and forth and brought an upscale neighborhood in and out of focus.

Tudor mansions on tree-lined boulevards.

Denver's rich and powerful.

Coventry didn't know this side of town that well and studied the signs.

Then, there it was—the street.

He turned right.

And saw nothing out of the ordinary.

Five minutes later, on his third pass, he spotted a dark shape on the ground, barely visible at the base of a row of pitch-black hedges—a shape that could be a body.

He slammed on the brakes and ran over.

Not even swinging the truck door shut.

Not caring if the interior got soaked.

There he found Dr. Leanne Sanders.

Laying face down.

Motionless.

In two or three inches of water.

He rolled her over to get her mouth off the ground, in case she was drowning, and felt wet goop at the back of her head. Thicker than water. He couldn't see it but knew it was blood.

Fresh blood.

Still flowing.

Meaning she was still alive.

TWO HOURS LATER he wound up Green Mountain to home, and found Ja'Von waiting up for him, watching *Body Double*. An empty wineglass sat on the coffee table. The stress on her face reminded him that a good amount of Leanne's blood had transferred to his clothes.

He kissed her and said, "That isn't mine."

Then he recapped the evening for her.

The highlights, anyway.

Halfway through, she interrupted him. "I don't ever want to lose you."

He held her at arms length and looked into her eyes.

The eyes of this mysterious woman he had only known for three days.

And couldn't imagine life without her.

"Me too," he said.

At first, he couldn't believe his own voice.

But as soon as he said it, he was glad.

"You too?"

He nodded.

"Right, me too."

"You're not just messing with me, are you?"

"To be honest, I don't think I've ever felt this way before in my whole life."

"You don't even know who I am," she said.

"I know enough," he said. "And I want you to appreciate something. I've never fooled around on a woman, behind her back. So if you want this to be an exclusive thing, starting right now—actually, starting since Monday when we met—just say the word."

She played with his hair, as if deciding, and then said, "The word." Two seconds later a mischievous expression washed over her face.

"What?" he asked.

"Do you remember what you promised me this morning?"

He tried to remember.

But couldn't.

"Do you want a hint?"

"Yeah, give me a hint."

"*Rug burns,*" she said.

Chapter Twenty-Eight

Day Five—June 15
Friday Afternoon

DYLAN JOOP WOKE UP in a bed that was too soft to be his. He opened his eyes, just a crack, enough to let some light in but not enough to hurt. Dark drapes were framed by a strong sunlight trying to break in from the outside. Next to him lay a woman, the stripper from last night, now showing an extra five pounds that he hadn't noticed before. She hadn't removed her makeup before passing out. Mascara and lipstick had drifted on her face during the night and now gave her the appearance of a Picasso painting.

Still very pretty though.

He muscled out of bed and staggered into the bathroom.

Then took a long piss.

The beer, so incredibly easy to swallow last night, had settled into the front of his head and now beat on his skull with little hammers. His mouth felt like a desert sandstorm.

Aspirin.

He needed Aspirin.

A truckload of Aspirin.

Jim Michael Hansen

Not in thirty seconds.

Right now.

He found some in the cabinet, tossed three to the back of his mouth and downed them with a full glass of water, followed by another, and a third.

There.

The healing was in progress.

In twenty minutes he'd feel semi-human.

He got the shower as hot as he could stand it and stepped in. When he came out ten minutes later, the woman was in the kitchen and the coffee pot was full.

He walked in with a towel around his waist.

"Morning," he said.

"Afternoon, actually."

What?

Really?

She handed him a cup of coffee.

"12:30," she said. "You were good last night. I'm glad you came over."

He was too.

And kissed her to prove it.

"If you want to see me again, you can," she added.

"You mean like a date or something?"

She nodded.

"Yeah, if you want," she said. "Or you can just come over and hang out and watch TV or something. Whatever you want."

He pictured it.

And liked the picture.

More than he thought.

She grabbed his hand, led him into the bedroom and shut the door, drawing the room into a deep darkness. Then she

140

dropped to her knees, slid her fingers up his thighs, slipped the towel off and said, "I just want to say thanks for last night." A few minutes later she paused for a heartbeat, looked up, and said, "My name's Bethany."

As soon as she said it he remembered.

"I know that," he said.

She paused again.

"Sorry," she said, "I think I forgot yours."

"Dylan."

"Glad to meet you, Dylan."

A HALF HOUR LATER, after throwing Bethany on her back and giving her the most intense oral stimulation of her life, he took a cab to the strip club to pick up the Audi, only to discover something weird.

The Audi wasn't there.

Maybe his memory was flawed, so he had the cabbie crisscross the area for a three-block radius.

Still no Audi.

So he had the cabbie drop him off at the loft downtown.

A call to the impound lot told him that the vehicle hadn't been towed, meaning it must have been stolen. That didn't surprise him, given the neighborhood. He was actually in the process of calling the police to report it missing when he remembered something.

Something bad.

Worse than bad.

The envelope was under the front seat.

The envelope with the pictures of Madison Blake inside.

His name and address were on the registration in the glove

box; on the insurance card too.

Damn it!

He stormed out of the loft, took a cab to Enterprise, rented a 4-door Nissan sedan, and drove into the mountains to the boxcars. When he got there, a car that he didn't recognize sat in the road in front of the gate, a car with no sign of life inside. Whoever had been driving it must have continued on foot.

He got out of the rental, slammed the door and huffed up the road, one foot in front of the other, as the little hammers pounded inside his brain.

Bang.

Bang.

Bang.

Chapter Twenty-Nine

Day Five—June 15
Friday Morning

PAIGE ALEXANDER HOPPED OFF THE TREK, chained it to a tree and walked inside the Starbucks. She spotted Ja'Von at a corner table, looking better than a human being had a right to, with two cups of coffee on the table, meaning one was for Paige. She hugged the woman, momentarily noted that her breasts were too firm to be real and too soft to be fake, and then got right to the point.

"I got up early and worked the phone," she said. "Do you want the good news or the bad news?"

"The good," Ja'Von said.

"Okay," she said. "Our Florida P.I., Rebecca Vampire, who disappeared *out of the country*, actually disappeared while she was on some kind of assignment in Bangkok."

Ja'Von slapped her hand on the table.

"I knew it!"

Then she stood up and danced.

Every man in the place watched.

Transfixed.

After Ja'Von sat down, Paige put a serious look on her face and said, "That's the end of the good news."

Ja'Von didn't care.

"The end?" she asked. "What more could we possibly need?"

"Lots," Paige said. "I haven't been able to uncover anything to suggest that she was working for a law firm, much less for Vinson & Botts. Also, no one I talked to recognized the name Bob Copeland. And unlike what happened to you, neither her office nor her house were ransacked."

"That doesn't mean someone didn't slip a file out of a drawer," Ja'Von said.

"Maybe, but that's speculation," Paige said. "Don't get me wrong, just the fact that the woman disappeared in Bangkok is enough to convince me that the same exact thing happened to her that happened to you. As far as a court of law goes, however, it's a whole different ballgame. We'll need a lot more connections before the court will admit any of it into evidence. Right now, from an evidentiary point of view, the fact that the woman is a P.I., and disappeared while in Bangkok, is nothing more than an irrelevant coincidence."

Ja'Von seemed undaunted.

"She's also hot."

Paige nodded.

"Okay, that too," she said.

"So what do we need?"

"We need to tie her to Vinson & Botts," Paige said. "If we can do that, then we'll have something."

"Then let's do it."

"How?"

"By taking a road trip."

"You mean to Miami?"

Ja'Von nodded. "That's exactly what I mean. There's only so much you can do by telephone." Then she stood up and grabbed Paige's hand. "Come on, darling, we're heading to DIA."

"You know I don't have money for that."

"Don't worry about it, it's going on my plastic."

Two hours later they were cruising at 35,000 feet.

Pointed east.

Maybe wasting their time.

Maybe not.

Chapter Thirty

Day Five—June 15
Friday Morning

COVENTRY CRAWLED OUT OF BED without waking Ja'Von, slipped into sweats, cranked out a three-mile jog, took a shower downstairs and watched her sleep as he brushed his teeth. He got to headquarters just as the sun cleared the horizon. He inhaled caffeine alone in the room and worked the computer to find out what he could about Mark Remington, the owner of the house that the Frenchman was scoping out last night before Leanne Sanders got blindsided.

Remington turned out to be a partner at Vinson & Botts, specializing in international law.

He had no record.

Not even an unpaid parking ticket.

Or a paid one, for that matter.

The clean didn't get any squeakier than his.

Why would someone from France come over here and pay attention to him? Had he crossed swords with the wrong opposing party? Or got on the wrong side of some foreign leader?

Coventry scratched his head.

The florescent light directly over his desk hummed like a madman. He ignored it as best he could, but the more he concentrated on not letting it bother him, the more it did.

So he climbed up on his desk and pulled it out.

And carried it into Chief Forrest Tanner's office and set it on his desk. Then stuck a yellow Post-It on that said, "This is how long my nose grows whenever I say something nice about you."

TWO MINUTES LATER HIS PHONE RANG and the voice of Leanne Sanders came through, framed by hospital sounds in the background. He could almost smell the antiseptic.

"When I dialed I was going to say thanks for saving me last night," she said. "But now I changed my mind."

He smiled.

"Oh?"

"So don't take this as a thank you," she said. "What I am going to do, however, is subtract one that you owe me."

Coventry considered it.

And found it fair.

"So how many do I still owe you then?—just for the record."

"You owed me five. Now you're down to four."

"Four, huh? That's the lowest I owe anyone."

"That's not a bragging point, Coventry."

He took a sip of coffee.

Found it lukewarm, dumped the cup in the snake plant and headed over to the pot for a refill.

"You scared me last night," he said.

"Scared you? You should have seen it from my point of view," she said.

"Did you see him, before he did it?" Coventry asked, referring to the Frenchman.

"No."

He frowned.

That meant they didn't have enough probable cause to haul him in.

He told her what he found out this morning about Mark Remington, the owner of the house that Frenchie had been so interested in.

"We should drop in on him," Leanne said. "You want to come down here and pick me up?"

"You good to go?"

"According to the docs, no. According to the stuff I need to get done today, yes."

Coventry looked at his watch.

8:15 a.m.

He knew he should be concentrating on Madison Blake, but couldn't think of anything concrete to do.

So he walked down the three flights of stairs to the parking garage and pointed the front end of the Tundra towards Denver General Hospital.

THE RECEPTION AREA OF VINSON & BOTTS looked like a museum. Leanne sat on a leather couch and sipped coffee from a fancy cup and saucer. She looked pretty good considering what she'd been through. Take the gauze wrap off her head and there'd be no evidence at all, except for the tiredness in her eyes.

Coventry sipped coffee from an equally fancy cup as he walked around and checked out the paintings.

The receptionist smiled every time he looked her way.

He smiled back.

The paintings bored him.

They lacked passion.

They had no freedom of movement.

Each brushstroke had been perfectly planned.

Too perfectly planned.

He kept hoping to find a wild stroke, a rogue splash of paint, a surprise color, something—*anything*—to show that the person holding the brush was an actual living human being.

But didn't find one.

He sat down next to Leanne and said, "The people who painted these things should have been engineers or doctors."

Leanne shrugged.

"They look okay to me."

Two minutes later they were escorted to the office of Mark Remington.

THE ATTORNEY HAD A PLEASANT FACE and looked a lot better in person than he did in the photo on the firm's website. For someone who rode a desk, he managed to stay in shape. He wore his tie loose and his hair shaggy. Instead of wingtips, he had soft leather loafers.

As they sat down he said, "I'm at a loss as to why you're here."

"Then thanks for seeing us," Coventry said. "There was a man on your street last night, a Frenchman by the name of Boudiette. Do you know him?"

For a heartbeat, Coventry thought he saw something flicker in the lawyer's eyes, but couldn't be sure.

"No," Remington said. "Who is he?"

Coventry took a sip of coffee.

"The word is, he was scoping out your house," he said.

"My house?"

Coventry nodded.

"Why would a Frenchman be scoping out my house?" Remington asked.

Coventry shrugged.

"We were hoping you could tell us."

Remington laughed.

"This is nuts," he said. "Did one of my partners put you up to this?"

Coventry shook his head.

"From what I understand, you do international law."

"That's correct."

"When was the last time you were in France?"

"France?"

"Right."

The lawyer searched his memory and said, "Twelve years ago."

"That's a long time," Coventry said.

Remington nodded.

"My next-door neighbor goes there all the time," he said.

Coventry raised an eyebrow.

Really?

To France?

"He's an interpreter. Big international companies hire him to be sure there are no miscommunications when deals go down."

"What's his name?"

Reynolds.

Pete Reynolds.

Peter, actually.

Peter Reynolds.

AS SOON AS THEY STEPPED OUT of the building an RTD bus sprayed them with a plume of diesel. Leanne grabbed Coventry's arm and pulled him back.

"So what do you think?" Coventry asked.

"I'll run down this Peter Reynolds just so the file's complete," she said. "But Boudiette was scoping out the lawyer's house, not the one next door."

"How can you be sure?" Coventry asked. "That street was pretty dark."

"Okay," she said. "I'm not *positive*."

"No one could be," he said.

But he had already lost interest.

This wasn't his fight.

He needed to get refocused on Madison Blake.

Right now.

This second.

Chapter Thirty-One

Day Five—June 15
Friday Afternoon

DYLAN JOOP DIDN'T HAVE A GUN OR A KNIFE with him—
they were in the middle boxcar—but he did have 209 pounds of
ripped muscle as he trotted up the dirt road to the boxcars. He
hoped he didn't have to kill anyone.

He really did.

His head pounded with too much beer pain to deal with the
hundred little details of the aftermath.

When the boxcars came into view, his worst fears came true.
A young woman was at the door of the boxcar that held Madison Blake, trying to pry the padlock off with a stick. On the
ground not more than two steps away sat a backpack and a large
plastic bottle of water. She wore green hiking shorts and a sun
visor. Joop slowed to a walk, concerned about spooking her.
When she spotted him, her face twisted in fear.

Be cool.

Just be cool.

Be another hiker.

"Hi," he said with his best smile. "Is this the way up to Lake

Jackson?"

She looked apprehensive.

As if she sensed a trick.

But she didn't bolt.

That was the main thing.

Joop concentrated on not scaring her as he closed the gap.

"I think I might be lost," he said. "Do you live here?"

"No," she said.

Beautiful.

Totally beautiful.

She was talking instead of running.

"I heard about a place up here with boxcars," he said. "But I always thought it was a story. Looks like I was wrong. How the hell did they get up here?"

"There's someone inside this one!" the woman said.

"What do you mean?"

"A lady's trapped inside."

He increased his pace.

And put a concerned look on his face.

"You're kidding, right?"

No, she wasn't.

She was dead serious.

Suddenly Madison Blake yelled, "That's him! Run! Do you hear me? Get out of here!"

The woman ran, but not fast enough.

JOOP GRABBED THE BACK OF HER HAIR, pulled it straight down as hard as he could—towards her ass—and snapped her neck. Even before she dropped to the ground, Joop wished he had smothered her instead. Because now she had been killed the same way as Madison Blake's friend, Samantha Rickenbacker.

Okay, think.

The important thing is that her body never be found.

Not in a million years.

He needed to get rid of her car too.

Where?

And when?

Now?

Or after dark?

SUDDENLY HIS CELL PHONE RANG. He looked at the incoming number, got himself as calm as he could and answered.

"It's me," the voice said.

"I know that."

"Your instructions at this point are to release the woman alive and unhurt, sometime tomorrow morning. Be sure there aren't any surveillance cameras around. And be sure she doesn't see you, your car or your license plate number when you're leaving. In fact, I'd suggest that you keep her tied and blindfolded the whole time. Just drop her by the side of a road where someone will eventually find her. Do you understand?"

Joop kicked the dirt.

Damn it!

"We had a complication," he said.

A pause on the other end.

A serious pause.

Joop swallowed.

"What kind of complication?"

"When that other woman showed up and forced me to deal with her, you-know-who ran and got all the way up to the street," Joop said. "My mask came off. We were under a street-light. She got a good look at me."

"She saw your face?"

"Like I said, it was because of that other woman. It's one of those things that just happens. You hope it doesn't but it does."

"Why didn't you tell me this before?"

"Because I thought you were going to tell me to kill her," Joop said. "Then it wouldn't matter."

Silence.

Joop exhaled.

"You should have told me."

True.

And equally true that he should report what happened just minutes ago—namely, that he killed a hiker.

But he didn't.

"This changes everything," the voice said. "Don't do anything until I can think this through."

"So don't release her?"

"No. And don't kill her either. Do you understand?"

"I understand, but why don't we just kill her and be done with everything?"

"It's not that easy," the voice said.

Then the line went dead.

INSIDE THE BOXCAR, barely audible through the steel, Madison Blake cried.

Joop picked up a rock and threw it at the door as hard as he could.

"Shut up!"

Then he threw another.

And another.

And another.

"Shut up!"

"Shut up!"

"Shut up!"

No sounds came from inside any longer.

He pictured her cowering in the corner.

Curled up in a fetal position.

Crying.

Stifling the sobs.

The entire mountain was silent.

Not a wing flapped.

Not a leaf rustled.

The only sound came from the air passing in and out of Joop's lungs. He exhaled, flung the dead hiker over his left shoulder, swooped up her backpack, and headed down the road.

Little hammers pounded in his head.

Bang.

Bang.

Bang.

Chapter Thirty-Two

Day Five—June 15
Friday Afternoon

THE SUN AND HUMIDITY assaulted Paige and Ja'Von the second they stepped out of Miami International Airport. "Watch close and you'll be able to actually see my hair curl," Ja'Von said. They rented a plain-vanilla Chevy coupe, the last one left, a black heat-magnet that had been parked on sticky asphalt all day. It took fifteen minutes for the air conditioner to make a dent.

Ja'Von drove.

After fighting with traffic for over an hour—traffic best described as crowded, fast and rude, meaning no different than Denver—they ended up at a South Beach nightclub on Collins Avenue called Outrageous.

The front entrance was locked.

They banged on it.

No one came.

So they headed around to the back.

That door was unlocked. After calling without response, they finally found a woman in an upstairs office, working the keyboard of a laptop with her back to them.

The woman jumped when they knocked.

"Are you Mackenzie Vampire?" Ja'Von questioned.

The woman nodded.

"That's me."

She appeared to be about thirty-four, in good shape, mildly but not wildly attractive, with a business attitude. She wore sandals, white shorts, an expensive blue blouse and lots of gold.

"You're the two from Denver, I assume," she said.

"We are."

After chitchat, introductions and universal agreement that Miami was too hot and sticky, the woman said, "So your theory is that my sister Rebecca got lured to Bangkok, as part of some pre-arranged thing, and then got taken into sexual slavery."

Ja'Von nodded.

"That's what happened to me," she said.

And then told her the story.

At the end Mackenzie asked, "Did you ever see Rebecca in this place?"

"Not that I remember," Ja'Von said.

"And you would remember another blond American, I assume."

"Absolutely," Ja'Von said. "But I know there were women there that I never met. It's possible that we were kept apart on purpose."

"She disappeared in May of last year," Mackenzie said. "That's thirteen months ago. Could anyone survive in that place that long?"

Ja'Von frowned.

"Do you want the truth?"

"Probably not."

"It would be hard," Ja'Von said. "But not impossible."

Mackenzie retreated in thought.

"She's ten years younger than me," she said. "I helped raise her."

THIRTY MINUTES LATER they pulled into the driveway of Mackenzie Vampire's house, a stucco ranch in a neighborhood west of Coral Gables. The garage was filled with boxes.

"This is it," Mackenzie said. "All of Rebecca's files."

She pulled one down and carried it into the living room.

Ja'Von and Paige did the same.

"So what are we looking for, exactly?"

"Anything that relates to Bangkok, Denver, law firms, Bob Copeland, cash retainers, or anything else out of the ordinary. We'll need all her bank statements, day timers, phone records, credit card statements, and stuff like that too. We also need to get into her computers, plus access her emails, if we can."

Mackenzie's fingers shook.

"What's wrong?" Paige asked.

"She's still alive," Mackenzie said. "I can feel it."

Ja'Von patted her hand.

"Me too."

They hugged.

Then looked at Paige and pulled her in for a group hug.

"Enough girl stuff," Ja'Von said. "Let's get busy."

Chapter Thirty-Three

Day Five—June 15
Friday Afternoon

BRYSON COVENTRY WALKED INTO WONG'S on Court Street and immediately spotted Shalifa Netherwood in a booth. Two of the waitresses zigzagged over to say hello and pat him on the arm as he walked across the restaurant.

"How'd you spot me so fast?" Shalifa questioned as he slid in.

Coventry raked his hair back with his fingers. It hung in place for a heartbeat and then flopped back down over his forehead.

"What do you mean?"

"I was watching you when you walked in," she said. "You spotted me right away."

He shrugged.

"I don't know, I just did," he said.

"Okay, then," she said. "Let me tell you how."

"All right—how?"

"Because I'm the only black person in here," she said.

Coventry looked around.

She was right.

"I didn't notice that," he said.

"That's because you're not black," she said. "The next time we have lunch, we'll do it in Five Points. Then you'll notice more."

He chuckled.

Ming walked over, a beautiful little doll of a thing who also happened to be a straight-A graduate student at C.U. Denver, and asked, "The usual?"

Coventry smiled.

"Please."

Shalifa ordered the same and then said, "You should try something different once in a while."

"Can't," he said.

"Why not?"

"I'm not wired that way. By the way, thanks."

She cocked her head.

"For what?"

"For whatever it is that I haven't said thanks for before," he said. "So take one off the list I owe you."

She laughed.

"I don't even know where that list is anymore," she said. "It got so big I had to move it out of the house."

He grinned.

"Well, if you ever find it, scratch one off."

She leaned across the table and said, "I'll scratch two off if you pay for lunch."

He paused.

Giving it ample consideration.

Then he said, "One is enough for right now. I don't want to upset the balance of the universe."

OVER THE BEST CHINESE FOOD IN DENVER, Shalifa told Coventry an interesting story. She finally managed to get a chance to talk to the person who lived across the street from Alan Ewing, the pilot who got butchered in his bedroom. According to the neighbor, a busybody named Bunny Something-Or-Other, Ewing may have been under surveillance.

"Really?"

Shalifa nodded.

"The same car came down the street slowly on several occasions," she said. "It didn't belong to anyone who lived on the street. It slowed down to a crawl whenever it passed in front of Bunny's house, meaning Ewing's house too. At first she thought he was checking her out, but when she started to pay more attention she found that he always had his face pointed to Ewing's place."

"He?"

"Right—a man."

"Can she ID him?"

"No."

Coventry considered it.

Then Shalifa made a face at him.

Which meant that he was chewing with his mouth open.

"Is there any surveillance in the area?"

"I didn't notice any."

Shalifa put an inquisitive look on her face.

"What?" Coventry asked.

"So what's going on with your new squeeze?"

"Ja'Von?"

"Right."

"I was going to ask her to move in with me this morning but she was still asleep when I left."

"You're kidding, right?"

No he wasn't, not a bit.

"She's the one," he added.

She laughed. "*The one?*"

"Right."

"Well that's corny. You sound like a soap opera. *The one,*" she repeated. "*The one.* As in *the* followed by *one.*"

Coventry grinned. "Corny or not, that's how I feel."

"You just met her on Monday."

"That's how I know."

"Let me rephrase it," Shalifa said. "You just met her on Monday, *after she stalked you.*"

He shrugged and said, "I've always wanted my own personal stalker."

"And now you have one," Shalifa said.

"Right, now I have one." He leaned across the table and lowered his voice. "But no matter what, I'll never forget that night when I bounced a quarter off your ass, if that's what this is about."

She smacked him on the arm.

"You promised to never bring that up."

He grinned. "So now I owe you an apology."

"Yes you do."

"Put it on the list," he said.

"That means the list is right back to where it started."

"Figures," Coventry said. "That's the way my life works."

TWO MINUTES LATER COVENTRY'S PHONE RANG. He talked

for a moment, hung up and said, "That was Ja'Von. She's in Miami working on a case, and may or may not be back this evening."

"Which means no sugar in your coffee tonight," Shalifa said.

He chuckled.

True.

But it also freed him up to work on Madison Blake.

He looked at Shalifa and said, "Excuse me a minute," and dialed Ja'Von.

"Got a question for you," he said.

"Shoot."

"Do you feel like moving in with me?"

She laughed.

"I already did. Didn't you notice?"

Chapter Thirty-Four

ACCORDING TO HER DRIVER'S LICENSE, the dead hiker was a 20-year-old named Brandy Zucker. The name rang a bell but Joop couldn't place it. She had an upscale Cherry Hills address, meaning she came from money.

That wasn't good.

Not at all.

Kill a whore—what happens is that some underpaid civil servant sniffs around for a couple of days and tries to look busy while he scratches his ass. But kill a rich young white drama queen, and what happens is a whole different kind of hunt.

The kind with teeth.

Snap.

Snap.

Snap.

He needed to get her and her vehicle off his property now. Waiting for nightfall was too risky. So he put the woman in the trunk of her car, drove to an old abandoned mine near Idaho Springs and dumped her and her precious little backpack down a narrow vertical shaft. Judging by the sound, she bounced off the walls for at least a hundred feet before landing with a thud.

He drove her car another sixty miles west on I-70, all the way to Vail Pass, and pulled into the edge of a rest area where he had plenty of breathing room. He wiped his prints off everything as best he could and then spotted a female out-of-state trucker. Using his best smile, he talked her into giving him a lift to Vail, another twenty miles west.

From Vail he took the train back to Denver.

Paying cash.

Then he took a cab to Morrison at the base of the front range, bought a mountain bike, and peddled all the way up Highway 74 to the boxcars.

Everything was as he had left it.

Including Madison Blake.

Perfect.

NOW HE NEEDED TO GET MADISON BLAKE the hell out of there, and fast. The place was too hot. The hiker—Brandy Zucker—could have told someone where she was going, meaning the cops might come sniffing around.

But where could he stash her?

Not at his loft.

Not at a hotel, even a seedy one.

It had to be somewhere remote.

Where no one went.

Or even had a right to go.

Think!

Think!

But he couldn't.

166

What he should really do is kill her. He'd have to do that in the end anyway, since she'd seen his face. There was absolutely no way to get around it.

Yeah.

He should just kill her now and get it over with.

Then dump her somewhere.

And be free.

He picked up a rock and threw it at a tree, missing, but not by more than a foot. The second time he hit it; and the third and the fourth. Then he hiked over to the boxcar with a spring in his step, anxious to ask Madison Blake how she wanted to die.

Gunshot.

Knife.

Or razorblade.

Her choice.

The time had come.

Chapter Thirty-Five

Day Five—June 15
Friday Afternoon

———————

THE FIRST PASS THROUGH REBECCA VAMPIRE'S FILES lead to nothing except one frustrating dead-end after another. Everything seemed legit. None of the folders held any evidence of a connection to Bangkok, Vinson & Botts, Denver, Bob Copeland or oversized incoming cash.

Paige closed her last file and looked at Mackenzie.

"What are the chances there was a file but someone got to it?"

Mackenzie wrinkled her forehead and said, "It's possible, I suppose. They were in her office for three weeks before we brought them over here."

Ja'Von stood up and stretched.

"She might have taken it with her to Bangkok," she said. "Or not made a file at all. Either way we're SOL. I'm starved."

Paige's stomach growled.

Loud.

Ja'Von said, "It looks like I'm not the only one."

True.

Mackenzie worked the phone and thirty minutes later two large bags of halfway-decent Chinese arrived. They ate in the kitchen and, halfway through, Mackenzie wanted more details about what the men had done to Ja'Von.

"You really don't want to know," Ja'Von said.

"It's not a matter of *want*," Mackenzie said.

Ja'Von finished chewing.

Weighing it.

"ONE OF THE ROOMS HAD A WALL CONTRAPTION," she said. "It was basically a vertical wooden wall about two or three inches thick that went from the floor to the ceiling. It was about eight feet wide. There was an opening in it three or four feet off the floor, big enough for a head. What they would do is make me bend over and stick my head through. Then they slid a piece of wood down so I couldn't pull out. Picture something like a guillotine. So when they were on one side of the wall, all they saw was my head."

Paige pictured it.

And swallowed.

"On the other side of the wall they had my body, bent over at the waist," Ja'Von said. "They would usually put a spreader bar on my ankles and then tie my arms, usually behind my back, but sometimes they'd cuff my wrists to the wall or to my knees. When they were on the body side of the wall, I could handle it. It's when they came over to the head side that I lost it."

Why?

What did they do?

"When your face and head are totally vulnerable and immobile, and you can't distract them by wiggling your ass or something, it's the most helpless feeling in the world. Sometimes they would do breath-control. That's where they would gag me and then pinch my nose and watch me turn blue. The other thing they liked to do was pry my mouth open with a wire spreader and then ram their cocks in my mouth. I'm not talking about oral sex. I'm talking about mouth rape." She paused and then added, "I'm sorry to be so graphic."

Mackenzie wrinkled her forehead.

"Thanks," she said. "I'd rather know than not."

Ja'Von nodded and then looked at Paige. "I can't let Coventry get a mental picture of me like that."

Paige understood.

She really did.

But said, "Maybe you're not giving him enough credit."

"Maybe. But I don't want to find out just yet."

WHILE REBECCA VAMPIRE'S P.I. FILES DIDN'T HELP, her bank statements did—*maybe*. It turned out that the woman made three cash deposits into her operating account during the week preceding her Bangkok trip.

Monday: $4,000.

Wednesday: $4,000.

Thursday: $2,000.

"That's $10,000 total," Ja'Von said. "The same as I got. She probably deposited it in chunks to stay under the radar of the IRS."

"It could have come from existing clients," Mackenzie said. "She got lots of cash payments. When husbands had their wives followed, they couldn't exactly write a check from the joint account."

"I appreciate that," Ja'Von said. "What we need to do is reconstruct her billing records."

They did that.

Over two bottles of wine.

With the radio turned to a hip-hop station.

Making a spreadsheet of active clients, invoices, payments received, deposits made, and the like. In the end, they tied numerous smaller cash deposits to existing clients but couldn't tie the three bigger deposits to anyone.

It was mystery money.

"It came from Vinson & Botts," Ja'Von said. "I'd bet my life on it."

Paige grunted.

"You already have," she said.

Chapter Thirty-Six

Day Five—June 15
Friday Afternoon

BRYSON COVENTRY DIDN'T HATE every Friday afternoon but did hate most of them. That's because on Friday afternoons the universe got poised to party, meaning he had less support for the next few days.

And made less progress.

Ordinarily he didn't mind that much.

But this afternoon was different.

This afternoon Madison Blake was still missing.

Which is why a layer of stress wrapped around him as he paced next to the windows and stared blankly at the cars going down Cherokee Street.

A couple of kids on bicycles caught his eye.

So innocent.

So young.

So wonderfully naïve.

Suddenly his shin exploded with pain and the snake plant toppled over and crashed to the carpet. Faces turned and Coventry said, "I had the green light." Ten heartbeats after he muscled the stupid thing upright and scooped the last of the dirt back into the pot, his phone rang.

Thirty seconds later he swung by Shalifa Netherwood's desk, grabbed her by the arm and said, "Come on, we're taking a field trip."

She had that deer-in-headlights look for a split moment.

Then snatched her purse and fell into step.

"Where are we going?"

"Down the stairs," he said, rushing past the elevators and heading into the stairwell.

She sped up enough to catch him. Then she smacked him on the back of the head.

"Don't be a smart ass."

"Fine," he said. "West."

"What?"

"We're going west."

A pause.

"Why?"

"Because that's the quickest way to get to where we're headed."

Another pause.

"You're pressing your luck, Coventry," she said.

He turned and smiled over his shoulder as he pushed through the metal fire door into the parking garage. Then he broke into a trot for the Tundra.

LUCKILY THE RUSH-HOUR NUTS hadn't jammed up the 6th Avenue freeway with bumper-to-bumper insanity yet. Coventry guided the Tundra at four over the limit into one side of Lakewood and out the other while Shalifa punched the radio buttons, only to discover that Coventry had reset them.

"Hold it!" Coventry said. "Go back."

When she did the song turned out to be what Coventry thought—Robert Palmer's "Addicted to Love."

"Leave it there," he said.

Shalifa listened for a few seconds and then punched to the next station.

"Hey!" Coventry said.

She ignored him and said, "Remind me to sit down some day and drag you into this century."

He chuckled.

"You can scream and kick if you want," she added. "No extra charge." Then she reprogrammed the stations to hip-hop.

They looped onto C-470, got off at the Morrison exit, doubled back and then pulled over to the side of the road at the base of Green Mountain, coming a little too close to three people from a highway trash crew wearing florescent orange vests.

The shortest one—an older woman with rounded shoulders and a tanned, wrinkled face—carried a manila envelope.

Coventry hopped out and introduced himself as the woman handed him the envelope.

He opened it.

Inside he found six photographs.

He sucked in his breath.

And then pointed the pictures at Shalifa.

"You said your name was—"

"—Danielle Witherspoon—"

"—Right, Danielle. You done good, Danielle."

"So that's actually her? The missing woman?"

Coventry nodded.

"It is."

The woman smiled.

"I was almost positive she was the one I saw on the news," she said.

"Well you were right," Coventry said.

"What's her name again?"

"Madison Blake."

"Madison Blake?"

"Right."

She shook her head.

"Wow."

"Show me exactly where you found this," Coventry said.

"Right over here," she said, walking. "We marked the spot with a rock."

Coventry followed.

With the corner of his mouth turned up ever so slightly.

"That's the best way to mark spots," he said. "I used to use Kleenex but it was hardly ever there the next day."

The woman looked at him.

Not knowing if it was a joke or whether he was serious.

Then she looked at Shalifa.

Who wrinkled her face and said, "Picture being around him all day long."

Chapter Thirty-Seven

Day Five—June 15
Friday Afternoon

MADISON BLAKE CHOSE TO DIE BY GUNSHOT to the back of the head. At her request, Joop left her alone in the boxcar for fifteen minutes to make her peace. Then he opened the door, holding the .357 SIG in his right hand, and said, "It's time."

She got out of the boxcar.

Crying.

Broken.

Resigned to her fate.

Joop actually felt a little sorry for her and asked, "Is there any particular place you want to do it?"

She looked around.

"Can we do it by that tree?"

Joop nodded.

"Yeah, sure."

She walked over, timidly, with Joop three steps behind, and stopped at the base of a forty-foot Ponderosa. Then she turned and looked at him, unsure what to do next.

"Kneel down and face the tree," Joop said.

There was no sternness in his voice.

She complied.

Joop took the safety off.

"I'm sorry it has to be this way," he said. "It's my fault. I shouldn't have let you see my face."

She cried.

"This won't hurt," Joop added.

Then he brought the barrel to the back of her head.

His finger tightened on the trigger.

His cell phone rang.

THE SOUND BROKE HIS CONCENTRATION. He lowered the weapon, pulled the phone out of his pocket, looked at the incoming number and decided he better answer.

"Okay, here's what we're going to do," the voice said. "We're in a situation. We have no choice but to release the woman even though she's seen your face."

Joop waved the gun in the air.

"But—"

"We know that puts you in jeopardy," the voice said, "so we're going to relocate you. We have openings in Hong Kong and Western Europe, meaning you can base yourself in London, Paris, Rome, Amsterdam, wherever you want. Take through Monday noon to cash out your bank accounts and do whatever it is you're going to do to get ready. Don't worry about the big stuff like your loft and cars. We'll pay you the value of everything you can't take with you, so you won't loose a cent. We're also kicking in a relocation bonus."

Joop took ten steps away from Madison Blake and lowered his voice.

"How much of a relocation bonus?"

"Two fifty."

Two fifty.

Not a lot.

But not something to sneeze at either.

Especially if he chose Hong Kong.

"Let us know by tomorrow where you want to go. We'll have a flight lined up for you for Monday afternoon." A pause. "The other thing you can do is retire, if you want, and go wherever you choose. You still get the two-fifty."

Joop played with the idea.

Maybe head to Mexico.

Live on the beach.

Or Rio.

Or, hell, just wander the world.

Sample the pleasures of all the nooks and crannies.

"We won't release the woman until after you get to your new country," the voice said. "Until then, just be sure she doesn't escape."

The face of Brandy Zucker jumped into Joop's brain.

"I'm not sure where I have her is all that secure," Joop said.

"Why?"

"Nothing specific," Joop said. "I just don't like being in one spot too long."

A pause.

"Do you have another place?"

"Not at my fingertips," Joop said.

"Then just stay there," the voice said. "Moving her around is too dangerous."

A bluebird landed on a branch directly above Joop's head.

He studied it for a second.

And then moved over a step so he didn't end up with something unpleasant on his head.

"Amsterdam," he said.

The decision surprised him.

But he didn't take it back.

"Good choice."

HE WALKED OVER TO MADISON BLAKE who still kneeled on the ground, facing the tree. "I have a proposition for you," he said. "If you can convince me that you will never ever tell anyone about me under any circumstances, and if you can convince me that you will never ever assist the police in any way in finding me, I might just let you go."

She wrinkled her forehead and studied him.

Trying to determine if this was one last cruel trick before he killed her.

But she must have seen the truth in his eyes.

"I won't," she said. "I promise. Not ever."

"Get up," Joop said.

She complied.

"I just want my baby to be born," she said. "I'll do anything you want. Just let us live, please."

Joop put on a pensive face.

As if weighing the words.

"I'll never tell anyone about you," the woman added. "I swear to God. Not a soul."

Joop looked at her hard.

"If I let you go and find out you lied to me," he said, "you won't get a second chance."

"I'm not lying to you," she said. "I promise."

Joop smelled urine.

The woman's pants were soaked.

"We better get you a shower," he said.

She lowered her eyes, embarrassed.

Then she peered up demurely and said, "I'm sorry to be such a bother."

"You're not a bother," he said.

AFTER THE SHOWER he gave her a clean T-shirt. Then he let her sit on a boulder, under a cloudless Colorado sky, and get sun on her face as she watched him shoot the bow.

She studied his every move.

"You're good," she said.

"Thanks."

"I'm not just saying that," she said. "You really are."

Joop knew that.

Almost every shot had been within five or six inches of the bull's-eye.

"I've been doing it a long time," he said.

"Still—"

"It's not that hard," Joop said. "You want to try?"

She looked hesitant.

Then said, "Sure, if you want."

His thoughts turned to Bethany, the stripper.

Maybe he'd take her with him to Amsterdam.

Chapter Thirty-Eight

Day Five—June 15
Friday Evening

IN MIAMI—UNLIKE DENVER—THE WARMTH of the day didn't evaporate when the sun went down. The heat stayed, then the mosquitoes came, looking for blood and ending up with lots of Paige's. And that was just during a short walk around the block to clear her head.

When she got back to the house, Mackenzie Vampire and Ja'Von had broken out another bottle of wine and seemed to be celebrating.

"Bingo," Ja'Von said, handing Paige a piece of paper.

A cellular phone bill, to be precise.

"What am I looking for?" she asked.

Ja'Von put her finger on a line halfway down the page and said, "That."

An incoming phone call.

From a 303 area code.

Meaning from the Denver metropolitan area.

Eight days before Rebecca Vampire left for Bangkok.

"And that and that and that," Ja'Von said.

Sure enough.

More calls.

All from the same Denver phone.

"I'll be damned," Paige said.

"True, but not relevant," Ja'Von said.

"Is this the same phone that you got your calls from?"

Ja'Von shook her head.

"Negative."

"So is it a Vinson & Botts phone?"

Ja'Von looked amused, pulled her cell phone out and dialed the number. As it rang she said, "Let's find out."

Ring.

Ring.

No answer.

Ring.

Ring.

"Hello?"

"Hello," Ja'Von said. "Who am I talking to?"

"Security."

"Security?"

"Right."

"Security for what?"

"Building security."

"Which building?"

"Republic Plaza. Who is this?"

"I think I might have the wrong number," Ja'Von said. "Is this the number for a law firm?"

"No it's a lobby phone."

"You mean a public payphone?"

"Right."

"In the lobby of the Republic Plaza Building?"

"Right."

"Thanks," Ja'Von said. "Now I understand. I have the wrong number."

She hung up and looked at Paige. "Where's the Republic Plaza Building?"

Paige searched her memory. "I think it's on the 16th Street Mall, or between the mall and Broadway, someplace down around Court Street."

"How far is it from the Vinson & Botts building?"

"I don't know. Two or three blocks, maybe."

"Is it a big building?"

"Yeah, huge."

Ja'Von frowned.

"So we definitely have a Bangkok connection coming from Denver, but maybe not from Vinson & Botts after all. We need to find out what law firms reside at the Republic Plaza Building." She looked at Paige. "How do we do that?"

Paige shrugged.

Then she said, "We can check the directory in the lobby."

Ja'Von patted her on the back.

"That's the first thing we do tomorrow morning," she said.

THEY CAUGHT A REDEYE BACK TO DENVER and slept most of the way. At one point Paige said, "Maybe we should take what we have to the police."

Ja'Von moaned.

"The police? You have to be kidding."

"Why?"

"Because we'd be giving up our only advantage."

"Which is—?"

"Which is, being small and invisible. We need more information, a lot more information. At this point, no one knows that we know about a Bangkok connection. We need to keep it that way."

Paige chewed on it.

And agreed.

WHEN SHE GOT BACK TO HER APARTMENT, something felt off, almost as if someone had been inside. The feeling was so strong that she pushed down the need to flop immediately into bed and instead walked around, studying the details.

Looking for something that had been moved.

Or taken.

Or left.

In the end she found nothing.

Not a single thing was a millimeter off from where she remembered it, other than a paperback book called *Night Laws* which might be slightly over from where she set it, although she couldn't be sure. Just for grins she booted up her laptop to see if anyone had logged on in her absence.

No one had.

She turned off the lights, got into bed and briefly pictured Ja'Von's head sticking through a 3" wooden wall while some freak rammed his dick in her mouth.

She forced the visual out of her brain.

And fell asleep before it could get back in.

Chapter Thirty-Nine

Day Five—June 15
Friday Afternoon

THE HIGHWAY TRASH CREW had collected four bags of litter by the time they stumbled on the envelope with the pictures of Madison Blake. Bryson Coventry had them sign chain-of-custody forms and then threw all four bags in the back of the pickup and headed back to headquarters.

His thinking was simple.

There was a good chance that whoever took Madison Blake and killed Samantha Rickenbacker had handled the envelope and/or the pictures. If they could pull prints maybe they'd find the same prints on some of the other refuse, which in turn might tell them something they didn't know already.

And maybe even contain DNA.

Say a pop can.

Or a cigarette butt.

Traffic was thick on the 6th Avenue freeway, even heading into downtown, where gridlock was almost certain. Everyone in the city was trying to be somewhere else.

"Too many cars," Shalifa said.

185

Coventry nodded.

"May as well be in L.A."

She looked at him.

"Ever been there?"

Yes he had, once, about ten years ago.

"And?"

"*And*, they got beaches, we got mountains. What I'm wondering is if Madison Blake somehow got herself caught up in something that involves more than one person."

Shalifa wrinkled her forehead.

"What do you mean?"

"I mean, if there's only one person involved, why would he have a half-dozen photographs of her? He already knows what she looks like. The more I think about that envelope, the more I'm convinced that it's the kind of package that you give to a hit man, someone who doesn't know the target. *This is what she looks like.*"

"Good thought except for two things," Shalifa said.

Coventry hit the brakes to keep from running up the ass end of a white coupe that suddenly cut him off.

Jerk.

Then he looked at Shalifa.

"Two things," he said. "One and two, or A and B?"

"A and B," she said. "A, on a scale of importance to the universe, Madison Blake hardly registers. She doesn't warrant a hit man even under the wildest scenarios. And B, it's the hit man who would end up with the photos. Like you said, *this is what she looks like.* Could he really be so stupid as to throw them out the car window while he's driving down the freeway? I just don't see it happening."

She had a point.

Two points in fact.

"So how do you explain the envelope?" he asked.

She shrugged.

"I don't. I just shoot down your theories."

SHE PUNCHED THE RADIO SCANNER and landed on The Beach Boys' "Fun, Fun, Fun." Coventry pulled her hand away before she could skip past. She let it play and said, "So what did your new squeeze do with all the money?"

"What money?"

"You don't know about the money?"

"No."

"Well, she owns a house in San Francisco. You know about that, right?"

No.

He didn't.

"Anyway, she took out an equity loan not too long ago."

"For how much?"

"Three hundred."

"Thousand?"

"Yep."

"How do you know?"

"I'm still checking up on her for you."

He gave her a sideways look and said, "I asked you not to do that."

She chuckled.

"How long have we known each other?"

"I don't know. Two years—"

"So what makes you think I'm going to start listening to you now?"

AT HEADQUARTERS, COVENTRY TOOK THE STAIRS two at a
time to the sixth floor and managed to catch Paul Kubiak just as
he was about to escape. Coventry must have had a look on his
face like he needed Kubiak's help and needed it now, because
Kubiak frowned and said, "Two minutes; if I had just left two
minutes earlier."

Coventry handed him an evidence bag and explained about
the envelope and photos inside. "I need everything in here
printed ASAP, as in, *Do you have it done yet?*" he said. "Whoever
handled it may be the one who took Madison Blake."

Kubiak cocked his head.

"You have no idea how starved I am," he said.

Coventry looked at his watch.

5:23.

"I'll have some pizza delivered," he said.

"Your treat?"

Coventry nodded.

"You're not going to look in your wallet after it gets here like
last time and say, *Gee, I could have sworn I had a twenty in there.*"

"That was a one time deal," Coventry said. "Plus I said I'd
pay you back."

"But you never did."

"But I said I would."

Kubiak rolled his eyes.

"Tell you what," Kubiak said. "Let's have a look in your wallet right now, just to be sure."

"What? You don't trust me? Just because of one little innocent mistake?"

"Sure I trust you," Kubiak said. "But why don't we have a

tiny little look-see anyway?"

Coventry pulled out his wallet.

And opened it to show he had money.

Except he didn't.

Two dollars.

That was it.

"I knew it!" Kubiak said.

Coventry chuckled.

"Hey, I'm as surprised as you," he said. "So I'll tell you what, I'll order the pizza and pay, except you'll need to advance me the money."

"Unbelievable," Kubiak said. Then he put a somber look on his face. "Are you serious about the prints?"

"Deadly," Coventry said. "Come on. We're wasting time."

Chapter Forty

Day Six—June 16
Saturday Morning

JOOP CHAINED MADISON BLAKE in the boxcar, just to be good and sure she couldn't escape, and wound down Highway 74 out of the mountains under a cerulean Colorado sky. He picked up a large cup of caffeine at the Conoco in Morrison, then headed for the Denver skyline and got to his LoDo loft by 9:00 a.m.

He had a lot to do today.

But first, he got the coffee going.

And took a hot shower.

Then he got on the Internet and researched Cayman banks. He opened an account by phone and then wire transferred all the funds from his checking and savings accounts.

$4.2 million.

When he checked his Cayman account on the Internet an hour later, all the funds were reported as received.

Perfect.

He didn't envision his departure to Europe as necessarily permanent. If he chose to come back to the U.S. in a couple of years, it wouldn't be a problem to get a new identity and disappear into the masses of New York, even if Madison Blake cooperated with the cops.

Which she would, of course.

Once she was safe and the police pressured her.

He killed Samantha Rickenbacker. Who knows how many other poor innocent women he'll kill if you don't help us stop him. Do you really want all that blood on your hands?

She'd crack in an hour.

No, thirty minutes.

So what?

It wouldn't matter.

HIS CONTACT CALLED AT 11:00. Forty-five minutes later, $250,000 was wire transferred into his Cayman account, reportedly from a Hong Kong bank—payment of his relocation bonus.

He felt better knowing it had arrived.

It showed good faith.

He needed exercise.

Right now.

So he dropped to the floor and did three sets of fifty push-ups. Then headed outside for a five-mile run, breathing deep, letting the air clean his lungs.

HE'D JUST WALKED IN THE DOOR, still out of breath, when his phone rang; the landline, not the cell. He didn't recognize the incoming number but answered anyway. A man's voice came through. "Is this Dylan Joop?"

It was.

"Well, Dylan Joop, a friend of mine told me he drove off in your car by mistake the other night. He was at a strip club and got pretty drunk. The car's an Audi. The registration in the glove box indicates it's yours. Is that true?"

Drove off by mistake?

What a crock.

The doors were locked.

The keys weren't in the ignition.

"Yeah, that's mine," Joop said. "Where is it?"

"We can bring it to you if you want."

"Okay, good."

"It will need to be later this afternoon," the man said. "That will give you time to get to the bank."

The bank?

"What is this, a shakedown? You steal my car and now you think you can sell it back to me? You little punk—"

The man laughed.

"Steal," the man said. "Such a strong word. I don't know if you ever watch the news, but they've been airing this story about some poor woman named Samantha Rickenbacker who got killed Tuesday night. Her roommate, a sweet young thing named Madison Blake, disappeared. The police are searching like crazy, but so far they haven't been able to come up with that one critical clue that they need so bad."

Joop paced.

Knowing where this was going.

"Go on," he said.

"The weirdest thing happened. It turns out that there's an envelope under the front seat of your car," the man said. "Inside that envelope are pictures of the woman who disappeared—

Madison Blake. We thought you probably wouldn't mind having those pictures back. We can bring them, if you want, when we drop off the car. But we were wondering if you had a reward out for them."

Joop kicked a chair.

It fell over.

"Stop being cute," he said. "How much?"

"We were thinking that a hundred thousand is a nice round number, that is, if there's a reward out for them. We hope there is, because then you get them back and we never saw them."

Joop didn't know who was on the other end of the line.

But he did know one thing.

It was the next person he would kill.

Chapter Forty-One

Day Six—June 16
Saturday Morning

WHEN THE EARLY RAYS OF DAWN worked their way into the bedroom, Paige Alexander reminded herself that she didn't get to bed until two in the morning because of the redeye, and that it was way too early to get up. But the anticipation of the upcoming day wouldn't let her get back to sleep.

So she threw off the sheets and took a shower.

Wearing shorts and a pink T-shirt, she peddled the Trek to the McDonald's on Alameda, sat down at a corner table and propped herself up with caffeine. She no longer had any doubts that a human trafficking conspiracy existed and that it emanated from Denver.

But where in Denver, exactly?

Vinson & Botts?

At first she had thought, yes.

Absolutely.

Based on a number of things: Ja'Von had a feeling that the firm who called her was large. The call came from a payphone in the lobby of the V&B's building. V&B was in the process of

194

opening an office in Bangkok. Thomas Fog was willing to cough up twenty grand without much of a fight. Fog wanted a comprehensive release, one broad enough to wipe out torts, conspiracies and any other type of action. Someone ran Paige off the road on her bike, and maybe even tried to kill her, not long after she made contact with V&B. Someone slashed Ja'Von's tires.

But now she had new information.

The calls to Rebecca Vampire had come from the lobby of a different building. That didn't mean that someone from V&B hadn't walked over there and made them, but it did raise at least a shadow of a doubt.

Enough to make Paige focus on the flip side of the V&B "evidence."

ANYONE COULD HAVE USED THE PHONE in the lobby of V&B's building. It wouldn't be unreasonable for V&B to agree to pay an alleged claim by a P.I., even if it was highly questionable, if for no other reason than to avoid the cost, time and embarrassment of a trial. Twenty grand was chump change. If V&B was going to pay an alleged claim, it also wouldn't be unreasonable to ask for a standard release. Finally, there was no telling who ran Paige off the road. It could have been some drunk or someone who just didn't see her. Teenagers could have slashed Ja'Von's tires.

The more she thought about it, the more she realized just how thin the case against V&B was.

No, thin wasn't even the word.

Microscopic.

If she filed the case at this point, the court would have no option but to bounce it out on its ass, and would probably assess attorney fees against her for bringing it.

Not good.

JA'VON PICKED HER UP AN HOUR LATER, looking like the winner of the genetic gene pool. She wore an aqua tank top and abbreviated white shorts that showcased tanned muscular legs. Unlike yesterday in Miami, when she had her hair in a ponytail, it now hung loose and full.

Very exotic.

"How's Coventry?" Paige asked.

"He scares me," Ja'Von said.

What?

Why?

"If he's reckless with me, I'm going to break."

Paige nodded.

"That's the problem. The higher you go, the farther you fall. It's called gravity. The secret is to pack an emotional parachute, just in case."

"How do you do that?" Ja'Von asked.

"I don't know. Just be sure you don't dump all your friends, I guess."

"I want you to meet him."

"Really?"

Ja'Von nodded.

"Yeah. Would you mind?"

No, she wouldn't.

Not at all.

They found a free 2-hour parking spot near 10th and Bannock and then headed over to the financial district, an easy fifteen minute hike. When they got to the Republic Plaza Building, they found a cluster of public payphones. Ja'Von dialed the number that had been used to call Rebecca Vampire.

No ringing.

They found another cluster.

Same thing.

No ringing.

They finally located the phone they were looking for on the fourth try. It turned out to be near a restaurant at the north edge of the building.

"Maybe someone from V&B was over here at another law firm for depositions or something. He ate at the restaurant and made the calls either before or after," Ja'Von said.

"Were the calls made around the noon hour?" Paige asked.

Ja'Von shrugged.

"I don't remember. We'll have to ask Mackenzie."

THE BUILDING DIRECTORY listed hundreds of tenants. Ja'Von pulled a small spiral notebook out of her purse and began writing down every one that could be a law firm.

Then something weird happened.

Two Asian men walked across the lobby.

Immaculately dressed in suits and ties.

Looking like lawyers.

Intense.

On a mission.

Carrying leather briefcases.

Ja'Von squeezed Paige's elbow and said, "Follow them!"

Chapter Forty-Two

Day Six—June 16
Saturday Morning

MADISON BLAKE'S BODY HADN'T SHOWN UP YET, at least as of last night. Until and unless it did, Coventry was prepared to treat her as alive even though lots of contemporaries would say that he was trying to blow smoke upwind. He got up an hour before daybreak and jogged in the dark.

Ja'Von's perfume hung on him.

Barely perceptible.

But strong enough to pull up the memory of last night, when she got back from Miami and crawled into bed at two in the morning.

Horny.

Not in the mood to be denied.

As if he could or would.

Ja'Von.

Ja'Von.

Ja'Von.

Who was she?

Where was she taking him?

He picked up the pace, letting his legs stretch and his lungs burn. What he really needed was a full workout at 24-Hour Fitness every day for a month, but that hadn't happened in over three years when he took over as the head of the homicide unit.

Back home, he smelled coffee.

Ja'Von was in the kitchen making pancakes.

Wearing one of his T-shirts.

"You're going to abandon me today," she said. "I can already tell."

He walked over and pulled up the shirt to see if she wore anything underneath.

She didn't.

So he slapped her ass.

It hardly even moved.

"Got to," he said. "But I'll make it up to you tonight."

"How?"

"I don't know. We'll do whatever you want."

"Whatever I want?"

"Right." He poured a cup of coffee, headed for the shower and added over his shoulder, "Up to ten dollars." She stuck her tongue out. "By the way, did I say thanks for the coffee?"

"No."

"I will," he said.

HE ATE PANCAKES FROM A PLATE IN HIS LAP as he drove to headquarters. The FBI profiler, Dr. Leanne Sanders, was sitting at his desk working on something when he walked into the room—a surprise. The aroma of caffeine floated in the air.

She glanced at her watch and said, "You used to get up early."

He gave her a sideways look and headed for the pot.

As he poured a cup he said, "The first rule of the forest is, don't mess with Sasquatche before he's had his coffee."

She grinned.

"Good analogy, except we're not in a forest, and you're not Sasquatche."

Then she chuckled as if she had just heard a joke.

"What?" he asked, curious.

"I almost added, *Notwithstanding the similar IQs.*"

He grinned.

"But you didn't say it, because you're so nice."

"Exactly," she said. "That and the fact that I don't want to insult Sasquatche."

He laughed and then asked, "So what's the latest and greatest with your Frenchman? What's his name—?"

"Boudiette."

"—Right, Boudiette."

"He hasn't resurfaced since he attacked me," she said. "He's still technically checked in at the Adams Mark Hotel downtown, but he's un-technically AWOL."

"Is he still in Denver?"

"My best guess is yes," she said. "We still think that the lawyer, Mark Remington, is his target. So we're tracking him, hoping to catch Boudiette in the act."

"Do you think that will work?"

"Probably not, but you never know."

"Why is Frenchie after the lawyer?"

"We don't know."

He studied her.

"How's your head?"

She shook it, as if to test whether it was there.

"It's still attached."

HE SHOWED HER COPIES OF THE PICTURES of Madison Blake and explained how the originals had been found by a highway trash crew. She confirmed that they were the kind that would be given to a hit man.

"Maybe Frenchie," Coventry said.

"Right," she said. "Except he wasn't in Denver yet."

He chuckled.

"You sure know how to ruin a good theory with facts."

"Here's another fact," she said. "A hit man wouldn't throw pictures of a target out a car window. That's what shredders are for."

"So what do you make of them?"

She took a closer look.

"They were definitely taken with a telephoto lens," she said. "And you can tell by her face that she didn't know it was going down. So they were definitely taken surreptitiously. Any prints?"

Coventry held his hands up in surrender.

"A few," he said. "Most belonged to the woman from the trash crew who found them. But we pulled a couple of others too. Unfortunately they didn't match up to anyone."

"They never do."

SUDDENLY HIS CELL PHONE RANG and the voice of Jena Vernon came through. Most people along the front range knew her as the charismatic roving reporter from the Channel 8 TV news. Coventry knew her from the old high school days back in Fort Collins when she was the ticklish tomboy down the street.

"Do you know Dick Zucker, our weatherman?" she asked.

"Not personally," he said.

"I know not personally, but you know who he is, right?"

He did.

"Well, he has a 20-year-old daughter named Brandy Zucker. She didn't come home last night. She's been missing since yesterday afternoon and isn't answering her cell phone." Jena said. "Dick's totally freaking out."

"The girl's probably out partying somewhere," Coventry said. "You were twenty once, remember?"

"I know Dick," she said. "He doesn't exaggerate. Can you talk to him or something?"

Coventry winced.

"The timing couldn't be worse," he said.

"I'd consider it a personal favor," Jena said. "If you do it, I'll let you tickle me again the next time we're down by the river."

Coventry pulled up a high school memory.

One he hadn't thought of in years.

Sunday afternoons down by the river.

With Jena and Jana.

Wrestling and goofing around.

"I don't get down there much anymore," he said.

"It doesn't have to be at the river," she said.

He chuckled.

"Be careful," he said. "I'm going to call your bluff one of these days."

"So you say."

Chapter Forty-Three

Day Six—June 16
Saturday Afternoon

———————

JOOP WOUND UP BEAR CREEK CANYON with the river on his left and the radio off, trying to decide if the man blackmailing him with the photos was a problem or not. The police would know Joop's identity as soon as he released Madison Blake. She'd be able to describe being held in a mountain setting with three boxcars. Even a dumb-ass civil servant detective would be able to locate the place sooner or later.

And trace ownership of the property to Joop.

Plus his fingerprints were everywhere.

He couldn't remove them in ten years.

Not even with an army of Molly Maids.

So, within a very short time, Joop's name would be on an arrest warrant for the murder of Samantha Rickenbacker and the abduction of Madison Blake, followed by an insanely intense manhunt. The blackmailer didn't really pose much of an additional threat. More evidence, yes. But the cops would already have all the coffin nails they needed.

The blackmailer was shooting blanks.

But didn't know it.

The important thing at this point was to keep him from going to the cops before Joop got out of the country.

Meaning he needed to leave today if possible.

Or stall him until Monday.

Or pay him.

Or kill him.

Of course, there was one other option. That was to kill Madison Blake and kill the blackmailer too, if he could. That would get Joop out of the cop net. But then he'd be in direct disregard of his orders to release Madison Blake. At a minimum, he'd have to spend the rest of his life looking over his shoulder and wondering if a rifle was pointed at the back of his head.

How did everything get so complicated?

And then there was the stripper, Bethany.

If he took her with him to Europe, she'd probably end up bolting after she found out he was wanted, meaning the only way he could have a future with her was to not get wanted in the first place, meaning he would have to kill Madison Blake and the blackmailer.

He passed Idledale.

Then turned onto his road, kicking up a trail of dust.

The gate was locked, as it should be.

And the twig that he put on top of the lock was still in place.

Good.

He passed through, relocked the gate behind him, and then headed up the road.

JUST AS THE BOXCARS CAME INTO SIGHT, his phone rang and the voice of Bethany, the stripper, came through. She sounded nervous.

"Some guy's been stalking me," she said.

"Who?"

"I don't know," she said. "My only guess is that he's someone from the club."

"Why? What's he been doing?"

"Every time I turn around he's there," she said.

"You've seen his face?"

"Yeah, but I don't recognize him." She paused and then added, "I'm scared."

Joop knew what she wanted.

The timing couldn't have been worse.

But he couldn't deny her.

"I'll take care of him for you," he said.

"He's big," she warned.

AT THE END OF THE ROAD he killed the engine and looked through the windshield to be sure Madison Blake's boxcar was still locked.

It was.

Perfect.

He stepped out of the vehicle and stretched as he walked.

Still trying to sort everything out.

Amsterdam would be a good place to live. Damn near everyone there spoke English. He could get an apartment on one of the canals. Both Paris and London were only a short train ride away. He could vacation on the French Riviera and play blackjack in Monte Carlo. Maybe spend a week or two in Greece every now and then—get some culture.

He pictured Bethany with him.

Why?

He didn't know.

There was just something about her.

No sounds came from Madison Blake's boxcar.

Joop pictured her passed out.

And numb from being on the hard floor for so long.

"Lucy, I'm home," he said in his best Ricky voice.

No response.

As he pulled the key out of his pocket, something whizzed past his ear, not more than an inch away, and ricocheted off the lock.

A bullet.

He turned and spotted a movement on the side of the mountain, more than two hundred yards off.

And dove under the railroad car.

Chapter Forty-Four

Day Six—June 16
Saturday Morning

PAIGE ALEXANDER FOLLOWED the two Asian men into the elevator and watched as they pressed floor thirty-nine. Everyone faced the front and said nothing on the way up. When the men got out, one of them turned and looked at her.

Not towards her.

At her.

Their eyes locked.

And for some frightening reason she felt like prey being studied by a predator.

The man turned away almost immediately.

But had memorized her face.

The door shut.

The elevator ascended.

She looked down to see what was wrong with her hands and found them trembling.

Back in the lobby, Ja'Von Deveraux said, "Well?"

"They got off on floor thirty-nine."

The building directory reported three tenants on the thirty-ninth floor, including one law firm—Thung, Manap & Deringer, Ltd. Ja'Von wrote down the name and said, "If they have a Bangkok office, we've found our connection."

Paige nodded.

Maybe.

Ja'Von pulled a $20.00 bill out of her wallet and handed it to Paige. "Do you want to see if you can find us some coffee while I finish up with my list?"

JUST OUTSIDE THE BUILDING, on the 16th Street Mall, Paige found a Starbucks and got at the end of a line ten long. The man in front of her looked like a 28-year-old rock star in a business suit—extremely attractive. He twisted his wrist every ten seconds to look at a black designer watch. He wore his hair straight, blond, parted in the middle and halfway down his back.

Something about him oozed sex.

He ordered an espresso, took a sip and then went to pay.

His wallet wasn't in his left jacket pocket.

Or his right.

Or his pants.

"This is really embarrassing," he said. "I think I left my wallet in the car." He chuckled. "I don't suppose you take IOUs."

The man behind the counter wasn't amused.

Paige surprised herself and said, "I got it."

The rock star looked at her.

With the bluest eyes she had ever seen.

"Thanks, I'll pay you back."

"Don't worry about it."

He looked at his watch and headed for the door. "Thanks again," he said.

Then he was gone.

Walking back to the Republic Plaza Building, Paige spotted him again, talking intently into a cell phone and pacing back and forth near the fountain. He noticed her, walked over and said into the phone, "Hold on a minute." Then to Paige, "You need to let me say thank you. I'm thinking lunch."

No.

That wasn't necessary.

"But thanks anyway."

"Wait a minute," he said. "What's your name?"

"Paige."

"Michael Dexter," he said. "I'll tell you what. I'm going to be standing right here at noon. If you show up, we'll do lunch. If you don't, then my loss."

FROM THE REPUBLIC PLAZA BUILDING, Paige and Ja'Von went straight back to Paige's apartment to drink more coffee and run Thung, Manap & Deringer, Ltd. through Google.

"Bingo!"

The law firm maintained offices in three Thailand cities—Bangkok, Chiang Mai and Krung Thep—as well as satellite branches in Hong Kong, Paris and Denver.

According to the Denver office website, the man in the elevator who looked at Paige was an attorney by the name of Virote Pattaya, Esq., a specialist in intellectual property law.

They printed page after page from the Internet.

And roughly organized things in manila file folders.

Totally absorbed.

Paige looked at her watch.

11:40.

She hadn't planned on meeting the rock star for lunch.

But suddenly had to.

"Can you run me downtown?"

Ja'Von must have sensed urgency in her voice because she said, "Sure, when?"

"Right this second!"

THEY WERE ALMOST OUT THE DOOR when Paige ran back, grabbed a pair of fresh khaki pants and a crisp white blouse, and then fell back into step. She waited until they were on the 6th Avenue freeway and then changed in the car. A trucker spotted the show and honked with approval.

Then he tried to keep up but couldn't.

"He'd run someone over just to see your panties," Ja'Von said.

"Men."

"They're animals," Ja'Von added.

Paige laughed.

"What?" Ja'Von asked.

"Here's a secret. Right now, so am I."

Paige looked at her watch: 11:50 and they hadn't even reached Sheridan yet. "Step on it." Ja'Von checked for cops, saw none and brought the vehicle up to 78. Suddenly Ja'Von's cell phone rang and she answered it. Paige hardly paid any attention to the conversation as she frantically brushed her hair and painted her lips.

Ja'Von hung up and said, "That was my assistant, Hannah. I've had her doing research to see if she could find any other female investigators who have gone to Bangkok and disappeared."

Paige looked at her and said, "And?"

"And she found one."

Paige stopped fussing with her hair and looked over.

"Are you serious?"

"Dead."

"Who?"

"Someone named Susan Wagner from Cleveland."

"Does she fit the profile?"

"Meaning tall and blond?"

"Right, and hot."

"I forgot to ask," Ja'Von said. "But I'm guessing yes, otherwise Hannah wouldn't have been so excited. I think I better call her and see if I can get her out here to Denver."

"*Her* meaning Hannah?"

"Right."

"Good idea."

"I'll call her while you're screwing Mr. Rock Star," Ja'Von said.

Paige laughed.

Then got serious.

"He's someone important," she said. "He's not going to be interested in a waitress."

"You're not a waitress, sweetie. You're a lawyer. Stop forgetting that."

Chapter Forty-Five

Day Six—June 16
Saturday Noon

THE WOODEN TABLE in the conference room had enough scratches on it to stretch from Denver to Aspen. Coventry set his coffee cup down and slipped into a seat. Dick Zucker—the Channel 8 weatherman—took a seat on the opposite side, looking older than he did on TV. Ten seconds later Sergeant Kate Katona walked in, sat down and said, "Morning."

"Morning back to you."

She had a pleasant face, an easy smile, and short wash-and-go hair.

As usual, Coventry did his best to not drop his eyes to her world-class chest, currently encased in a T-shirt with a yellow smiley-face.

He checked his watch.

And found he forgot to put it on this morning.

Then twisted Kate's wrist so he could see hers.

11:43 a.m.

Damn.

Where had the morning gone?

Coventry looked at Zucker and said, "I'm going to be honest with you, we're up to our asses in alligators around here. If it wasn't Jena Vernon who called, we wouldn't be talking right now. That doesn't mean we don't understand your situation and your concern as a father. And it doesn't mean we don't sympathize. It just means that you need to understand our time constraints and the fact that this really isn't even in our jurisdiction. But if we can grease some skids for you we will. Actually, Kate will, which is why she's sitting in. With that, tell us what's going on."

Zucker told them the story.

Brandy, age 20, still lived at home.

She left the house yesterday to go for a hike.

She never came back.

"Go for a hike where?"

"We don't know for sure," Zucker said. "She was talking about somewhere around Morrison or up Bear Creek Canyon. Last night we called everyone she knows and no one knows anything. We got up at the crack of dawn this morning and drove up and down Highway 74 but couldn't find her car anywhere."

"She's probably just lost," Coventry said.

"No," Zucker said. "She always took her cell phone with her. Everyone in our family has the same plan. The reception is good in that whole area. If she got lost she would have called."

They talked for another ten minutes.

At the end Coventry said, "Here's what we'll do. We'll open a missing person's file right now and get a BOLO out for her vehicle."

A BOLO?

Be On Look Out.

Oh.

"Kate will help you coordinate with the parks department and the forest service. Is that good enough?"

Yes.

"Thank you. Thank you so much."

Coventry cocked his head.

"Does she have a credit card?"

"Several."

"Get us the numbers," he said. "We'll see if any of them have been used." He looked at Kate and added, "Also check with her cell phone company, find out who she talked to in the last 24 hours, and see if they know where she is."

Kate nodded.

Coventry looked at Zucker and said, "In exchange, we expect good weather from now on."

AFTERWARDS AT THE COFFEE POT, Coventry told Kate, "Sorry to stick you with this."

"I have to admit, I'm not too motivated," she said. "We both know she'll wander home sometime this afternoon either hung over or with rug burns on her ass."

"Maybe," Coventry said. "But Channel 8 has helped us out a lot over the years. This is called payback. I just wish it had come at a better time."

"So you want me to really follow through?"

Yes he did.

TWO HOURS LATER DR. LEANNE SANDERS CALLED. "I thought I'd let you know I'm loosing my target."

"You mean the Frenchman?"

"No, his target, the lawyer."

"Why? What's going on?"

"The lawyer is getting on a plane to Bangkok."

"Bangkok?"

"Right."

"Why? What's in Bangkok?"

"I don't have a clue," she said. "We're monitoring all flights at this point. If the Frenchman follows him, I'm going to be in tow."

"Do you think that's smart? He's already attacked you once and you'll stick out like a sore thumb over there."

"I don't think he ever really got a good look at me," she said.

"Yeah, well I don't think you're giving him enough credit."

"Maybe not," she said.

The line went dead.

Bangkok.

That's where the pilot, Alan Ewing, had been just before he got butchered in his bedroom.

Coventry called Leanne back.

"Be careful," he said.

She chuckled.

"Always."

"I mean it."

Chapter Forty-Six

AS SOON AS THE BULLET RICOCHETED, even before Joop dropped to the ground, he knew he'd been set up for a hit. At the backside of the railroad car, he got low to the earth and stuck his head out just far enough past a wheel to where he could see the mountainside.

No one was running down towards him.

He saw trees.

And boulders.

And fallen logs.

But nothing human.

The air stood deathly quiet.

What to do?

In the middle boxcar he had a gun, plus his bow. But they might as well be on the moon. He was lucky enough that his hunter missed once. It wouldn't happen again. Was the man coming for him to finish the job or was he getting the hell out of there?

He was coming.

Joop saw nothing to indicate that.

But could feel it.

That's what he would do.

Think.

Think!

HE BACKED AWAY FROM THE BOXCAR and, still hidden from view behind it, got to the base of a forty-foot lodgepole pine. On the backside, he shoved four or five good throwing stones in his pants pocket and then climbed up the trunk until he was thirty feet off the ground. Then he got his breathing as shallow and quiet as he could and waited.

Nothing happened.

Ten minutes passed.

Then another ten.

And another.

Then what happened took him totally off guard. A man with a rifle came down the mountain, behind him. All this time he must have been circling around.

Joop was in plain view.

He held his breath.

The man wasn't going to pass under him. Joop couldn't jump down on him, even if there weren't twenty branches in the way. The man passed, stopped ten feet short of the boxcars, and bent down to see if Joop was hiding underneath.

Joop swallowed hard and then started to climb down.

Chapter Forty-Seven

Day Six—June 16
Saturday Noon

THE ROCK STAR WAS STILL WAITING at the designated spot when Paige Alexander trotted up, out of breath, fifteen minutes late. He looked at his watch and said, "I was only going to give you one more hour."

"Thanks for waiting," she said.

"Two at the most," he added.

She smiled.

"Then I'll consider myself two hours early. I'm starved."

"What are you in the mood for?"

"What are my options?"

"Anything you want, and I even remembered my wallet."

"Anything?"

"Yes."

"Okay, but remember, you said."

She grabbed his hand, led him over to a street vendor and ordered a $1.00 hotdog and diet coke. He grinned and said, "Two." They ate as they walked down the 16th Street Mall.

"True confessions," she said. "I got dressed up for you."

"You look nice."

"Liar," she said. "This is as good as it gets. I don't own a dress."

He chuckled.

"Full disclosure," he said. "I like that."

"Nor do I want to." She took a bite, chewed and said, "So disclose something about you."

"Like what?"

"Are you married?"

He laughed. "No."

"Girlfriend?"

"No."

"No?"

"No."

"Why not?"

"Because I've been waiting for someone to come along who likes hotdogs better than lobster," he said.

"That's not necessarily me," Paige said.

"No?"

"Well, it may be or it may not be," she said. "I've never had lobster, so I can't tell you with any honesty one way or the other."

"You've never had lobster?"

She shook her head.

"Never ever?"

"No."

"In that case, we need to make a stop at Fisherman's Wharf one of these days."

"Where's that?"

"San Francisco," he said.

She laughed.

"I usually don't go that far to eat."

"Me either."

"You'd be hungry again by the time you got back," she added.

He agreed.

"That's the downside."

They were approaching a homeless woman sitting on the sidewalk in the shade. The rock star pulled a $10.00 bill out of his wallet, put it in her hand and closed her fingers around it. She looked up, took a moment to focus and then smiled. "Thank you, Michael."

"You're welcome."

"She knows you?" Paige asked.

He nodded.

"How?"

"That's not important," he said. "What is important is that I want to see you again. I already know that so I'm just going to get it out in the open. You don't have to say yes, but don't say no."

She studied him.

And found the words sincere.

"Yes," she said.

JA'VON PICKED HER UP AT 2:30 and must have seen something on her face because she said, "Someone's in lust." Paige's first thought was to deny it, but she didn't.

"*Possible* lust," she said.

"Lust," Ja'Von repeated.

Paige grinned.

"Okay, lust."

"Details."

Paige gave them and added, "There's only one downside."

"What's that?"

"He's a lawyer."

Ja'Von chuckled.

"FYI girlfriend, that goes in the plus column, not the minus."

Paige felt herself get serious.

"Usually, yes," she said. "But he's not your ordinary lawyer."

"So what is he?"

"He's a lawyer with Vinson & Botts."

"Vinson & Botts?"

"Right."

"You've got to be kidding me."

"I wish I was."

"Well that's a pretty big coincidence."

Paige nodded.

She already knew that.

"Let me ask you something," Ja'Von said. "When you met this guy this morning, was he already in line or did he sort of hop in there right in front of you?"

Paige didn't know.

She hadn't been paying attention.

Ja'Von retreated in thought.

Then looked at Paige and said, "I'm not saying it's a setup, but I'm not saying it's not a setup either."

Paige understood.

"You've been to Fisherman's Wharf, right?"

Ja'Von had.

Hundreds of times.

"Do they have good lobster there?"

"Good is an understatement. Why?"

Paige shrugged.

"Just curious."

THEY DROVE IN SILENCE. Two blocks before Paige's apartment, Ja'Von said, "Assume it's not a setup. Are you going to be able to do this?"

"Do what?"

"You know."

"You mean go for blood against V&B at the same time that I'm all hot and bothered over one of their attorneys?"

"Right, that."

Paige looked at her.

"Maybe V&B isn't our target," she said. "Maybe it's Thung, Manap & Deringer. Either way, I won't let you down. I promise."

Ja'Von studied her.

And apparently didn't see the need to press.

But she added, "It's not just me at this point. In fact, I'm all safe and sound back here in the U.S. I'm more concerned about the other women who will disappear down the road if we don't do something."

Paige nodded.

And understood all too well.

Chapter Forty-Eight

Day Six—June 16
Saturday Night

COVENTRY WAS SOUND ASLEEP when his cell phone rang. He twisted and looked at the red digits of the alarm clock on the headboard—10:02 p.m., meaning he had only been out for a half hour. Next to him, there was no Ja'Von. Then he remembered that she was picking up a friend at the airport, someone named Hannah.

"Got some job security for you," Barb Winters said.

Coventry grunted.

"Tell them to be dead in the morning. I'm too tired."

She chuckled.

"I'll see what I can do."

Thirty minutes later he squeezed the Tundra into a parking spot on Broadway and walked over to a small public parking lot in the middle of the downtown's financial district.

A sign with the rates caught his eye.

Outrageous.

What is this, New York?

Someone had already taped off the entire lot, very impressive. Better to have a crime scene too big than the opposite. One of the responding officers turned out to be John Root, a hang glider fanatic who got slammed into the side of Lookout Mountain last summer and broke a bunch of bones.

Coventry shook his hand and said, "Still flying?"

"Oh yeah," Root said. "In fact, last week I caught this absolutely crazy wind, took it way the hell up there and stayed up for four hours."

"Four hours?"

"Yep."

"How do you—?"

"What?"

"You know, go."

"You mean to the bathroom?"

Coventry nodded.

"You just unzip and go for it," Root said.

Coventry pictured it and said, "Man, I'd have to be really high to do that."

Root looked puzzled. "Why?"

"Well, I wouldn't want to be dragging that bad boy on the ground."

Root pushed him.

"In your dreams, buddy."

"It reminds me of the Ohno bird," Coventry said.

"What's that?"

"You never heard of the Ohno bird?"

No.

Root hadn't.

"Well," Coventry said, "the Ohno bird is about the size of a vulture, and it's the only bird species in the world where the size of the male's member is actually longer that its legs. Every time it comes in for a landing it makes the same sound—oh no, oh no, oh no!"

Root laughed in spite of himself.

"Bad, even for you."

"You love it," Coventry said. "You'll tell it ten times."

THE VICTIM TURNED OUT TO BE A WHITE MALE, early 30s, slumped over in the passenger seat of a Jeep Commander, with no visible signs of physical trauma.

"Overdose?" Coventry asked.

Root shrugged.

"The paramedics said it seemed like he had a broken neck."

Coventry must have had an expression on his face because Root asked, "What?"

"Nothing, except that I just had a broken neck case," Coventry said. "A woman named Samantha Rickenbacker."

Root looked blank.

He hadn't heard about it.

"You don't get that many of them," Coventry added. "Guns and knives. That's the bread and butter."

Root pointed to an Avis sticker on the rear passenger window of the vehicle.

"A rental," he said.

"Can you do me a favor? Call Avis, find out who rented it and have them fax me over a copy of all the paperwork, including the guy's driver's license." Coventry handed him a business card. "Use that fax number."

"Done," Root said.

Five minutes later Root returned and said, "A guy by the name of Jean-Paul Boudiette rented the car from the DIA

Avis."

Boudiette.

Coventry recognized the name but couldn't place it.

"Word is he's a Frenchman," Root added.

Coventry nodded.

Remembering now.

The INTERPOL guy.

He was pretty sure that the victim was Boudiette rather than some third person, but put on gloves and pulled the man's wallet out of his pants pocket.

It turned out he was right.

Then he called Dr. Leanne Sanders.

"You're still looking for the Frenchman, right?" he asked.

She was.

Very much so.

"I'll bet you a steak dinner that I can find him before you do," he said.

A pause.

"You know where he is," she said.

"Maybe," he said. "Do we have a bet?"

"Where is he?"

"I can't tell you unless we have an official bet."

"That's so low."

"True. But do we have a bet?"

"Fine, we do."

"A steak dinner," he said.

"Agreed."

THE FBI PROFILER showed up twenty minutes later carrying a thermos and two disposable cups. She looked for a bullet in the back of Boudiette's head, saw none and said, "I'll be damned. It's him. How'd he die?"

"Broken neck, from what we can tell."

"Too bad, he was such a nice guy." She looked at Coventry and said, "I'll make you another bet."

"What kind of bet?"

"I'll bet that you want what's in this thermos more than you want that steak dinner," she said.

He chuckled and said, "I'll bet you're right."

"So I'm officially off the hook?"

"Yes, but only because you play dirty."

He poured while she held the cups.

Some kind of chocolate flavor.

Piping hot.

"It's decaf," she said.

Good.

Coventry nodded at the body and said, "Does our buddy here have any ties to Bangkok?"

Leanne wrinkled her forehead.

"Not that I know of, why?"

"Something's been nagging at me ever since you told me that the lawyer, Mark Remington, got on a plane to Bangkok. I have another case involving a pilot named Alan Ewing who got stabbed in the back a bunch of times in his bedroom, right after he got back from a flight to Bangkok."

"When did that happen?"

Coventry searched his memory.

"That would have been Monday."

"Boudiette wasn't in Denver yet, if you're implying that he did it," Leanne said.

"Right, I know that," Coventry said.

"Remington was though, I assume," she added.

Coventry nodded and took a drink of coffee.

"So who killed your Frenchman?"

"I don't have a clue," she said.

"Then let me give you one," he said. "*Someone strong.*"

Chapter Forty-Nine

Day Six—June 16
Saturday Night

JOOP'S CONTACT LIVED in a stately Riva Chase mansion on a primo 5-acre cul-de-sac lot with a stream. Deer, elk, fox and coyotes abounded, yet downtown Denver was a mere twenty-minute jaunt down the freeway.

Right now he wasn't home.

So Dylan Joop waited in the dark.

With the lights off.

Down the road.

Behind the wheel of the Nissan rental.

Not knowing yet if he would kill the man or not.

On the seat next to him sat a manila envelope, the envelope that Joop found inside the center console of the Frenchman's vehicle. Inside that envelope were several photographs of Mark Remington. Of greater interest, however, were the photographs of Joop himself.

The photographs meant one thing and one thing only.

Namely that Mark Remington and Joop had both been targets.

But why?

Headlights suddenly reflected from the rearview mirror into his eyes. A car approached. Joop's heart beat faster and he ducked down as the lights swept past. The driver was alone and headed for the driveway. Joop cranked over the ignition and followed with the lights off. By the time the other vehicle pulled to a stop, Joop was right behind it.

"Good evening," Joop said as he got out.

No response.

Then the man said, "This is squarely against protocol."

"So was the hit man who paid me a visit. The *dead* hit man, to be precise."

"I was afraid something like this might happen," the man said. "Come inside."

THE MAN WALKED ACROSS A LARGE VAULTED ROOM to a wet bar, poured whiskey into two crystal glasses and handed one to Joop, who took it but didn't drink.

The man swallowed half the glass and said, "Go ahead and drink. You're not going to kill me."

Joop swirled the liquor.

And then looked at the man.

"We haven't established that yet," he said.

The man laughed. "Damn, man, you're strung tight."

Joop handed him the envelope and watched as the man removed the photographs of Mark Remington and Joop and looked at them.

The man studied them and said nothing.

Joop pulled the .357 SIG out of his coat jacket and pointed it at the man.

"Talk," he said.

He expected the man to tremble but he looked more like he was trying to solve a puzzle instead. "The Frenchman is your Western Europe counterpart. He's either gone rouge or someone's pulling his strings. We're not sure which yet."

"Go on."

"We just recently found out that he was after Mark Remington," the man said. "But we had no idea he was after you."

How?

How did they know he was after Remington?

"He was hanging around outside Remington's house Thursday night," the man said. "It turned out that a female FBI agent was tailing him. He doubled back and attacked her—a stupid thing, but a thing he did, nonetheless. The next morning, the agent and a homicide detective by the name of Bryson Coventry paid a visit to Remington to find out why he was a target. Remington told me about the visit."

"Then what?"

"Remington got on a plane to Bangkok."

"So then the Frenchman turned his attention to his second target—me," Joop said.

The man nodded.

"It sure seems that way."

"He tried to snipe me but missed," Joop said. "When he came in to finish up, things didn't go the way he planned."

"You killed him?"

"Yes. I snapped his neck."

THE MAN REFILLED HIS GLASS. Joop pondered the situation for a few moments, then lowered the gun, drained half his glass, and let the man top it off.

"So why was he after Remington? And me?"

The man held his hands out in surrender.

"We don't know," he said. "He went AWOL three months ago. A month after he dropped off the radar screen, his counterpart in Hong Kong—and your counterpart—showed up dead. We have every reason to believe he did it but don't know why. That's why there's an opening in Hong Kong, like I was telling you about before. And the opening in Western Europe is to replace him, obviously. That's the slot you'll be filling."

Joop took a solid drink of alcohol.

It dropped hot and tingly into his stomach.

"Has the Frenchman taken out anyone else, besides Hong Kong?"

The man nodded.

"A man named Gordon Smyth, in London. A damn fine guy." He sipped the liquor. "What did you do with the body?"

"I put it in the passenger seat of his car and parked it in a parking lot downtown."

The man looked dumbfounded.

"Why?"

"Well, I thought Remington might have been behind it somehow. The body was meant to be a warning shot across the bow."

"I wish you hadn't done that," the man said.

Chapter Fifty

PAIGE ALEXANDER WORKED HER SHIFT at Sam's Eatery from four to nine and miraculously encountered only one customer from idiot-land. She kept having a vision of the rock star, Michael Dexter, walking in with a bunch of friends and accidentally bumping into her, but that didn't happen. She got home at ten and logged on to the Colorado Bar Association website to see if any new jobs had been posted.

None had.

She twisted a pencil in her fingers.

Then snapped it in two.

Ja'Von knocked on the door ten minutes later. With her was a woman—mid-20s, five-ten, incredibly attractive, athletic, short black hair, jeans, sandals and a green long-sleeve shirt.

"This is my assistant, Hannah," Ja'Von said.

Paige shook her hand.

And liked her immediately.

Ja'Von held up a bottle of white wine and said, "Brought another friend too."

They sat at the kitchen table—a cheap folding unit—and Hannah filled Paige in on what she knew so far about Susan Wagner, the private investigator from Cleveland who disappeared in Bangkok approximately eighteen months ago.

She was a solo practitioner.

Twenty-three.

Attractive.

Blond.

And made a $7,500 cash deposit into her checking account.

"I'm heading to Cleveland in the morning," Hannah said. "I actually had a layover in Denver, so it isn't costing any money to be here."

PAIGE GOT UP, pulled fresh ice cubes from the freezer and plopped them in her wine. Both of the other women held their glasses up and she did the same for them.

Then she sat down and twisted a pencil in her fingers.

"What we need at this point more than anything else is a direct evidentiary link to either Vinson & Botts, or to Thung, Manap & Deringer," she said. "We need to trace a phone call to their office, or get evidence that they hired a messenger service to have the cash delivered, or trace an email to or from one of their lawyers, or get a connection between them and Bob Copeland, anything like that."

"Exactly," Ja'Von said.

"I don't care how small it is," Paige added. "It's driving me nuts not knowing which one is the target."

"What does your new lawyer friend from V&B know about any of this?"

"Michael Dexter?"

"Right."

Paige snapped the pencil in two.

"I don't know and I'm not going to ask him," she said.

Ja'Von patted her hand and said, "You're rough on stuff. Do you know that?"

Paige grinned.

"I'm going to do a background check on him," Ja'Von added.

"Michael Dexter?"

"Yes."

"Why?"

"Because if he's married or has a girlfriend or something like that, then the whole meeting-you-thing was a setup, meaning that V&B is our target."

Paige didn't like the idea.

But couldn't disagree with the logic.

"Just don't do anything illegal," Paige warned. "If we do end up suing V&B, we don't want them to have a counterclaim against you. That would destroy your credibility, not to mention putting the entire case at risk."

Ja'Von cocked her head.

"Fine. If we need to bend the rules, we'll have Hannah do it."

"No," Paige said. "No one bends the rules."

Ja'Von looked at Hannah and said, "Feisty, isn't she?"

"Apparently so."

HANNAH SPENT THE NIGHT AT PAIGE'S APARTMENT. They talked for an hour in bed and then Hannah gave Paige a backrub before they went to sleep.

Chapter Fifty-One

Day Seven—June 17
Sunday Morning

———————

ON SUNDAY MORNING, COVENTRY swung by the Marriott West in Golden, picked up Leanne Sanders, and drove back down to the parking lot crime scene while the profiler punched the preset radio buttons.

"It's all hip-hop," she complained.

Coventry grunted.

"Shalifa," he said.

"You let her reset them?"

"I don't let her do anything," he said. "She just does it."

"Well two can play at that game," Leanne said.

And then reset everything to easy listening. "This is what it sounds like inside an elevator," she said.

"No wonder I never go in them."

AS THEY PASSED BANNOCK STREET and entered downtown, Kate Katona called and said, "Got a hit on our BOLO."

What BOLO?

Brandy Zucker's car.

Right.

He remembered now.

"It showed up parked at the rest stop at Vail Pass," she said.

"Vail Pass?"

Right.

"That's a long way from where she was supposed to be hiking," he said.

"That it is," she said. "What do you want to do?"

He considered it.

"Has she shown up anywhere yet?"

"No."

"Okay, let's err on the side of caution and treat the car as a crime scene," he said. "Call Paul Kubiak and have him send someone up there to process it."

"That's eighty miles," Kate said.

"I know, but if she was abducted and there are prints in the car, I want them," he said. "I also want to know if the car is running fine or broken down. Have you called the weatherman yet?"

"No, I wanted to talk to you first."

"Go ahead and call him and get him up to speed."

"He's going to freak," Kate said. "He's already a rubber band stretched to the limit. Should we wait until after we process it?"

Coventry considered it.

"If I was in his shoes, I'd want to know now."

IT BEING SUNDAY MORNING, the traffic was actually sane. That didn't mean some idiot couldn't take them out at any moment, but at least the odds were less.

"I had a strange thought last night," he told Leanne.

"Did it involve a naked woman, a donkey and a midget?"

He chuckled.

"No."

"Then go ahead and tell me about it," she said.

"By no, I mean no midget. Still want to hear it?"

She rolled her eyes.

"Go on."

"Okay," he said. "The Frenchman was after the lawyer."

"Remington."

"Right," Coventry said. "Remington knows this, because we paid him a visit. Now the Frenchman turns up dead. Did you note the location?"

"You mean, not too far from Remington's office?"

"Right," Coventry said. "Now, ordinarily Remington would be my prime suspect. Except you said he went to Bangkok."

"Right, he did."

"Are you sure?"

"Yes."

"So if Remington didn't kill Frenchie, the question is whether Remington hired someone to do a preemptive strike. That makes sense in a way, because Frenchie was in the passenger seat, meaning he was probably killed somewhere else and then driven there. Maybe so that Remington would see that the job had been done."

"I doubt it," Leanne said.

"Why?"

"He's not in town to see it for one," she said. "Plus there are a lot safer ways to show that a hit's been completed. Especially since Remington knows that we know that he and the Frenchman are somehow connected."

They were at the crime scene now. Coventry parked on Broadway and they took advantage of the light of day to check the surrounding buildings for security cameras.

There were several in the area.

But none pointed at the parking lot.

A dead end.

They checked the ground in the parking lot.

And found nothing new of interest.

Coventry pulled the tape off the perimeter and threw it in the back of the Tundra.

There.

The scene was released.

FROM THERE, THEY SWUNG BY THE 7-ELEVEN on Santa Fe, refilled Coventry's thermos with caffeine, and headed over to the Adams Mark Hotel where Boudiette had initially checked in.

To see if the room had any secrets.

If it did, it wasn't coughing them up.

Not that Coventry cared that much.

His thoughts were on Samantha Rickenbacker.

Dead since Tuesday night.

And Madison Blake.

Missing since Tuesday night.

"The Frenchman had a snapped neck," Coventry said. "A woman by the name of Samantha Rickenbacker got killed that same way on Tuesday night."

Leanne studied him.

"You told me that before," she said.

"Oh, sorry. I guess it just keeps bouncing around in my mind."

"That's okay."

"I made a promise to her," he added.

"The dead woman?"

"Right."

"I didn't think you did that anymore."

He didn't either.

BEFORE THEY LEFT THE ADAMS MARK HOTEL, Coventry returned the key to the front desk and said, "We're releasing the room. Go ahead and rent it if you want to." He turned to Leanne as they walked across the lobby and asked, "Now what?"

"That depends."

"On what?"

"On whether you know any judges who are sympathetic to the cause," she said. "Because if you do, I wouldn't mind getting a search warrant and spending the afternoon in Mark Remington's house."

Coventry chewed on it.

"We can use the theory that Remington hired someone to kill the Frenchman as a preemptive strike," she added.

Coventry grunted.

"That's awfully thin," he said.

"Maybe we'll find something to point to who the neck snapper is," she added.

Coventry's eyes narrowed.

"Let's get going."

Chapter Fifty-Two

Day Seven—June 17
Sunday Morning

WHEN HE GOT BACK TO THE BOXCARS last night from his contact's house, Dylan Joop grabbed a flashlight and checked on his captive, Madison Blake, who was pounding on the door and screaming. She couldn't take the isolation any longer and begged him to let her go. So he made a compromise and told her she could spend the night in his bed if she wanted.

"You mean for sex?" she asked.

No, he didn't.

Just for company.

If she wanted.

Her choice.

She'd have one side.

He'd have the other.

She bit her lower lip and said, "Okay."

He let her shower and then they drank beer. She told him about camping trips as a child, a 4th grade play in which she had a singing part, driving on the wrong side of the freeway once, a boyfriend who got a finger blown off with an M-80, and on and on and on. When it was time to go to bed, he let her use the facilities, then chained her ankle to the bed frame and made sure there was nothing she could reach to use as a weapon, even if she got out of bed and stretched to the end of the chain.

He didn't care about her hands.

She couldn't use those to hurt him.

Even if she attacked him while he slept.

But he wanted to be sure she couldn't get her little fingers on anything sharp or heavy; or on his cell phone, for that matter.

She promised to behave herself.

Then they slept.

She slept well.

He didn't.

Instead he flipped and pitched half the night with two things on his mind—one, what his contact would say today regarding the request that Joop gave him last night; and two, how to best handle the guy blackmailing him with the pictures.

SUNDAY MORNING, JOOP LET MADISON BLAKE sit in the sun and watch him shoot the bow. When his phone rang, he gave her a warning glance and then answered.

It turned out to be the call he'd been waiting for.

His contact.

"I've been giving a lot of thought to your request to come up with a way to keep you in the United States," the man said. "There's only one way that I can think of to make it work. Obviously, first of all, you'd have to kill Madison Blake. That means she won't be released like we wanted. That won't be as much of a problem as we initially thought if a man named Porter Potter happens to die."

"Who's Porter Potter?"

"He lives here in Denver and will be an easy target," the man said. "The key is, though, it will have to look like an accident. We can't have anyone even begin to think that he was murdered. If you can pull that off, then you have our permission to kill the woman and stay in Denver."

Joop grinned.

"I already have a plan," he said.

"So that's the route you want to go?"

"Absolutely."

"Potter has to die before the woman though," the man said. "If she dies first and he finds out about it, which he will, that will cause us more problems than you can even believe."

"Okay."

"Say it," the man said.

"Potter goes first," Joop said.

"Then and only then can you do the woman."

"Then the woman," Joop said.

"I'm dead serious," the man added. "The order is critical."

"Why?"

"That's need-to-know," the man said. "I'll call you back in an hour with the information on Potter."

"Be sure you get me his vehicle descriptions and license plate numbers."

"Done."

WHEN JOOP HUNG UP, Madison Blake looked at him with kind eyes. He had been good to her lately. And had told her he would be releasing her as soon as he was absolutely convinced that she wouldn't help the police.

"Thanks for letting me be outside," she said.

"No problem."

"It really means a lot to me."

"Don't worry about it."

A hawk circled above, riding a wind current on outstretched wings, scouting for food. Joop's heart raced as he suddenly realized something. He had been counting on releasing Madison Blake, which meant that the police would find out who he was, which meant that the blackmailer with the photographs wasn't a real threat since he wouldn't be telling the police anything they didn't already know. But now that he would be killing Madison Blake, the blackmailer was a huge problem.

A problem that needed to go away.

Permanently.

And fast.

Today if possible.

Chapter Fifty-Three

PAIGE ALEXANDER WOKE SUNDAY MORNING when the mattress moved. A deep recessed survival gene immediately forced her arms over her face for protection. Then she saw that the movement came from a woman.

Hannah Trent.

Breathing deeply.

Paige shifted onto her back and closed her eyes.

Five minutes later she forced herself out of bed, turned on the hot water for the shower, and used the facilities while the water came up to temperature. She lathered her legs with soap and shaved them in the shower while the spray splashed on her back. Fifteen minutes later she was in the kitchen wearing a T-shirt with her hair combed but still soaking wet. She got the coffee pot in motion, fired up the Gateway laptop and pulled the blinds to the side to see what the day looked like outside.

The sun broke over the horizon.

A cloudless sky floated above.

Nice.

The shower turned back on.

And Hannah joined her in the kitchen thirty minutes later, clean and refreshed. Her short hair had almost dried. She looked slightly embarrassed and said, "Sorry about last night."

Paige had a pretty good idea what she was referring to.

But feigned ignorance.

"What do you mean?"

"I mean the backrub," she said. "I guess the wine just got to me."

"It's okay," Paige said. "It felt good."

"You're probably wondering if I'm gay," she said. "I'm not, at least that I know of."

"Well I'm totally straight, but it felt good, so thank you."

"You're not mad?"

Paige walked over and hugged her.

Quick but tight.

Then kissed her on the cheek.

"You're a nice person," she said. "I'm glad you stayed over last night."

Hannah smiled.

"I just didn't want to appear inappropriate."

OVER BREAKFAST, PAIGE HAD A WILD IDEA and immediately called Ja'Von Deveraux. "Here's what I'm thinking," Paige said. "We know you never saw the man who hired you."

True.

That had all been done by telephone.

"But obviously he has some type of a connection to Bangkok," Paige said.

"Right."

"I mean, he's embedded there deep enough to not only know about the place where you were taken, but also to get women for the place. That means that whoever runs the place trusts him. And no one's going to trust him unless they know him pretty well."

Agreed.

"So how do they know him?"

Silence.

"I don't know."

"Me either," Paige said. "But I do know one thing. He's definitely been to the place."

Agreed.

"More than once."

Agreed.

"And when he goes there, they'd treat him like royalty."

Agreed again.

"Meaning that he'd have his pick of the women," Paige said. "Not necessarily for S&M—we don't know if he was into that or not—but at least for a good blowjob."

True.

"Which means that you might have seen him there," Paige said. "In fact, it's even possible that he chose you in the first place to have you personally service him in Bangkok. You might not have been as random as we thought. So the bottom line is this: even though you didn't see the guy when he hired you, you might have seen him in Bangkok."

"That makes sense."

"So here's what we do," Paige said. "We get on the website of Vinson & Botts, pull up the bios of the lawyers one at a time, and see if you recognize anyone."

"You're brilliant," Ja'Von said. "I'll be over in fifteen minutes."

SHE ACTUALLY ARRIVED IN FOURTEEN, wearing green shorts and incredible legs. Following hugs all around, they pulled up V&B's website on the Gateway. Ja'Von said, "They have 175 lawyers. This is going to take some time."

True.

Which gave Paige a chance to walk down to King Soopers and pick up a few groceries. Her phone rang as she pushed a shopping cart down the frozen food section.

Ja'Von's voice came through.

"We got a hit!" she said.

"You're kidding me."

"Does it sound like I'm kidding you?"

No it didn't.

Not at all.

"Who?"

"A guy named Mark Remington."

"You actually saw this guy in Bangkok?"

"Yes."

"Are you positive it's him?"

Ja'Von got serious.

"I'm so positive that you can't even believe it. I'll never forget him," she said. "He was a mean little freak."

"You're absolutely positive?"

"Let's put it this way," Ja'Von said. "His dick's five inches long, circumcised, and bends slightly to the right. He also has a tattoo down there, on his right thigh, of three or four foreign letters or symbols. Something in Thai, no doubt."

Paige couldn't help but smile.

"You can't get any more positive than that," she said.

"No you can't," Ja'Von said. "So get your pretty little face back here so we can start planning on how to wipe this law firm off the face of the earth."

Chapter Fifty-Four

Day Seven—June 17
Sunday Afternoon

CLAY PITCHER, THE ASSISTANT D.A., FROWNED when he handed Bryson Coventry the search warrant for Mark Remington's house. "We just barely skated by on this one, buddy boy," he said. "If anyone besides you was doing the investigation, I don't think the judge would have been too interested in signing it."

"Which judge?" Coventry asked.

"Anderson."

Coventry put a puzzled look on his face. "I haven't even been in his courtroom for more than two years."

"Well you must have made an impression," Clay said.

Leanne Sanders chuckled. "He *always* makes an impression."

Clay grinned. "I know. But this time it must have been a good one."

"What are the odds?"

"Slim to none," Clay said. "And Slim just left town."

THIRTY MINUTES LATER, Coventry and the FBI profiler arrived at Mark Remington's house. "Remember that spot?" Coventry said, pointing to where Leanne had been attacked on Thursday night.

She scratched her stitches and grunted.

When they knocked on Remington's door no one answered. Coventry didn't feel like making a mess, especially since the search was on thin ice to begin with, so he phoned a locksmith and waited on the front steps.

"So how are you and your new squeeze coming along?" Leanne asked.

"Ja'Von?"

"Right."

"I like her," Coventry said.

Leanne shook her head as if that didn't matter.

"You always like them," she said. "What does Shalifa think of her?"

He raked his hair back with his fingers.

It stayed up for a second and then fell.

"Shalifa?" he asked. "You know Shalifa, she never likes any of them. As usual, she's snooping around and finding all kinds of red flags and conspiracy theories."

"Maybe that's because she likes you," Leanne said.

"She's too smart for that."

"Have you ever slept with her?"

He looked at her as if she was crazy.

"Of course not, she's my partner."

"She's an attractive woman," Leanne said.

"Agreed but not relevant. Even I have a couple of boundaries."

THE THERMOS WAS ALMOST EMPTY when the locksmith arrived. Inside, they found a spotless, uncluttered interior, with an extremely open floor plan. A large oil painting caught Coventry's eye—a scene looking down from the hills onto a coastal town, portrayed with an impressionistic brush and realistic colors. Soft lavender clouds hung over the ocean, thirty miles away.

"I thought so," he told Leanne as he looked at the signature. "Gregory Hull."

"Is he someone?"

"He's a plein-air painter out of California," Coventry said. "One of my heroes, actually."

"That looks like Laguna Beach."

"Could be."

He turned and scouted the interior.

Where to start?

They did a non-destructive search.

Putting everything back as they found it.

Room after room.

The house didn't cough up any obvious evidence, which wasn't a big surprise. Remington had somehow gotten himself on the radar screen of Jean-Paul Boudiette. That wouldn't happen without something deep and dark going on. That's not the kind of thing that gets written down on a piece of paper and left sitting on the kitchen countertop, especially by someone as smart as Remington.

Deep and dark things get well hidden.

Nothing with the name Jean-Paul Boudiette showed up.

No evidence that Remington had hired someone to kill Boudiette showed up.

No evidence of anything that would warrant Remington being marked for death showed up.

And most importantly, there was no evidence of a connection to Madison Blake.

"This is a big dud so far," Leanne said.

True.

But that's what they suspected.

The secrets, if anywhere, would be in Remington's computers, telephone records and bank statements.

So they took all of those.

And then left.

ON THE DRIVE BACK TO HEADQUARTERS Leanne said, "It'd be nice to know who killed Boudiette, but I can't justify throwing any more time at it unless INTERPOL puts a serious squeeze on us," she said. "The main thing is that he's dead."

"So you're heading back?"

She nodded.

"I'm going to have to leave you in charge."

He chuckled.

"That's a scary thought."

She smiled.

"The equivalent of Freddy Krueger," Coventry added.

"I was thinking more along the lines of King Kong."

Coventry nodded.

Yeah.

King Kong.

EXCEPT HE DIDN'T FEEL LIKE KING KONG. He felt more like the guy that King Kong picks up and throws at the T-Rex.

He needed to find Madison Blake.

The afternoon had been a bust.

Somehow Madison Blake had gotten her picture taken.

The kind of picture that gets handed to a hit man.

Boudiette was a hit man.

Boudiette had been after Remington.

Meaning Remington was somehow connected to Boudiette.

Meaning he might be connected to Madison Blake.

Maybe directly.

Maybe indirectly.

Which is the main reason Coventry wanted to search Remington's house.

But the search had turned up nothing. Coventry would press forensics to get into Remington's computers first thing tomorrow morning but was already bracing himself for the fact that it would probably be a bust.

In the meantime he was back to square one.

With another day slipping away.

Chapter Fifty-Five

Day Seven—June 17
Sunday Afternoon

DYLAN JOOP HAD SO MUCH TO DO in such a short period of time that he hardly knew where to start. He needed to kill the blackmailer and get the photographs back. He needed to kill some stranger named Porter Potter. He needed to kill Madison Blake. He needed to have a heart-to-heart with Bethany's stalker. Somewhere down the road, he needed to figure out why the Frenchman had been after him, and deal with the root source of that problem to be sure it didn't happen again. And he had to do it all without making any further messes.

How did everything get so complicated all of a sudden?

The most pressing problem was the blackmailer.

He needed to address that first.

He stuffed Madison Blake back in the boxcar, to her dismay, and waited for the call, which didn't come until early afternoon. Joop explained that he couldn't get the money until tomorrow when the banks opened. The blackmailer said, "Tomorrow's your last chance," and hung up.

PORTER POTTER, a 45-year-old who rode a desk for a living and wore a spare tire around his gut to prove it, lived alone in a nice house on the 11th hole of the Denver Country Club.

Dylan Joop, wearing one of his many disguises, drove past the house several times in the afternoon and then took a leisurely walk behind it on the golf cart path.

The plan solidified.

The perfect plan.

That evening after dark, shortly before ten, Joop snuck through the fairway under a moonless Colorado night. He wore black jeans, a black T-shirt, an even blacker sweatshirt and latex gloves. His persuader—the .357 SIG—was holstered under the sweatshirt.

The pudgy man was still awake.

The colored lights of a TV flickered in the upstairs bedroom.

Good.

Joop muscled up the redwood deck to the upper level and snuck towards the target on cat feet. The sliding glass door was open and sitcom sounds squeezed through the opening. The screen portion of the door was closed. Joop tested it, ever so slightly, to see if it was locked.

It wasn't.

The fat man was in a chair.

With his back to the door.

Watching a Cheers rerun.

With the gun in hand, Joop slid the screen door open with a quick motion and stepped inside.

HIS TARGET TURNED, more curious than frightened, as if to confirm that he really hadn't heard anything. Joop closed the gap with three quick steps and had the gun jammed against the back of the man's head before the jerk even got twisted all the way around.

He had a half-drained glass of whiskey in his hand.

And smelled like a bar.

"Don't do anything stupid," Joop said.

A pause.

"Okay."

Joop surveyed the room.

It had no ceiling lights.

Plus the floor had carpeting.

"Don't move," Joop said.

"Okay."

Joop stepped into the master bathroom and flicked on the lights. The space looked like something out of a magazine, with double sinks nestled in a granite countertop, an enclosed steam shower, a Jacuzzi tub, tile flooring and rich textured towels. What grabbed his attention, though, were the two light fixtures above the sinks.

Particularly the left one.

The one with one of the four bulbs burned out.

"Where are your replacement bulbs for this thing?" Joop asked.

"What thing?"

"Get your ass in here!"

The fat man obeyed.

"That," Joop said. "Where are your replacement bulbs?"

Confusion filled the man's face.

"I think I have some spares in the linen closet. I don't under-stand—"

"Shut up and show me!"

FIVE MINUTES LATER THE FAT MAN had a tragic accident while changing the light bulb in the bathroom before going to bed. It seems he had been standing on the sink and slipped off, probably because of the whiskey.

The poor man hit his head on the tile floor.

And cracked his skull wide open.

Chapter Fifty-Six

PAIGE ALEXANDER AND HER CLIENT Ja'Von Deveraux arrived at Vinson & Botts at 9:15 a.m. without an appointment, and requested a meeting with Thomas Fog. Now, a full hour later, they still waited in the reception area.

Ja'Von kept her face stuffed in one magazine after another.

Not talking.

With her legs crossed.

Rocking her right foot up and down.

Obviously stressed.

Paige was equally frazzled but also equally determined to not let it show. For the most part, she kept her focus on the upcoming meeting, trying to anticipate Fog's reactions and possible moves. But something more sinister tugged at her; namely the fact that the meeting would take the case from the chest-beating level to the full-combat level. There might well be an attempt on either her life, or Ja'Von's, or both.

One other thing crept into her thoughts.

The money.

She had the case on a one-third contingency fee.

If the case was as big as they believed it to be, it could mean millions. She could be on the verge of putting her one-bedroom apartment—and her one-bedroom *life*—in the rearview mirror forever.

She shook the thought out of her head.

Stay focused.

Don't count your chickens.

A half hour later, Fog's personal assistant walked into the reception area and said, "Mr. Fog is sorry you've had to wait so long, but he's had clients. He can see you now if you still want."

They stood up and looked at each other.

Then followed Fog's assistant into the same conference room as before.

THOMAS FOG SHOWED UP TEN MINUTES LATER wearing gray pinstriped pants, a crisp white shirt and a blue silk tie pulled loose around the neck. "I am so sorry to keep you waiting," he said. "This has been the day from hell." He took a deep breath as if to calm himself. "So what's on your mind?"

Paige had prepared for this moment twenty times.

And now went blank.

Ja'Von, who had been looking at Fog, turned her head.

Then nudged Paige.

"You're up," she said.

"Right," she said. Then to Fog, "You remember what we talked about before, about how Ms. Deveraux had been hired by a law firm to follow a man to Bangkok."

He nodded.

"And you thought the firm could be ours," he said. "Even

though I checked and found no evidence of any such thing."

Paige swallowed.

"Right," she said. "What we didn't tell you about the last time we were here is what happened to Ms. Deveraux after she arrived in Bangkok."

He looked puzzled.

And held his hands out in confusion.

"Okay," he said. "So what happened?"

"We'll tell you," Paige said. "I'm treating this meeting as a Rule 408 settlement negotiation. I assume you're doing the same."

That meant that neither party could use anything said by the other party as evidence in court. It's as if the meeting never happened.

He shrugged.

"Sure. I have no problem with that."

Paige looked at Ja'Von and asked, "Do you want to tell him the story or do you want me to?"

Ja'Von looked calmer now.

In fact, defiant.

"I'll tell him," she said.

WITH THAT, THEY TOLD HIM EVERYTHING. How Ja'Von had followed the target, Bob Copeland, into a BJ bar where her drink got spiked. She ended up in sexual slavery where inhumane acts were perpetrated upon her on a daily basis. She was eventually purchased for a snuff but gained her freedom following a freak traffic accident.

"When did this happen?" Fog asked.

Ja'Von searched her memory. "I got there on April 11th and

got out about a month later."

"When exactly?"

Ja'Von went deep and then said, "May 10th."

OTHER FEMALE PRIVATE INVESTIGATORS were also lured to Bangkok where they disappeared.

"Who?" Fog questioned.

"We're not saying at this point," Paige said.

"Why?"

"In case they're still alive."

"What does that mean?" Fog questioned.

Paige leaned across the table. "It means we don't want them disappearing."

Fog scowled at her.

She didn't flinch.

"One of the men who paid a visit to Ms. Deveraux is an attorney from this law firm," she said.

Fog looked flabbergasted.

"Who?"

"Mark Remington."

"Mark Remington?"

Paige nodded.

Fog chuckled.

"Are you nuts?"

"I wish we were," she said. "Here's the bottom line. This law firm is, at a minimum, engaged in the illegal trafficking of women for sexual slavery."

Fog looked dumbfounded.

"Honey," he said. "We're the biggest law firm in the world. Why in the hell would we do anything as stupid as that?"

"Because you're the biggest law firm in the world," she said. "And therefore you think you can. We'll see you in court."

They stood up.

Fog shook his head in bewilderment and motioned them back into their seats.

"Here's what I'll do," he said. "I'll talk to Mark Remington and check into this."

"Today," Paige said.

He nodded.

"Of course," he said. "I'm a hundred percent positive that I'm going to find out that this law firm is not involved in anything like this, not in a million years. If it turns out that Mark Remington is as dirty as you make him out to be, then be warned in advance that he was doing it all on his own, without the knowledge or consent of this law firm. I can see dollar signs bouncing around in your eyes. My advice to you is to get them out. Even if all your wild theories are true, which they're not, you end up with a case against a rogue lawyer acting outside the scope of his employment. But not a case against this law firm. I repeat—not against this law firm."

Paige stood up.

But so did Thomas Fog.

"THERE'S ONE MORE THING you should be crystal clear about before you leave this room," he said. "I consider your allegations to be defamatory. If you go public with them, then you are both going to get slapped with a slander suit so fast and so big and so heavy that you'll never recover from it. Not in ten lifetimes. Mark my words."

Paige leaned across the table and stared him in the eyes.

"Here are our demands," she said. "We want the name of every single woman who has been lured to Bangkok. We want every single one of them released and returned to the United States immediately. We want every person involved in this to voluntarily surrender themselves to the police and to confess to their crimes. And we want full financial redress for all of the pain and suffering and injuries and losses sustained by each and every one of the victims and the families of the victims who have been subjected to these horrible acts."

Fog looked flabbergasted.

"And we want an apology too," she added. "Either get it done yourself or we'll get a judge and jury to get it done for you."

Fog slammed his hand on the table.

"You have no idea who you're dealing with," he said.

"Then we're even."

THEY HUFFED OUT OF THE CONFERENCE ROOM, down the hall and into the reception area, where something happened that Paige didn't expect.

The rock star Michael Dexter came through the space.

So preoccupied with a file that he actually bumped into her.

Totally shocked.

"What—?" he started to ask.

She pushed him away, ran towards the door and said over her shoulder, "Don't call me."

"Paige!"

"You heard me!"

Chapter Fifty-Seven

Day Eight—June 18
Monday Noon

———————

PAUL KUBIAK COPIED MARK REMINGTON'S hard drives Monday morning. Bryson Coventry jumped into them with lots of caffeine-laden enthusiasm, but after hours of plodding through the mundane, his altitude and attitude dropped.

Ja'Von called and asked if he had time for lunch.

She sounded stressed.

He looked at the oversized industrial clock on the wall.

11:29.

Ouch.

Where did the morning go?

"Okay," he said. "But it'll need to be somewhere close and quick." He thought about it and said, "Meet me at Wong's on Court Street, high noon."

"I know why you like that place," she said. "All the waitresses have a crush on you."

"I tip 'em," he said. "That's all."

He got there ten minutes late and spotted Ja'Von in a booth.

Something was wrong.

He could tell, even at a distance.

He slid in and said, "Something's wrong."

She nodded.

"It's time for full disclosure," she said.

"What's that mean?"

"It means that the car you thought was new actually has a lot of miles on the odometer," she said.

Huh?

He took her hand and said, "Talk to me."

WITH THAT SHE TOLD HIM A STORY ABOUT BANGKOK, and sexual slavery, and horrible things that had been done to her. She studied his eyes the entire time, trying to gauge his reaction.

"I couldn't tell you before because I didn't know how you'd react," she said.

"What do you mean?"

"Well, most men wouldn't want a woman who has been through all that."

He squeezed her hand.

"Why would it matter?" he asked. "You were a victim. I'm not going to think less of you because of something that happened to you beyond your control."

She cried.

Silently.

Barely detectible.

But with tears.

"Do you still want me?"

He came around to her side of the table and put his arm around her shoulders.

"Of course I still want you."

"I'm sorry," she said. "I'm embarrassing you."

"Never."

AS THEY ATE, SHE TOLD HIM MORE. She had retained an attorney by the name of Paige Alexander. Their investigation traced the initial Bangkok assignment as coming from Vinson & Botts.

"Vinson & Botts?" Coventry asked.

She nodded.

"That's not possible."

She disagreed.

"We had a kick-'em-in-the-balls meeting with the head of the firm this morning, a guy named Thomas Fog," she said. "We told him everything we knew and demanded lots of stuff. They won't comply—I already know that—which means we'll be filing a lawsuit within the next couple of days. It's all about to hit the fan, big time. That's why I'm telling you now. You're going to find out about it in a day or two, and I'd rather you hear it from me."

Coventry frowned.

"What?" she questioned.

"They'll throw an army at the case," he said. "They'll take your deposition for days just to screw with you. Your life is about to be a living hell."

"I think you underestimate them," Ja'Von said.

"What does that mean?"

"It means that for someone's life to be a living hell, first they have to have a life."

Coventry didn't follow.

"Think about it," she said. "What if I wasn't alive to testify?"

"What do you mean, not alive? Are you trying to suggest that they'd actually kill you?"

She nodded.

"That's insane," he said. "Law firms don't kill people."

She ignored the words.

Then looked directly into his eyes.

"It'll look like an accident," she said.

Chapter Fifty-Eight

Day Eight—June 18
Monday Morning

WITH PORTER POTTER DEAD, Joop was now free to kill Madison Blake. He almost did it when he got home last night from the scene of Potter's unfortunate accident. Then he changed his mind. It would be better to deal with the black-mailer first because if the guy did go to the police, Joop would rather be charged with the abduction of Madison Blake as opposed to her murder.

The contact called Joop shortly before noon and sounded like he had just stepped off a roller coaster.

"Whatever you do, don't kill Porter Potter yet," the man said.

"Why?"

"Something came up this morning," the man said.

"Your timing sucks," Joop said.

"What are you saying?"

"It's already a done deal."

"When?"

"Last night."

"Damn it."

"Madison Blake's still alive," Joop added.

"I don't give a rat's ass about her," the man said.

"So you don't care if I complete the plan?"

"No. In fact it would probably be even better that way." The man paused as if in thought and then added, "In fact, if you're going to do it, do it quick. I'm pretty sure I'm going to have another job for you and I'm going to want your full attention on it."

Another job meant another pile of money.

"Not a problem," Joop said. "When?"

"Maybe as early as tonight. I have to think it through."

THE BLACKMAILER CALLED TEN MINUTES LATER. "Today's the day," he said. "Don't tell me that you don't have the money, because if you tell me you don't have the money, I'm going to find myself in a very bad mood."

"I have the money," Joop said, which was true.

"All of it?"

"Yes."

"Good boy," the voice said. "Now write down these directions—"

"No," Joop said. "You listen to *my* directions. Meet me at the Red Rocks Park Amphitheater at two o'clock. I'll be sitting on the 20th row, which is nice and public. Neither one of us will be able to kill the other one. We'll make the exchange face to face. That's the only way I'm going to do it. Be sure you bring the pictures and don't be late."

Joop flipped the phone closed.

There.

Done.

Now to see what happens.

FIFTEEN MINUTES BEFORE THE APPOINTED TIME, Joop parked the rental in the lower lot, hiked up to the Amphitheater, walked up to the 20th row and sat down. A light wind shuffled black-bellied clouds in from the west, warning of possible rain this evening.

He sat down and faced the stage.

But kept the brown leather briefcase on his lap.

He didn't look around.

Either the guy would come or he wouldn't.

At exactly two o'clock a man walked down the rows from above and took a seat next to Joop. He held an envelope.

"Nice day," the man said.

Joop recognized the voice.

It was him.

"I don't know," Joop said. "It looks like rain."

He turned and looked at his blackmailer—a skinhead covered with tattoos, about twenty or twenty-one, no more than 150 pounds. Joop could grab the man's throat with one hand and choke the life right out of him without even breaking a sweat.

"This was a good idea," the man said. "Meeting in a public place and all." He held his hand out to shake and said, "My name's Paul."

Joop shook his hand and said, "Paul what?"

"Paul Youngfield."

"Show me your driver's license," Joop said.

"Why?"

"Because this whole thing is going to be even. You know where I live. Now I'm going to know where you live."

The man grinned.

Unafraid.

And slapped Joop on the back.

"Sure, why not."

Joop studied the license.

Paul Youngfield.

Marion Street.

Denver.

"Did you bring the photographs?"

"We had a complication with the photographs."

JOOP FELT HIS CHEST TIGHTEN.

And did his best to not kill the man with his bare hands right then and there.

"What kind of complication?"

"Well, when I stole your car, I found them under the front seat," the man said. "But I threw them out the window while I was driving down C-470. It wasn't until the next morning, when I saw the picture of Madison Blake in the Rocky Mountain News, that I realized who she was. I went back to get them but they were already gone."

"You're lying," Joop said.

"I'm not and the pictures don't mean a rat's ass anyway," the skinhead said. "What you're buying is my silence. Hell, even if I had the pictures and gave them to you, I could have made a hundred copies first. The actual pictures don't mean squat. But since I don't have them, I'll tell you what I'm going to do. I'm going to cut the price in half."

"Meaning fifty thousand," Joop said.

The skinhead nodded.

"I know who you are and now you know who I am," the skinhead said. "What we're going to do is both walk away from this a winner. You got a little sloppy and left the pictures in your car, but I'm giving you a chance to correct that mistake. I got a little lucky finding those pictures, but I'm not a greedy man. You give me the fifty thousand and you'll never hear from me again. I'll take this whole thing to my grave. Honor among thieves and all that."

Joop considered it.

"What did you do with my car?"

"We just rode around in it for a while," the man said. "It's parked on Clarkson Street, just north of Colfax."

Joop knew the location.

"So do we have a deal or not?" the skinhead asked.

Joop opened the briefcase, kept the money hidden from stray eyes, counted out fifty thousand and gave it to the man.

Then they walked away in separate directions.

Joop stopped and said over his shoulder, "You caught me in a good mood. Don't catch me again because your luck won't be as good."

The man laughed.

Blew him a kiss.

And walked away.

JOOP WALKED BACK TO HIS CAR, simultaneously relieved that it was over and infuriated that he let some punk steal his car, get his money and then blow him a kiss.

"You shouldn't have done that kiss," he muttered.

In any event he was now free.

Free to kill Madison Blake.

And get on with his life.

Chapter Fifty-Nine

Day Eight—June 18
Monday Afternoon

PAIGE ALEXANDER WAS TAKING AN ORDER at Sam's Eatery from a man with two kids when her cell phone rang. She didn't answer. Men with kids were the best tippers and she didn't want to spoil it. So instead she let the phone ring and smiled at the man as if he were the most important person in the universe. After she got his order in the cook's hand, she went to the restroom where the boss couldn't see her, checked the missed number, didn't recognize it and punched *Call*.

"Sarah Woodward," a woman said.

Paige didn't know the voice or the name.

The woman turned out to be one of the senior partners at Vinson & Botts. "I'd like to meet with you and Ms. Deveraux if that's possible."

Paige looked at her watch.

3:30 p.m.

She was scheduled to work until 9:00 with a break at 5:00.

"When?"

"The sooner the better," the woman said. "You name the

275

time."

"How about 5:15?"

"That'll work just fine."

"Subject to my client's availability," Paige added. "If you don't hear back from me, we'll be there."

OF COURSE, PAIGE GOT JAMMED UP with orders exactly when her break came up. She finally got out of the Eatery at ten after five, pulled off her apron and peddled the Trek as fast as she could through the rush hour mess into the heart of the city's financial district.

When she arrived at the bottom of the elevator bank at 5:30, Ja'Von was already waiting for her.

Pacing.

Nervous.

"We're late," Ja'Von said.

"That's okay, it's their turn to cool their heels."

On the elevator ride up, Ja'Von pulled a brush from her purse and worked on Paige's hair. Then she wiped a stray splash of mustard from Paige's chin.

"There, all pretty again," she said.

"Yeah, right," Paige said. "Just point me to the beauty contest."

Ja'Von hugged her.

Paige wore jeans, a T-shirt and tennis shoes, none of which were exactly pristine. As she stepped off the elevator and pushed through the doors into the reception area of Vinson & Botts, she felt more like someone arriving from a cleaning crew than an attorney about to have a meeting.

The receptionist was still at her post.

A surprise.

She smiled and waved as they walked towards her.

Then punched a button and said, "Sarah, your guests are here."

Thirty seconds later a woman appeared.

SHE TURNED OUT TO BE A PLEASANT LOOKING WOMAN, about forty-five, dressed crisp and nice but not in-your-face expensive, with long brown hair that she tended to flick with her head.

Paige liked her immediately.

The woman smiled, introduced herself as Sarah Woodward, said "Thanks for coming," and shook their hands warmly with both of hers.

They ended up in her office.

A corner unit three times larger than it needed to be.

With incredible views of both the Rocky Mountains and the city.

Diplomas hung on the wall.

Two from Brown.

One from Harvard.

A paperback book called *Fatal Laws* sat on her desk.

"I understand that you had a rather unpleasant meeting with Thomas Fog this morning," she said. "I apologize for that. Tom's an alpha-male. In this business that's usually a good thing, but not always. I'm going to be heading things up for the firm from this point on."

Paige nodded.

"Good."

"This is a Rule 408 settlement negotiation, by the way,"

277

Sarah added.

"Agreed."

"Tom's filled me in on all the details," Sarah said. She leaned across the desk, patted Ja'Von's hand and said, "My heart goes out to you."

Ja'Von said nothing.

But her eyes were moist.

"Mark Remington is in Bangkok right now," Sarah said. "We had a chance to talk to him this afternoon. He denies everything." Sarah looked directly at Ja'Von and said, "But I'm going to proceed at this point as if he's lying. I'm going to assume that you're telling the truth and that he really did do what you said he did."

Ja'Von looked grateful.

As if someone besides Paige finally believed her.

"Thank you."

Sarah patted her hand again.

"You're welcome." Then to Paige, "What we need right now is some time to investigate the matter. And I'm going to make a promise to you, right here and right now. If we find out that there are other women in Bangkok, and that they're still alive, we will find a way to get their freedom and bring them back to the United States. We'll do that whether or not Mark Remington was involved, simply because it's the right thing to do and we're positioned as well as anyone else to get it done. Is that fair?"

Both Paige and Ja'Von nodded.

"In the meantime," Sarah said, "we ask that you hold off on any lawsuit. Is that fair too?"

Yes.

It was.

They shook hands.

"I'm going to keep you informed every step of the way," Sarah added.

OUTSIDE, AN **RTD** BUS THREW A PLUME OF DIESEL at them. They backed out of it and Ja'Von asked, "So what do you think? Do you trust her?"

"Right now, yes," Paige said. "At least enough to hold off on filing a formal lawsuit."

"So are you going to give her Rebecca Vampire's name, like she wants?"

Paige nodded.

"I'm going to talk it over with her sister first," Paige said. "If she says okay, then I will."

"She'll definitely say okay if there's even one chance in hell that Rebecca can actually be found alive," Ja'Von said.

Paige nodded.

She knew that.

"But if all this is just another layer of lies and deceit, and Rebecca Vampire is actually located alive, she'll be killed so the firm won't ever have to worry about her dragging them down." Paige looked at Ja'Von. "It all comes down to whether Sarah Woodward is being honest or not."

"We almost have to assume she is," Ja'Von said, "because if Rebecca Vampire is actually alive, it isn't by much in any event."

"Agreed."

Chapter Sixty

Day Eight—June 18
Monday Afternoon

PRIOR TO LUNCH WITH JA'VON TODAY, Bryson Coventry had two curious connections to Bangkok: the pilot, Alan Ewing, returned from Bangkok the night he got stabbed to death in his bedroom; and the Frenchman's target, Mark Remington, recently boarded an airplane to Bangkok.

Now he had even more connections.

Serious connections.

Namely Ja'Von got enslaved there.

And Mark Remington abused her during that enslavement.

The freak.

In some sick twisted way everything was intertwined. It had to be. But the more Coventry tried to figure out how, the further away he seemed from an answer.

MID-AFTERNOON, COVENTRY FILLED A THERMOS with decaf and headed over to the D.A.'s office. Clay Pitcher, Esq., a man with a barrel chest and yellow cigar teeth, looked up from his desk when Coventry walked in and closed the door behind him. Clay used to be a tireless prosecutor but now had half an eye on retirement. Still, he could get riled up and cross swords with the best of them when he got motivated enough.

Six apples sat on his desk.

"What's with the fruit?" Coventry questioned.

Clay rolled his eyes.

"The wife keeps putting them in my lunch," he said. "She says they're good for me."

"But you don't eat them?"

"No. I hate apples."

"So why don't you tell your wife to not pack them any-more?"

"Because she thinks I'm eating them."

"But you're not."

"Right, but she *thinks* I am. That translates to less flak when I eat a cookie or something like that."

"What are you going to do with them?"

Clay shrugged.

"I don't know. You want 'em?"

Sure.

Why not?

Then Coventry told him about Ja'Von's enslavement in Bangkok and the fact that a Denver attorney named Mark Rem-ington paid her a visit in Bangkok, a very rough visit. "My ques-tion is this," Coventry said. "Can we bring charges against the lawyer here in Denver? For assault or rape or something?"

Clay scratched his head.

"I haven't come across a situation like this before, where one American assaults another one in a foreign country," he said. "I'd have to dig into it a little. My gut tells me no, but like I said, let me check. The bigger problem is this—even if the U.S. courts have jurisdiction, there's no proof. It's a he-said she-said case. No judge in his right mind is going to let it get to a jury."

"Thanks. Keep this conversation private, especially the part about what happened to Ja'Von."

Clay pulled an imaginary zipper across his lips.

Coventry scooped up the apples and headed for the door.

"Coventry, wait a minute," Clay said.

He stopped and turned.

"Don't do anything stupid."

"You mean like put on a ski mask some dark night and beat the life out of Remington myself?"

Clay shrugged.

"Yeah, that."

"It never crossed my mind," Coventry said. "Thanks again for the apples."

HE DROVE BACK TO HEADQUARTERS with the radio on, getting a string of good songs—"Hungry Like the Wolf," "Beat It," "Like a Rolling Stone." Halfway through yet another good one—"Cheeseburger in Paradise"—a disturbing thought entered his brain.

If Mark Remington visited Ja'Von in Bangkok, maybe the pilot—Alan Ewing—did too.

Maybe Ja'Von somehow traced him to Denver.

And then killed him.

For doing whatever it was that he did to her.

He pulled up a picture of Ja'Von hiding in the dark in Ewing's bedroom and then stabbing a knife into his back, again and again and again.

Chapter Sixty-One

Day Eight—June 18
Monday Afternoon

DYLAN JOOP WAS FEELING GOOD. Better than good, actually. Everything was falling into place. Porter Potter was dead. The blackmailer was history—at least short-term. And Madison Blake would be dead by midnight.

Yeah, baby.

He went to Clarkson Street and found the Audi parked where the blackmailer said it would be. The passenger window had been busted in with a rock and a slew of wires had been pulled out from under the dash. Otherwise the vehicle was in good shape. He had it towed to the Audi dealership on Broadway, greased the guy behind the counter fifty dollars to get it fixed by the end of the day, and picked it up shortly before six.

There.

Another issue resolved.

Bethany called while he was driving up Highway 74 through Bear Creek Canyon. "Come by the club tonight," she said.

"Sure."

"Really?"

"Yeah."

"You promise?"

He did.

"Will you take me home, afterwards?"

"If you want."

"I want."

"Then done deal."

"I'm horny as hell," she said.

"Good. Keep it that way."

"You're not messing with me about taking me home, are you?"

"No."

"Because I'm going to take a cab to the club, if you're going to take me home."

"Do it."

"Okay but I'll be really bent if you don't show up."

"Relax," he said. "I won't let you down but I probably won't get there until about midnight. Is that guy still stalking you?"

"I don't know, I've been sleeping all day."

AT THE BOXCARS, Joop let Madison Blake cook supper—a simple chili with ground meat, kidney beans, onions and celery. They ate outside on the deck stairs as a westerly wind pushed increasingly darker clouds across the sky.

"I've made up my mind," Joop said. "I'm going to let you go. But remember, no cops—ever."

She studied his face.

Searching for a trick.

"Really?"

"Yes really."

"When?"

"Tonight."

She hugged him.

And he hugged her back.

An expression washed over her face that actually made Joop jealous. He couldn't remember ever being as happy as she was at this moment.

Later he had her take three sleeping pills.

"Just to keep you relaxed," he said. "When you wake up you'll be somewhere safe."

"Where?"

"I don't know yet exactly. I have to play it by ear. You'll be safe though, so don't worry about it. Remember, no cops."

"Don't worry."

SHORTLY BEFORE DARK, he put her sleeping body in the trunk of the Audi and headed down the road.

Soon she'd be dead.

Her body would never be found.

And Joop would be at the club getting drunk by midnight.

It started to rain.

A drizzle at first.

Then heavy.

Chapter Sixty-Two

Day Eight—June 18
Monday Night

PAIGE ALEXANDER GOT OFF WORK at 8:00 p.m. to an ominous rainy sky that turned her to a sloppy mess by the time she got halfway to the bus stop. The stop had no shelter so she hugged a building until the RTD came. She put her bike on the front rack as fast as she could and took a seat directly behind the driver, where weirdoes were less likely to bother her.

Water dripped from her head.

A chill worked its way into her bones as Colfax rolled by.

When she got off at Simms, the bus driver must have forgotten about her bike, because he pulled away with it still in the rack.

Her apartment was more than two miles up the road.

Meaning a long walk.

Especially in the rain.

Not to mention that she had been on her feet all day.

She hung around the stop for a few moments to see if the driver figured out what he did and was swinging back. But no bus came and she headed down the street on foot.

Halfway home her cell phone rang.

The voice of the V&B attorney, Sarah Woodward, came through. "We just got some news and I thought you should know about it right away."

"What kind of news?"

"Mark Remington hung himself in his hotel room," she said.

"He did?"

"Yes."

"Are you sure?"

"Yes."

"Why?"

"We don't know yet for certain," Sarah said. "The word is that he didn't leave a note."

Paige pondered it.

And then said, "He knew it was all coming his way and took the easy way out."

"Maybe," Sarah said. "I'm hoping to have more information tomorrow."

WHEN PAIGE CALLED JA'VON and told her the news, Ja'Von said, "I see three possibilities. He's actually still alive and the whole thing is a charade so that V&B can say it tried to investigate but couldn't. Or V&B killed him so he couldn't drag them down. Or he really did kill himself because, as you say, it was all about to hit the fan."

"So how do we figure out which it is?" Paige questioned.

A pause.

"I don't know right at this second," she said. "I'll have a better handle on it by the morning. Let's plan on meeting for coffee."

Paige almost hung up but said, "Are you still there?"

Ja'Von was.

"If he was murdered, you might be next," Paige said.

Ja'Von already knew that.

"Or you," she said. "I'm staying at Coventry's tonight. Maybe you should join us. In fact, I insist on it. It's time you two met anyway. So pack your stuff because I'm swinging over to get you in a half hour."

"You don't think Coventry will mind?"

"No, he won't. But I'll give him an extra good blowjob tonight just to be sure."

Paige chuckled.

"That's more information than I need."

TWO MINUTES LATER MICHAEL DEXTER CALLED. Paige recognized the incoming number and almost didn't answer, but changed her mind at the last second.

"What the hell is going on?" he asked.

"You don't know?"

"No. Know what?"

She took a moment to collect her thoughts and said, "Look, I'm sorry about this morning. I sort of had a heat-of-battle thing going on. I took it out on you when I shouldn't have."

"I want to see you," he said.

"Tonight's bad," she said. "How about tomorrow?"

"Tomorrow's too long."

She chuckled.

"How am I supposed to survive until then?" he added.

"See you tomorrow," she said.

A BLOCK LATER SHE CALLED HIM BACK. "Tonight's bad because I can't be alone. I'm going to spend it with friends."

"Spend it with me."

"You don't even know me."

"And I never will if you don't give me a chance."

A pause.

"Okay."

"Yeah?"

"Yeah."

She hung up, called Ja'Von and said, "Thanks for the invite, but I'm going to spend the night at Michael Dexter's."

Silence.

"Okay, but remember, he could be the enemy."

"If he kills me, you'll be the first person I tell."

"I'm serious."

Chapter Sixty-Three

Day Eight—June 18
Monday Night

THE 1967 CORVETTE IS THE COOLEST CAR ever made, hands down, end of story, period. Coventry owned a red one, convertible, numbers matching, second flight. True, it was a small-block and paled by comparison to its older sibling the 454, but it still had 300 horses under the hood and turned heads with the best of them.

He kept it in the garage with the top down and the front end facing the street.

Shortly after dark it rained.

Light at first.

Then heavy.

Then downright mean.

Perfect.

Ja'Von followed him around the house, sipping a glass of wine, as he closed windows.

"Nice ass," she said.

He chuckled.

"What?" she asked.

"Shalifa says I don't have an ass. She says I just have a place where an ass is supposed to be." He grabbed her hand. "Come on."

"Where we going?"

"To the all-time best place in the world."

He swung by the kitchen, grabbed a cold Bud Light, and headed for the garage. They ended up sitting in the Corvette with the garage door open, watching the storm through the windshield. "This is my favorite thing," he said. "Don't tell anyone."

"Favorite?" she asked.

He chuckled.

"Okay, second favorite."

"It's dark," she said.

True.

They could hardly see each other.

The rain pummeled straight down.

Thunder crackled over Green Mountain, rolled over their heads and got swallowed up somewhere to the east.

Coventry took a long drink of beer.

Damn good stuff.

"I have to admit, this is sort of cool," Ja'Von said.

"If this doesn't recharge your batteries, nothing will."

"So are your batteries getting recharged?"

"Yes they are."

"Good," she said. "You're going to need the energy later."

HE DIDN'T KNOW HOW TO EASE GRACEFULLY into the next subject so he just went for it. "Hey, do you remember the night we met, and you waited in the truck while I responded to that pilot who got stabbed in the back?"

Yes she did.

"The guy's name was Alan Ewing," he said.

Right.

He mentioned that once before.

"It turns out that he was in Bangkok," Coventry said. "In fact, he was just getting back from there on the night he got killed."

"Small world," she said.

"I wonder if you'd recognize him if you saw him," Coventry said.

"What do you mean?"

"Maybe he was someone who went to that place where you were kept," Coventry said.

"You think?"

Coventry shrugged.

"I don't know," he said.

"Do you have a picture of him?"

He did.

In his laptop.

"Let's have a look," she said.

COVENTRY SWALLOWED THE LAST OF THE BEER, crushed the can in his hand and opened the door. "Be right back," he said. "You want some more wine?"

She handed him the glass and said, "Go ahead and top me off if you want."

Coventry returned two minutes later with fresh liquor and the laptop. He fired it up and showed her several pictures of Alan Ewing. She studied them and said, "If he ever went to that place, I never saw him."

Coventry exhaled.

And found no lies in her voice.

"Are you sure?"

"Positive," she said. "We didn't get that many Americans. Plus everyone who spoke English is etched in my mind."

Coventry closed the laptop, twisted around and set it in the back, feeling better than he had all day.

Lightning flashed.

Directly overhead.

Followed immediately by an explosion that brought them both out of their seats.

Chapter Sixty-Four

Day Eight—June 18
Monday Night

———————

THE AUDI'S WIPERS SWISHED BACK AND FORTH at high speed but still couldn't keep the slop off the windshield. Dylan Joop drove with both hands on the wheel, forward in the seat, as he twisted farther and farther into the mountains on a pitch-black road.

The radio was off.

Madison Blake was in the trunk.

Alive but not for long.

Up ahead he saw something weird on the road.

Red lights.

They looked like taillights.

But they didn't hang together like the lights of a car. They weaved back and forth, coming closer to one another and then drifting apart. Then he figured it out.

Motorcycles.

Three of them.

Caught in the storm and going slow. What idiots. Joop had ridden cycles in the rain before. The problem wasn't so much the loss of traction as the loss of vision. In a storm this violent and this dark, it's a wonder that the idiots could even see the road.

They had to be drunk.

Or stupid.

Or both.

They disappeared to the right around a twist in the road, then reappeared, then disappeared to the left, then reappeared. Joop took his eyes off the road long enough to look at the speedometer.

35.

The motorcycles couldn't be doing more than 25.

Naturally.

Joop would either be stuck behind them for miles or he'd have to pass. Passing would be problematic at best. They were riding single file, well separated. The closer he got the more he could tell that they were all over the road.

Bunch of damn drunks.

He had to be careful to not clip one of them.

That's all he needed with Madison Blake in the trunk.

He pictured three leather-clad freaks on Harleys, maybe even part of a gang. The cycles had to be Harleys instead of crotch-rockets, because kids rode crotch-rockets and they'd be too smart to be out in a mess like this. No, the bikes would be Harleys and the riders thought they were bulletproof.

Joop closed the gap even farther.

Then, damn!

A forth bike appeared.

From out of nowhere.

Directly in front of him.

It had no taillight.

No headlight.

No nothing.

A Harley.

Joop slammed on the brakes and brought every muscle in his leg to bear down. The driver turned and waved an arm, frantic.

A woman.

Wearing a red bandana.

Then he hit her.

Hard.

Directly on the back wheel.

The bike flew to the right.

The woman came over the hood, hit the Audi's windshield and disappeared over the top of the car.

The Audi slid to a stop.

JOOP TWISTED AROUND TO FIND THE WOMAN but saw only darkness. He powered down the window but heard nothing except the pounding of the rain on the asphalt. He opened the door, ran to the back of the vehicle and saw nothing.

He shouted into the blackness, "Are you okay?"

No response.

"I said are you okay?"

No response.

He looked up the road.

The three motorcycles were turning around and doubling back.

HE JUMPED BACK INTO THE CAR and slammed the door. Then he jammed the stick into first gear, made a violent turn to the left into the opposing lane, stopped just short of running off the road, backed up, and then turned again to the left.

Now pointed back the way he came.

He floored it.

A quick glance in the rearview mirror showed three head-lights approaching fast. When he brought his eyes back to the road he couldn't believe what he saw.

The woman was directly in front of him.

Broken but trying frantically to crawl out of his way.

She waved her arm.

Total fear gripped her face.

Before Joop could react, the Audi pounded into the woman and forced her underneath.

She got hung up on something under the engine.

And dragged for a hundred yards.

Maybe more.

Then disappeared.

Chapter Sixty-Five

Day Nine—June 19
Tuesday Morning

PAIGE ALEXANDER ROLLED OVER IN BED and drifted out of sleep just far enough to register that the mattress was firmer than usual and that someone was taking a shower. She opened her eyes to find herself in a strange dark bedroom. Two heartbeats later she remembered where she was.

And recalled the sex.

The incredible sex.

The rock star sex.

So vivid she could still taste it.

She rolled onto her back and stretched her arms above her head, feeling more like a complete person than she had for a long time. She had let herself go without someone else in her life for too long and now realized what a huge mistake that had been.

Michael Dexter walked out of the bathroom with wet hair and a towel around his waist, trying to figure out if she was awake.

"Hey there," she said.

"Hey there back."

When he walked over, Paige grabbed his towel and pulled it down. He looked just as good as she remembered. Michael must have read her mind because he said, "I have an eight o'clock meeting."

"Too bad because you're going to be late."

She licked him until he got hard.

Then the rock star took her.

Wildly.

Like an animal.

Afterwards, while throwing on clothes at light speed, he said, "You shouldn't have done that."

"Why?"

"Because now I'm addicted."

WHEN PAIGE GOT OUT OF THE SHOWER, Michael had already gone. A full pot of coffee waited for her in the kitchen. Next to it was a note: *I mean it—addicted! I'll call you later. PS—If you snoop around, don't look in the bottom drawer of my bedroom dresser, whatever you do.*

She poured a cup of coffee, stirred in a touch of skim milk, and sipped it as she walked into the bedroom.

Delicious.

Banana-nut.

Nice and hot.

She almost set the cup on the top of the bedroom dresser but realized it might leave a mark. So she set it on a paperback book called *Shadow Laws* and pulled out the bottom drawer. It was empty except for a pair of keys and another note: *These fit the Jeep. Enjoy.*

She walked to the front window and looked outside.

A white Wrangler with a black hardtop sat in the driveway.

Cool.

She resisted the urge to snoop around, drank one more cup of coffee as she read the paper and then got in the Jeep and headed home.

AFTER FULL DISCLOSURE, Rebecca Vampire's sister immediately and energetically gave Paige the go-ahead to give Rebecca's name to Sarah Woodward.

Then Paige called Sarah at V&B and told her.

Rebecca Vampire.

"Good," Sarah said. "Email over everything you have on her."

Paige hesitated and then said, "Okay."

Sarah said thanks and indicated that she had no further news about Mark Remington's suicide at this point. But she added, "We hired a Bangkok P.I. to sniff around and see if he could find the place where Ja'Von had been taken. He had heard rumors about such a place. He had also heard that it was somehow connected to a man named Niran Thung. Now do you want to hear something really interesting?"

"Absolutely," Paige said.

"This Thung guy is the brother of a lawyer named Aran Thung," Sarah said. "And Aran Thung isn't just any lawyer. He runs one of the most influential firms in Thailand, by which I mean that he has lots of political clout and business clout. He's the kind of man who could persuade people to look the other way if something bad was happening."

"Damn," Paige sad.

"Major damn," Sarah said. "Now do want to hear something else that's really freaky?"

"Shoot."

"The name of Aran Thung's firm is Thung, Manap and Deringer, Ltd., which probably doesn't mean anything to you, but here comes the freaky part. They have a branch office right here in good old Denver, USA. In the Republic Plaza Building to be exact."

"So you think they're connected to Ja'Von's abduction?"

"I don't know if I'm ready to jump that far yet, but they're the most prominent blip on the radar screen right now, that's for damn sure," Sarah said.

Chapter Sixty-Six

Day Nine—June 19
Tuesday Morning

AT DAYBREAK TUESDAY MORNING, Bryson Coventry pulled in front of the for-sale house and killed the engine. He unscrewed a thermos of coffee and topped off a half-filled disposable cup. Then he walked around the side of the house on squishy grass to the backyard and stood next to the spot where Samantha Rickenbacker died. He closed his eyes and pictured her lying there, with a broken neck that left her head twisted at a disturbing angle.

He spotted a dry area on the concrete patio.

Where he sat down and leaned against the house.

With his legs stretched out.

A slight morning chill still hung in the air. Robins were already hopping around in the grass, stalking insects. A dog barked nonstop, a block or two away, but still annoying. A couple of clouds hung in the sky from the storm last night, but not many. The early morning sun painted them yellow.

This is where Samantha Rickenbacker died.

And where Madison Blake disappeared.

Last Tuesday.

One week ago.

There was a time, early in his career as a detective, when he went back to the murder scene of every unsolved case on the one-week anniversary of the event.

As a reminder.

As an inconvenience.

As a time to reflect.

As an opportunity to remind himself that he had not yet done the job.

But in the last three years, after he got promoted to the head of the homicide unit, he hadn't gone back once. In his defense, he didn't have time—at least that's what he told himself. But now, sitting here and watching the day start, he realized that maybe there was something deeper at work. Maybe he was getting jaded. Maybe he was becoming like some of the older detectives on the force.

He stood up.

"Screw that."

He walked back over to where Samantha Rickenbacker died. He looked down at the spot where her body had been and said, "I renew my promise to you. And to Madison Blake."

Then he got in the Tundra and pointed the front end towards headquarters. On the way he called the realtor who had the listing for the rental house, got the man's voice recorder, and left a message for him to call back.

AT HEADQUARTERS, COVENTRY WALKED straight to the sixth floor to see if Paul Kubiak was in yet by some miracle.

He wasn't.

Of course.

Because that's how Coventry's life worked.

So he left a note on Kubiak's desk and then headed down to homicide. No one was there yet, meaning there was no coffee, so Coventry got it going. While the pot filled, Coventry called the FBI profiler and got her voice message service. He said, "Give me a call," and hung up. As soon as he did he realized he hadn't given his name or number. Hopefully she'd recognize his voice.

He pulled the Alan Ewing file and went through it.

Thirty minutes later Shalifa Netherwood showed up in a nice gray pantsuit.

"I hope you got a good night's sleep because we have a truckload of work to do today," Coventry said.

She headed for the coffee and gave him a sideways look.

"Do I know you?"

He ignored it and said, "The first thing I need you to do is get the flight logs of every trip that Alan Ewing took to Bangkok. I don't care about other places, only Bangkok. Get the names and phone numbers of the passengers on those flights. I want to talk to them."

"Why?"

"To see if they know anything about him going to a bondage place," he said.

"Why?"

"Because if he did, that could be related to why he's dead," Coventry said. He raked his hair back with his fingers. "Oh, another thing, too. Check his bank records and see if he made any cash withdrawals before his Bangkok trips."

"I'm sure he did."

"I'm talking about sizeable withdrawals," Coventry added.

"Why?"

"Because if he went to the place that I think he might have gone to, it's pretty pricey—and they don't take American Express."

SHE TOOK A SEAT IN FRONT OF HIS DESK, propped her legs up on the other chair, took a sip of coffee and looked directly into his eyes. "What place are you talking about? And what the hell is going on?"

He hesitated.

Unsure whether to talk or not.

Then he said, "This is confidential, meaning you don't say a word to anyone. Agreed?"

She nodded.

"Okay, if that's what you want."

"That's what I want."

"Okay then, so what's going on?"

"I've stumbled across a few things that could possibly suggest that Ja'Von killed Alan Ewing," Coventry said.

Shalifa wrinkled her forehead.

"Your Ja'Von?"

"Right, mine."

Then he told her the story of how Ja'Von had been enslaved in Bangkok.

"If Alan Ewing paid a visit to her there, and then she somehow tracked him after she got back to the U.S.—which isn't totally unfathomable since she's a private investigator—she'd have plenty of motive to kill him. She had opportunity too, since she was in Denver at the time."

"Damn."

"I need to confirm that Alan Ewing never paid a visit to her," Coventry said.

"Why don't you just ask her?"

"I did," Coventry said. "I showed her pictures of Ewing and she said she'd never seen him. I didn't detect any lies."

"But that doesn't mean she wasn't," Shalifa said.

"Correct," Coventry said. "So I need to prove she's telling the truth. I'm hoping to find that Ewing never made any big cash withdrawals before his Bangkok trips. I'm hoping that Ewing's passengers have evidence that Ewing spent all his time with them, or on tours, or whatever."

"What if you find the opposite?"

He shrugged.

"I don't know," he said. "I haven't gotten to that point in my mind yet."

She reached across the desk and squeezed his hand.

"I'm sorry you're going through this."

"Don't worry about it."

She looked as if she wanted to say something but was hesitant.

"What?" Coventry asked.

"Did Ja'Von describe what this place looks like?"

Coventry held his hands up in uncertainty.

"Just in general terms," he said. "She was embarrassed to get into specific details. She said she didn't want me to have too vivid of an image of her. She was afraid I wouldn't be able to get it out of my mind and that it would taint my feelings towards her."

Shalifa nodded.

"I can see her point," she said.

"But?"

306

"But, like I told you before, Alan Ewing has lots of bondage porn on his computer," she said. "Maybe he took some of those pictures himself. Maybe some of them came from this place where Ja'Von was. If you knew what the place looked like, you'd be better able to judge."

Coventry nodded.

"I remember you telling me about the porn," he said. "In fact, I stopped up at Kubiak's this morning to get into Ewing's computer and take a look at it firsthand. That's the first thing I'm going to check out this morning."

She looked hesitant again.

"What?"

"If he's got all this porn on his computer, I can't imagine him being in Bangkok and *not* spending time in bondage clubs," she said.

Right.

Coventry already knew that.

"That doesn't mean he knew about the place where Ja'Von was though," he said.

HALF AN HOUR LATER Coventry called Ja'Von and said, "I'm going to need you to describe this place you were taken to. You know, what the rooms looked like, what was in them, that kind of thing."

She hesitated.

"You know I don't want to do that."

"I know," he said. "But this is important."

A pause.

"I'll think about it. But if I say okay, we need to do it face to face."

"Tonight?"

"Sure, if I say okay."

KATE KATONA WALKED INTO THE ROOM, poured a cup of coffee and took a chair in front of Coventry's desk. He recognized the look of excitement on her face, so compelling that he hardly even glanced at her chest. It meant that she had a breakthrough in one of her cases.

"Got big news," she said.

"Shoot."

"This involves the Brandy Zucker case." Coventry recognized the name but couldn't place it. Kate must have sensed his confusion because she said, "The hiker, the weatherman's daughter."

Suddenly it came back to him.

"Right."

"Okay," she said, "you remember that we found her car at the rest stop on top of Vail Pass."

Coventry nodded and pulled up an image of the place. It was one of the main rest stops on that stretch of I-70, with lots of parking and lots of use. He couldn't remember a time he had ever passed it without stopping, thanks to the people who make coffee.

"Right."

"There were no fingerprints on the steering wheel or door handle," Kate said. "That tells me that the woman isn't the one who drove the car there. Someone else drove it and then wiped their prints off."

"That's how I'd read it," Coventry said.

"There's more. It turns out that this particular rest stop has a couple of videotape surveillance cameras," she said. "Unfortunately, neither of them pointed at the area where we found the woman's car."

Ouch.

Too bad.

"BUT," SHE ADDED, **"WE** DID GET SOME FOOTAGE of a truck driver, a female, actually. When she pulled into the rest stop she was alone. She went in and used the facilities. When she came back out, a man approached her at her truck. They talked for a little and then he got in the truck with her and they left. My thought is—this is the person who drove Brandy Zucker's car there. This was how he left."

Coventry nodded.

Impressed.

"How good is the tape?"

"I'm giving it to Paul Kubiak to do his magic," she said. "My gut feeling is that it's going to be good enough to put on the news."

"Nice going."

"Actually you deserve most of the credit."

Why?

He hadn't even done anything.

Except hand the whole mess to Kate.

"Because you jumped on this so fast," she said. "If we had waited even one more day, the tape would have been written over."

He grinned.

"So I did something right," he said.

"Yeah and you cost me a lot of money."

Huh?

How so?

"I had all my cash riding on September of next year."

Chapter Sixty-Seven

Day Nine—June 19
Tuesday Noon

DYLAN JOOP WOKE UP HUNG OVER IN BETHANY'S BED. He took a long piss and drank three large glasses of water to get the sandpaper off his tongue. The woman moaned, rolled to her other side, and then passed back out. When Joop got out of the shower, she still hadn't moved.

Last night had been a surreal mix of valleys and peaks.

The deepest valley was running over the biker woman. He could still feel her thumping and scraping underneath the car as she got mangled into human hamburger.

One of the three motorcycles stopped at the scene.

The other two chased Joop.

Driving like maniacs.

Somehow managing to stay on his tail for more than five miles through the storm before one of them went down and the other one stopped.

They couldn't have gotten his license plate number.

Not through all that rain.

Maybe, if they were lucky, they'd be able to identify the vehicle as an Audi.

But he doubted it.

And, needless to say, they never saw his face.

After he lost them, he circled over to I-70, then C-470 and then Highway 74, back to the boxcars. Even though he had no reason to be nervous at that point, he had second thoughts about killing Madison Blake so quickly. Just in case someone did find a way to track him, he didn't want to be found with a dead body. So he locked her in the boxcar.

Those were the valleys.

THEN THE PEAKS CAME. He took a shower, dressed, and made it to the strip club just before midnight. Bethany—stage name Phoenix—immediately took him to the private-dance area and positioned herself so that he could feel her up without being spotted by the bouncers.

Then he drank beer.

Lots and lots of beer.

Enough beer to drown out the vision of the biker woman being torn to shreds under his car.

Bethany's stalker wandered into the club an hour later.

A gorilla.

Six-four.

Able to swing from tree limbs.

Bulletproof.

Joop waited until the dickhead went to the restroom and then stuffed his head in the toilet and broke his ribs.

Then he drank beer until closing.

He and Bethany were both too drunk to drive, but he was drunker than her, so he let her take the wheel. Somehow they managed to get to her place without killing anyone.

Then they screwed like rock stars before passing out.

That was last night.

Now it was almost noon.

HE KISSED BETHANY AS SHE SLEPT and left a note on the kitchen table saying that he'd call her later. Then he popped three Tylenol and pointed the Audi towards the boxcars.

The grim reaper was calling Madison Blake's name.

It was time.

Past time.

Chapter Sixty-Eight

Day Nine—June 19
Tuesday Afternoon

PAIGE ALEXANDER WALKED ACROSS THE LOBBY of the Republic Plaza Building and spotted her client, Ja'Von Deveraux, strategically positioned where she could watch the comings and goings of the elevator bank that fed the law office of Thung, Manap & Deringer. The black-haired assistant who gave such good backrubs, Hannah Trent, was with Ja'Von—obviously back from her trek to Cleveland.

Both women wore baggy clothes, hats and dark sunglasses.

Paige wouldn't have recognized either one if she hadn't been expressly looking for them.

Staking out the Thung firm had been Ja'Von's idea, following the news from Sarah Woodward this morning that pointed to a connection between the Thung firm and the place where Ja'Von had been held captive.

The plan was simple.

See if Ja'Von recognized anyone.

No one had seemed familiar based on the firm's website.

But not all bios had photographs.

And even of those that were there, Ja'Von had trouble knowing if she'd seen the person before. What she really needed to do was view the men in person where she'd have the benefit of seeing their skin color, size, posture and mannerisms.

"HOW'S IT GOING?" Paige asked as she walked up.

"Not much action yet," Ja'Von said. "Things will pick up at 5:00."

Paige smiled and said, "I have big news."

They looked at her.

Eager.

"Yeah? What?"

"I told Sarah Woodward about that tattoo that you described on Mark Remington's thigh. She said she'd check into it. About a half hour ago she called and confirmed that Remington's body did in fact have such a tattoo."

Ja'Von gave her a high-five.

Hannah did too.

"Now she knows we're not lying about Remington having a session with me," Ja'Von said.

"Exactly."

"Major cool."

"She's a believer," Paige added.

"She better be."

"She is."

"That gives us an ironclad suit against V&B," Ja'Von added.

Paige frowned.

"Not exactly," she said.

"What do you mean?"

"It means we have a pretty good case against Mark Remington," she said. "What we still don't know is if he was a rogue attorney acting on his own."

Ja'Von looked confused.

"Tell me how that works."

"Okay," Paige said, "it works like this. If Remington was acting on his own, without the knowledge or participation of the law firm, then the law firm isn't liable for anything he does. He's liable, of course, but not the law firm."

"But Remington said he was representing a law firm," Ja'Von said. "He said the firm wanted dirt on Bob Copeland."

"It doesn't matter what Remington said," Paige said. "Nothing he says is binding on the law firm. The only way the law firm itself can be held liable is if it did something wrong. That can come in a number of ways. If, for example, the law firm provided the money that was given to you, or knew what Remington was doing and allowed it to continue, or knowingly profited from Remington's actions, or something like that, then the firm itself can be held liable. But if Remington was acting solely on his own, outside the scope of his employment, then the firm isn't liable."

"This is complicated," Ja'Von said.

"Just think of it in terms of basic fairness," Paige said. "If Remington was acting on his own, it wouldn't be fair to hold the firm responsible. If the firm was in on it somehow, then it would."

"Okay."

"Do you understand?"

"I think so."

Paige looked at Hannah.

"Do you understand?"

"Yes."

"Good."

"What if Remington was working with someone else in the law firm and that person helped him by giving him law firm money or something like that?" Ja'Von asked.

"That would probably be enough to make the firm itself liable," Paige said.

"Then I have only two things to say."

"What's that?"

"Thomas," Ja'Von said. "And Fog. That guy's dirty. I can feel it in my gut. We need to focus on him."

Paige chewed on it.

Then a wild thought came to her.

"We're been assuming that Remington was working with Vinson & Botts since that's who he's employed with," she said. "Maybe, in point of fact, he was working with Thung, Manap & Deringer the whole time."

Chapter Sixty-Nine

Day Nine—June 19
Tuesday Morning

ALONE IN A CONFERENCE ROOM, Bryson Coventry sipped coffee as he pulled up the bondage photographs from Alan Ewing's computer. There were fewer than he thought, only a couple hundred. His primary goal was to figure out if any of them had been taken by Ewing in Bangkok, and in particular, at the place where Ja'Von had been kept.

And whether Ja'Von was in any of them.

That answer came easy.

No.

All of the pictures had been downloaded from websites. In fact, most of them had the web name imprinted on them. They had been pulled from cyberspace more than three years ago over a period of six months.

Meaning they were stale.

So where was the fresh stuff?

HE FLIPPED BACK TO ONE OF THE PICTURES—an unusually

beautiful woman wearing only a thong, stretched tight in a spread-eagle position on a bed. It reminded him of that night with Darien Jade, when she tied scarves on her wrists and ankles and told him to tie her down.

He said no.

It was too weird.

But she insisted.

So he did.

Then he explored her body with a light touch, slowly and teasingly, for a long time, working her into an orgasmic frenzy but backing off before she came.

And starting all over again.

Controlling her every sensation.

Until there was nothing left in her universe except the need to come.

Then denying her that.

Making her want it even more.

Reducing her to pure animal lust.

SUDDENLY THE DOOR to the conference room opened, Shalifa Netherwood stuck her head in and then entered. "There you are," she said.

Coventry closed the picture on the computer.

And realized that the *little fellow* was in a half-happy state.

"Hey," he said, trying to appear normal.

"Getting anything good?" she questioned.

"This is all old stuff and none of it's from Bangkok," he said. "We need to find the new stuff."

"You think there's more?"

He nodded.

"This isn't tap water. You don't just turn the knob and shut it off."

SUDDENLY HIS CELL PHONE RANG and the voice of the FBI profiler, Dr. Leanne Sanders, came through. "You called," she said.

He did.

He did indeed.

"Did you hear about Mark Remington?"

No.

She hadn't.

"The word is he hung himself in his hotel room," Coventry said.

"In Bangkok?"

"Right."

"Interesting."

"Yeah, I thought you'd say that."

"Thanks, I appreciate it," she said. "Talk to you later, I'm already late for ten things. Every weirdo in the world is suddenly bubbling to the surface."

The line went dead.

Thirty seconds later she called back.

"How did you find out?"

"Ja'Von Deveraux told me," Coventry said.

"Your girlfriend Ja'Von Deveraux?"

"Right."

"How did she know?"

"It's a long story."

"Well I want to hear it, but not this second. What's the name of the hotel?"

Coventry didn't know.

"Can you find out?"

He could.

"Let me know," she said. "If I don't answer, leave it on my voice mail."

COVENTRY LOOKED AT SHALIFA and asked, "So what's going on?"

She handed him a pile of papers. "These are Ewing's flight manifests for his Bangkok trips. I cross-referenced the dates to his bank account statements." She frowned. "It's not good."

Coventry braced himself.

"Give it to me," he said.

"It seems he took a lot of cash with him every time he went," she said. "Three or four thousand at least. Nothing ever got re-deposited after he got back."

"Damn."

Shalifa looked sympathetic.

"We have the names and numbers of all his passengers," she added. "I didn't know if you wanted to contact them or wanted me to."

He thought about it.

"Neither right at the moment," he said. "First, let's head to Ewing's house and find the rest of his bondage pictures."

"You want me to go with you?"

He nodded.

Reluctantly.

"We're getting dangerously close to Ja'Von being an official person of interest," he said. "As soon as we cross that line I'm going to have to take myself off the case, meaning you'll be in charge."

Shalifa cocked her head.

"I don't think we're anywhere near that line," she said. "Remember, the neighbor across the street from Ewing saw a *man* casing the place. Now correct me if I'm wrong, but Ja'Von isn't a man—is she?"

"Not the last time I checked," he said.

She grinned.

"And you've been checking a lot, I assume."

"I have but remember she's a P.I."

"Meaning what?"

"Meaning that if she's going to stalk someone and kill him, she's going to be smart enough to wear a disguise."

Shalifa didn't seem impressed.

And punched him in the arm to prove it.

"You are so full of conspiracy theories sometimes," she said. "Come on. Let's find the rest of Ewing's pictures, confirm that none of them are from Bangkok, and move on."

Right.

Good idea.

Chapter Seventy

Day Nine—June 19
Tuesday Afternoon

ON THE WAY TO THE BOXCARS, DYLAN JOOP stopped at a carwash and sprayed the underside of the Audi. A lot more chunks of flesh came off than he anticipated. He thought that the rain last night would have splashed up and cleaned the vehicle pretty well. That assumption had clearly been wrong.

When he finished, he pulled the Audi out of the stall and inspected the ground. To his dismay, a couple of dozen hunks of flesh were on the concrete.

They weren't large.

Most were no bigger than a finger.

But with so many of them, they were clearly noticeable.

He put more quarters in the meter and washed the carnage down the drain.

A man walked past.

On his way to the change machine.

And gave Joop a weird look.

As if he was nuts for spraying the ground.

Joop tried to think of something to say, a quick explanation, but nothing came to mind so he turned his back to the man and continued working.

Then he hopped in the Audi and got the hell out of there.

A quick glance in the rearview mirror showed the man staring at him as he drove off.

He got to the freeway and brought the Audi up to speed.

But had a sinking feeling in his gut.

And his mind kept playing a movie. In it, the man stood in Joop's stall, talking into a cell phone. Two minutes later a cop car pulled into the carwash. The man waved at it. Two cops got out. Then all three of them stooped down and looked at something on the ground in Joop's stall. Then one of the cops said, "Let's get the grate off this drain and see what's in there."

Joop got off the freeway and doubled back to the carwash. He parked the Audi on a side street three blocks short of the place and then hoofed the rest of the way on foot.

The man was gone.

There were no cop cars.

Everything was normal.

Joop exhaled and got back on the freeway.

WHEN HE GOT OFF C-470 at the Morrison exit, a Conoco appeared immediately on his right, one of the last stops for travelers heading into the canyon. The sight made him check his gauge. What he saw he could hardly believe.

Almost empty.

He pulled in and filled up, paying with a VISA at the pump. Then he went inside to get a cup of coffee. As he waited in a line four deep to pay, the TV on the wall showed a man talking to a female truck driver at a rest stop. The man looked vaguely familiar. So did the woman. Then the man and the woman got in the truck and drove off. The newscaster said that anyone having any knowledge of who the man or woman were should contact the number at the bottom of the screen. Then a picture of Brandy Zucker filled the screen.

The missing woman.

Joop kept his face calm, paid for the coffee and walked out. The police must have found Brandy Zucker's car at Vail Pass. They must have figured out that she didn't drive it there. When they found videotape of Joop leaving with a trucker, they must have concluded that he was the one who ditched the victim's car.

And then hit the trucker up for a ride.

Unfortunately for the cops, the videotape was extremely poor quality. No one would be able to recognize either Joop or the driver.

Nothing to worry about.

HE HEADED INTO BEAR CREEK CANYON with a full tank of gas, punched the radio stations, stopped when he got "I'll Melt With You," and sang along. In twenty minutes or so he'd be at the boxcars.

Time to kill Madison Blake.

End of story.

Four miles later, in the heart of the canyon, he came around a twist in the road and slammed on his brakes to avoid running into the last vehicle of a long string of cars that had come to a stop.

What the hell?

Suddenly a cop car and an ambulance approached from behind with their lights on, swung around him, and disappeared up the road, driving the wrong way in the oncoming lane.

A minute later a pickup truck came around the twist.

Going too fast.

And slammed on the brakes.

By some miracle it stopped before it rear-ended the Audi.

The driver immediately jumped out, ran down the road and waved his arms to warn the other drivers. It worked, because six more cars pulled up into the line without a single crash. Another cop car came and told everyone to stay where they were and to not turn around. They were keeping the opposite lane open for emergency equipment.

Joop killed the engine.

People were out of their cars now.

Talking.

Trying to figure out what was going on and how long the jam would last.

Joop stepped out.

The truck driver immediately walked over and complained about the delay.

Then the word of what happened started to spread. A boulder the size of a bus dislodged from the canyon wall, probably because of the rain last night. It landed on the front end of a car, squashing the engine compartment and most of the interior. There were two adults and four children inside. Three of the kids were still alive. Rescue teams were frantically trying to extract them.

Suddenly a deep rumble bounced through the canyon.

And a news helicopter passed overhead.

Chapter Seventy-One

Day Nine—June 19
Tuesday Afternoon

HANNAH TRENT DISAPPEARED on a food hunt, leaving Paige and Ja'Von to hold up the fort. Five minutes later an Asian man emerged from the elevator bank and walked across the lobby of the Republic Plaza Building swinging an expensive leather brief-case. He had short black hair, a wide mouth and a very distinctive look.

"I know that guy!" Ja'Von said. "Come on!"

They followed.

Thirty steps behind.

"From where?" Paige asked.

"Bangkok."

"You mean the dungeon?"

"I don't remember where exactly," she said. "Maybe the dungeon, but not because of a session with me. *That* I would remember."

The man led them to P-2 where he got into a white Porsche 911 coupe and drove off. They didn't need to write down his license plate number. There was no forgetting HUNTR. Back in the lobby they found Hannah holding a white bag.

Ja'Von took it, looked inside and told Paige, "Salads."

They ate outside by the fountain under a perfect Colorado sky while Denver bustled around them. Every man that walked by stared at Ja'Von.

Then Hannah.

As for Paige, she may as well have been invisible.

She pulled her hair out of the ponytail and shook it loose.

Then raked it out with her fingers.

There.

Better.

Not quite so invisible.

Hannah pulled a brush out of her purse, ran it through Paige's hair and said to Ja'Von, "She's a cutie, this lawyer of yours."

"Yes she is."

Paige only half heard the words, too focused on the case. "I'm really glad we held off on suing V&B," she said. "I'm starting to get more and more convinced that V&B may end up being our best friend and that this Thung firm may end up being the real culprit."

THEY HEADED TO PAIGE'S APARTMENT, fired up the Gateway and settled back to see what cyberspace had to say about their new friend.

HUNTR.

The Porsche was registered to one of the Thung firm's Denver partners, Virotte Pattaya, who lived in upscale Greenwood Village. He was the same person who Paige initially followed into the elevator and got a strange look from. According to the photos on the firm's website, though, the man driving the Porsche wasn't Pattaya, but was a 42-year-old named Kiet, a partner in the firm's Bangkok office. He must be borrowing the vehicle while he was here in the States.

Suddenly Ja'Von beamed.

"What?"

"I remember where I saw Kiet," she said. "He was in the bar, the one that I followed Bob Copeland into the night I got abducted."

"Are you sure?"

"Positive."

Good.

Very good.

"He was in a booth," she added. "He had three or four women wrapped around him and he had his hands all over them. They were having a good time."

Hannah frowned.

"I'll bet the little freak was watching you the whole time to be sure everything went as planned," she said.

Ja'Von nodded.

"That's my guess," she said.

"He needs to be held accountable," Hannah added.

"Yes he does."

THAT EVENING AFTER DARK, the three women waited down the street from Virote Pattaya's fancy Greenwood Village estate to see if the Porsche made a move. Paige chuckled and said, "I'm going to rely on you two since stalking wasn't on the Bar Exam." Shortly after 10:00 the garage door opened, the 911 emerged with Kiet at the wheel and disappeared down the street.

They followed.

North on Colorado Boulevard to a strip club in Glendale called Shotgun Willies.

"One of us needs to go in," Ja'Von said. "It can't be me because he knows me." Then to Hannah, "Give me a number between one and ten."

"Four."

Then to Paige, "Your turn."

"Seven."

"It was nine," Ja'Von said. "Paige goes in."

They gave her money.

Then she headed in.

INSIDE SHE FOUND EIGHT OR NINE OR TEN STAGES, each one filled with a gyrating woman more striking than the other. None were in Ja'Von's league, or even Hannah's for that matter, but any one of them could break a heart with the blink of an eyelash. Kiet sat at one of the bars, facing the stages, with two lovelies already snuggled up to him.

Money.

The women must smell it.

Paige walked to the end of the bar and ordered a draft. A man appeared from out of nowhere and hit on her.

He wasn't bad looking.

Nicely dressed in a suit and tie.

Tipsy but not sloppy drunk.

He helped her blend in so she let him stay.

KIET SPENT THE NEXT HOUR GETTING LAP DANCES and then left. Paige got back in the car with Ja'Von and Hannah, and they followed him through the fringe areas of lower downtown where he pulled into a metered lot on Wazee and killed the engine. Ten minutes later a black sedan with deeply tinted windows pulled up next to him.

Kiet got in.

Then came back out almost immediately and took off.

Ja'Von stayed where she was.

"You're losing him," Hannah said.

"I'm going to follow the sedan," she said.

"Why?"

"I don't know," she said. "Instinct I guess."

They followed the sedan.

Chapter Seventy-Two

Day Nine—June 19
Tuesday Afternoon

COVENTRY WAS SITTING AT A RED LIGHT on 8th Avenue, tapping his hand to "Dancing in the Dark" and waiting to cross Colorado Boulevard, when Barb Winters from dispatch called and said, "Are you in the mood to look at a dead guy?"

Coventry frowned, glanced at Shalifa and muttered, "Another one." Then, into the phone, "Who is it?"

"Some guy named Porter Potter," she said. "The responding officers said it looked like he slipped and hit his head on the bathroom floor. Kate Katona's on her way over."

There was a time when Coventry went to every scene.

Day or night.

Rain or shine.

Someone dies.

He sees them.

But he simply didn't have that kind of time any longer.

Especially when first indicators pointed to nothing more than a garden-variety accident.

"Thanks for the call," he said. "Tell Katona I won't be able to make it."

"You're not heading over?"

"Can't," he said. "I'm up to my eyeballs in alligators."

"That's supposed to be ass," she said.

"What is?"

"The alligators," she said. "You're supposed to be up to your ass in 'em, not your eyeballs."

"Yeah, well, they passed the ass a long time ago."

Ten minutes later, with coffee in hand, Coventry and Shalifa walked in the front door of Alan Ewing's house.

THE FRESH BONDAGE PICTURES were probably on CDs. They started in the den, where Ewing's computer had been found. The only CDs there appeared to be store-bought. They bagged them anyway.

They expanded the search into the bedroom.

The basement.

The garage.

Time passed.

"Maybe they don't exist," Shalifa said.

Coventry kept searching without looking up.

"They exist."

An hour later they still hadn't found anything.

"I'm starved," Shalifa said.

Coventry was too.

So they headed over to Colorado Boulevard looking for something cheap and fast—a McDonald's or Wendy's or something like that—with "Surf City" on the radio.

"That's what I don't understand," Coventry said.

"What?"

"Some guys are Jan and Dean and spend their time checking out the parties for the surfer girls," he said. "I'm the guy stuck in a traffic jam, spending my time trying to figure out if my girlfriend is a murderer."

Shalifa punched the up button on the radio and "Surf City" instantly turned into Shakira's "Hips Don't Lie."

"There," she said. "Problem solved."

Coventry grinned.

"And tell that FBI profiler friend of yours to stop messing with the stations," Shalifa added. "All she's doing is making more work for me."

"She thinks she has rights," Coventry said.

"So do you," she said. "That doesn't mean she does."

He laughed.

A McDonald's popped up on the right. The drive-thru was jammed up nearly all the way to the curb but Coventry pulled in anyway. "Too many people in this city," he said.

BACK AT EWING'S, they found nothing. Then Coventry discovered something interesting, namely a wall safe hiding silently behind a painting in Ewing's bedroom. He said, "They're in here," and ripped it out using a sledgehammer and crowbar from the garage.

It fell to the carpet with a thud.

And was every bit of eighty pounds, not to mention awkward.

Coventry muscled it up into a bear-hug, did a Frankenstein walk out to his truck and got it into the bed.

Shalifa brushed plaster off his shirt.

Then they locked up and fought traffic on the way back to

headquarters, not getting a single good song on the radio except "California Dreaming."

BACK AT HIS DESK, cooling his heels until the lab could get the safe open, Coventry pushed papers and tried to not get too nervous. Kate Katona showed up mid-afternoon and took a chair.

"Sorry I couldn't join you," Coventry said. "What was the guy's name again?"

"Porter Potter."

"Tell me it was an accident," he said. "I don't want any more job security around here."

"It was," she said.

He nodded.

"Chalk up one for the good guys," he said.

"Right."

"Winters said he hit his head or something."

"He fell changing a light bulb," Kate said.

"Well that's dumb."

"Drunk is more like it."

Coventry grinned. "One more example of *Don't Drink and Do Stuff.*"

Kate laughed.

"The poster child."

Then a serious expression washed over her face.

"What?" Coventry asked.

"He might have been drinking because of his daughter," she said. "Do you remember that airplane crash at the Jefferson County Airport earlier this year? The one where six people died?"

No.

He didn't.

"She was on that plane," Kate said.

"That's a shame."

She nodded.

"He still has her pictures all over the place," she added. "Dozens of them. She looks a lot like Madison Blake."

"My Madison Blake? The Molly Maid?"

Kate nodded.

"They could have been sisters," she added.

Chapter Seventy-Three

DYLAN JOOP GOT ANOTHER HOUR OF HIS LIFE sucked away in the canyon traffic jam. Then the idiots in charge announced that the road wouldn't reopen at all. It would be closed for the indefinite future because the boulder needed to be blasted into manageable chunks to be removed. Also they were bringing experts in to look at the canyon walls to determine if other outcroppings were in danger of breaking off. Everyone had to turn around and squeeze through Morrison, which had been designed for horses and wagons instead of a New York rush hour.

Damn it.

Damn it.

Damn it.

Move your ass.

Get the hell out of my way.

Don't try to squeeze in front of me you jerk.

I'll take you down.

I'll take you down to Chinatown.

Joop was so frazzled by the time he finally punched through

all the congestion and got to the wide-open lanes of C-470 that he couldn't even sing along with Meat Loaf's "Paradise by the Dashboard Lights."

Plus the canyon closure was more than an inconvenience.

It was the death knell for one of the two escape routes from the boxcars.

Now there was only one way out.

And one way in.

Namely a long circular route of many miles up I-70, through Evergreen and then back down Highway 74.

What a pain in the ass.

But he had no choice, so that's the route he took.

THREE MILES FROM THE BOXCARS, Joop encountered a police roadblock. A baby-faced cop told him that the canyon ahead was closed due to an accident and possible rockslides, but then let Joop through when he told him he had a place up the road, this side of the accident.

"Just keep a lookout," the cop said.

"Will do."

Jerk.

How was Joop supposed to do that?

Be looking up as he drove?

Two miles later something weird happened. A helicopter sat on the canyon road. Two others circled directly above. The chopper must have just landed because there were no cars by it.

Three people stood outside, two men and a woman.

Joop recognized the woman.

Jena Vernon, the green-eyed TV 8 reporter.

Blond.

Very hot.

He actually had a dream about her once. They were making out in the backseat of a car at night. She was a dog in heat, insatiable, nothing more than a heaping pile of animal lust. She had Joop's cock in her hand and was trying to get him to put it in, but he was holding out, teasing her, making her beg for it. That's when a pack of flying monkeys showed up and carried the car into the sky, miles and miles above the earth, almost into outer space, and dropped it.

Weird.

JOOP PULLED UP TO THE CHOPPER AND STEPPED OUT.

"You guys okay?" he asked.

A man wearing jeans and T-shirt, no doubt the pilot, said, "We're fine. But if you're trying to get up the road, this bad boy isn't going anywhere for a while."

It turned out that they had been covering the car that got squashed by the boulder, developed problems and made an emergency landing. A mechanical crew was en route to evaluate the aircraft but probably wouldn't be able to repair it in place. That meant that a crane would need to be brought in to lift the aircraft onto a flatbed.

"We're looking at some serious time," the pilot said.

Joop half listened as the pilot talked.

And half focused on Jena Vernon, now sitting on the riverbank and tossing rocks into the water. She wore beige cotton pants and a short-sleeve white blouse, simple but sexy. He walked over and sat down.

"You see that boulder sticking out of the river over there?" he asked, pointing.

She did.

"I'm not going to tell you my name unless you can hit it with a rock."

She checked him out.

Then stood up and threw a rock.

Missed.

And threw another.

And another.

And another.

Then hit it, just barely, on the side, but a hit nonetheless.

She sat down and said, "Okay, so what's your name?"

"Dylan."

She shook his hand.

"I'm Jena Vernon."

"I know," he said.

Five minutes later her phone rang. She told Joop, "Excuse me a moment," and answered. Then, into the phone, "Bryson—no, I'm okay—honest—well, yeah, there is one thing you could do now that you mention it—get me drunk and take advantage of me—I *am* serious—"

She hung up and said, "An old friend of mine."

"Lucky guy," he said.

Chapter Seventy-Four

Day Nine—June 19
Tuesday Night

THE THREE WOMEN FOLLOWED THE BLACK SEDAN as it looped around towards Larimer Square but then lost it after getting stuck at a light. That was fine with Paige. Her watch said midnight and her body said sleep.

Twenty minutes later she was back at her apartment. She took a quick shower and stretched out face down in bed, wearing flannel pajama shorts and a tank top, barely awake. She didn't look up when Hannah turned off the living room lights and walked into the room.

"Long day," Hannah said.

"Mmm."

"What you need is a backrub," Hannah said.

Sure.

That would be okay.

Hannah straddled her and kneaded her shoulder muscles. "Feel good?" she asked.

Yes it did.

Paige kept her eyes closed and her head in the pillow. The

341

bed felt so incredibly good. Hannah felt like an old friend. Nothing else in the world existed.

Hannah's hands were under Paige's shirt now.

So nice.

It rode up higher.

Then Hannah said, "Let's get this off."

Paige didn't say yes.

But didn't say no.

And Hannah pulled it up and over Paige's head.

"That's better," Hannah said. "Now we have something to work with."

The woman's touch became lighter, more like a caress than a rub, and explored Paige's sides and underarms. Then she scooted down towards Paige's feet and massaged her ass.

Paige almost said something but didn't.

It felt too good.

"You may as well get the full body massage," Hannah said.

"Mmm."

Hannah went to work on her thighs.

And calves.

And feet.

Then back up her legs to her ass.

When Hannah pulled Paige's shorts off, she didn't protest.

A few minutes later Hannah said, "Time for the front."

To Paige's surprise, she rolled over onto her back.

Hannah straddled her stomach and stretched her arms above her head.

Paige let her.

And then left them there.

Vulnerable.

Open.

Curious.

Hannah ran her fingers down Paige's arms, slowly, and caressed her underarms and sides and stomach for a long time. Then she ran her fingers in little circles on Paige's nipples.

Little sparks fired in Paige's brain.

Then Hannah moved down, put her face between Paige's legs and used her tongue; her warm, wet tongue. After a few minutes she said, "I've never done this before. Does it feel okay?"

Yes it did.

Very okay.

Incredibly okay.

AFTER THE LONGEST AND MOST INTENSE ORGASM of her life, Paige got a drink of water. When headlights appeared in the parking lot, she took a quick peek to see who was keeping such late hours.

The headlights came from a black sedan.

It slowed as it went by.

And Paige felt mean eyes looking out from behind the deeply tinted windows. Then the vehicle sped up and disappeared out the other side of the lot.

She shivered and said, "We have company."

Chapter Seventy-Five

PAUL KUBIAK CALLED WITH BAD NEWS. Alan Ewing's safe
held car titles, insurance polices, and a small amount of cash,
but no bondage CDs. Coventry said thanks, hung up, and
slammed his hand on the desk. The coffee in his cup rippled.

Shalifa walked over and took a chair.

She looked tired.

"I got through to about half of Ewing's passengers so far,"
she said. "No one knows what he did with his free time. The
way it worked is, they would usually be there anywhere from
one to seven days. Ewing was on his own until it was time to
leave. A couple of the guys admitted to frequenting the blowjob
bars but said they never saw Ewing there."

"That means he's dirty," Coventry said.

"How so?"

"If he'd been doing normal things like sightseeing, it would
have come out."

Shalifa shrugged.

Maybe.

She didn't know.

When Coventry told her that Ewing's safe didn't have any CDs she said, "Then they don't exist."

Coventry disagreed.

"They exist," he said. "And the fact that he hid them so well tells me they're personal—pictures taken by him of his own victims."

"Come on, Bryson," she said. "We tore that place apart."

He shook his head.

"He's got a secret compartment somewhere."

She looked confused.

"What's going on here?" she asked.

He ran his fingers through his hair and said, "What do you mean?"

"It's almost as if you want Ja'Von to be dirty."

"That's ridiculous."

"Then how come whenever the evidence points the other way, you don't accept it?"

"Because not finding something isn't evidence," he said. "It's only evidence when you do find it and see what it says."

She cocked her head.

"That's bull and you know it," she said. "Personally I think you're just scared."

"Well you're right about that."

"Scared that she *isn't* a killer," Shalifa said. "Scared that you let her in your life. Scared that you're not the only one in control of you anymore."

He chuckled.

"I didn't know you had a degree in psycho babble."

She patted his hand.

"Well now you know."

HE ALMOST GOT IN THE TUNDRA and headed back to Ewing's, but couldn't think of where else to look. Ten minutes later Kate Katona cornered him at the coffee pot.

"We may have a break in the Brandy Zucker case," she said.

Coventry raised an eyebrow.

"What kind of break?"

"We got a call from someone named Mary Zang who's a waitress at a truck stop in Grand Junction," she said. "She saw the news report and thinks that the woman truck driver might be this lady who stops there once in a while."

"Run with it," Coventry said.

"How far?"

"Drop everything else," he said. "This poor girl's been missing too long. We either have a homicide or a homicide-in-the-making. Either way I want to nail this guy."

Kate retreated in thought.

"If you're really serious, then I'm going to hop in the car and follow the trail."

"You mean to Grand Junction?"

"Right."

He looked at his watch.

"If you leave now you'll be there by dark."

SHE GOT UP AND HEADED FOR THE DOOR. Then she came back and said, "I almost forgot to tell you. That guy that you and Leanne Sanders were so interested in, Mark Remington, was a lawyer with Vinson & Botts, right?"

He nodded.

"Yep."

"Did you know that our latest dead guy, Porter Potter, had his deposition taken by a Vinson & Botts attorney recently?"

No.

He didn't know that.

"Small world," she said.

TWO MINUTES LATER COVENTRY'S CELL PHONE RANG. It turned out to be the realtor, Jim Hansen, returning his call from this morning.

"This involves the murder of Samantha Rickenbacker at the house you have listed," Coventry said.

"I figured that."

"Before the night in question, did you get any strange calls? You know—someone who wanted to confirm that the owners weren't living in the house or something like that?"

The man hesitated.

"I don't recall anything like that."

Chapter Seventy-Six

Day Nine—June 19
Tuesday Afternoon

JOOP BACKTRACKED A QUARTER MILE, found a place off the road big enough to park the Audi, and hoofed it to the boxcars on foot—a forty-five minute trek. Madison Blake was apprehensive when he rolled open the door to her boxcar.

With good reason.

She was supposed to be free.

"Don't worry," he said. "We're still on track to set you free. Unfortunately we had a complication last night."

He held his hand out.

She took it and he helped her out of the boxcar.

"What kind of complication?"

He told her about the storm and the unfortunate event of running over the biker woman. "After that happened, I had to get the Audi off the road."

She cocked her head.

As if deciding whether to believe him or not.

"Today we had another setback," he said. "The road is blocked in both directions." At first she didn't believe it, but he gave her so many details that she had no choice.

"As soon as one way or the other opens up and I can get a car in and out of here, you're free," he said. "Until then we have to sit tight."

"I can't be in the boxcar anymore," she said.

He understood and said, "You don't have to while I'm here, as long as you behave yourself."

"You know I will," she said. "I've already proved that. I'm proving it right now. Can I take a shower?"

Sure.

SHE COOKED SUPPER and they ate on the deck steps. News helicopters flew back and forth. "See," he said, pointing. "Down that way they're covering the car that got squashed. The other way they're covering the news chopper that made the emergency landing."

She believed him.

After supper they shot the bow.

The woman was actually starting to show some skill.

Then they walked up and down his driveway until their legs ached.

After dark they put on long-sleeve shirts and drank wine.

Then he chained her in the bed with him.

And closed his eyes.

THE TV 8 HELICOPTER should be off the road by tomorrow.

Meaning Madison Blake would be dead 24-hours from now.

"Pleasant dreams," he said.

"You too."

Jim Michael Hansen

He thought about Jena Vernon and wondered if he could recapture his dream about her if he kept thinking about it before going to sleep.

No flying monkeys this time though.

Chapter Seventy-Seven

Day Ten—June 20
Wednesday Morning

THE RTD HAD NO KNOWLEDGE of what happened to the Trek after the genius bus driver disappeared with it on Monday night, so Paige took the Wrangler to work as a temporary solution. She parked it on the other side of Broadway in a free 2-hour spot and hoofed it six blocks to the Eatery. Then she spent the morning carrying plates of food to ungrateful people who thought a 50-cent tip was more than fair.

She hated being there.

But the rent was due in ten days.

During the morning break, she stepped outside and called Ja'Von. Hannah had already told her about the black sedan trolling past the apartment last night.

"Coventry told me something weird last night," Ja'Von said.

"What?"

"Apparently there's a guy named Porter Potter," she said. "He was changing a light bulb and managed to fall and crack his head open. It turns out that he had recently been deposed by a Vinson & Botts attorney. Also, he had a daughter who died in a plane crash earlier this year. It turns out that this missing girl who's all over the news—Madison Blake—looked a lot like this guy's daughter."

Paige chewed on it.

"So what's Coventry's take on all that?"

"Nothing," Ja'Von said. "He just thinks it's really weird that V&B keeps getting linked to bad stuff."

"He's right about that," Paige said.

"Other than that, there's nothing new from my end," Ja'Von said. "I'm at Coventry's, he's at work. There are no black sedans in sight."

"Watch your back."

"You too."

Okay.

They hung up.

Two minutes later Paige called back.

"Does Coventry have a copy of the guy's deposition?"

"Not that I know of, why?"

"It would be interesting to know what it was about," Paige said. "Maybe it has something to do with Bangkok."

"Want me to get a copy of it?"

"You can't," Paige said.

"Why not?"

"Only attorneys on the case can get them," Paige said. "They're not public documents."

Ja'Von laughed.

"I'll get a copy for you."

WHEN PAIGE GOT BACK TO HER APARTMENT after work, a copy of Porter Potter's deposition sat on her kitchen table. Hannah wasn't there and hadn't left a note. Paige took a quick shower, poured cheap white wine from a box into a plastic cup, and then settled back on the couch with the deposition, a pen and a yellow highlighter.

Emily Hand, Esq., took the deposition.

According to the firm's website, she was a senior associate in V&B's litigation department, seven years out of law school, meaning she was probably on the verge of becoming a partner.

The deponent, Porter Potter, was the Vice President of the Vanguard Group, a pharmaceutical research and development company. Vanguard was suing the Warren Corporation, a New Jersey company engaged in the research, development and manufacturing of drugs.

Vanguard's position in the case seemed to be that it had hired a Ph.D. professor named Randy Ice on a contract basis to develop a new drug to combat arthritis. It claimed that Ice conducted the research, gave faulty information to Vanguard, and then sold the proper information surreptitiously to Warren who was currently in the process of obtaining FDA approval.

The drug, once approved, would be worth billions.

Both the plaintiff and the defendant claimed entitlement to the drug.

The researcher, Randy Ice, died last year when he drove through a red light and got broadsided by a garbage truck.

So his testimony wasn't available.

Porter Potter had been the primary person at Vanguard to deal with Randy Ice. One of the central issues in the case was whether Potter had fired Ice for nonperformance, thereby freeing Ice to work for Warren. Thus Potter's testimony as to the nature of Vanguard's relationship with Ice was critical to the case.

The interesting thing was that Potter's deposition testimony actually helped V&B's client, Warren Corporation, a lot more than it helped Potter's own employer.

In fact, Potter would no doubt be V&B's star witness at trial.

With Potter's testimony now nailed down in his deposition under oath, V&B's client was almost certain to win at trial.

Meaning V&B would have no motivation whatsoever to have Potter dead.

In fact, quite the opposite.

Now, with Potter's death, V&B could only read the witnesses' testimony into the record at trial. That wasn't anywhere near as effective as calling the man live.

Further, there was no mention of Bangkok anywhere in the deposition.

Not even close.

THE PHONE RANG and Michael Dexter's voice came through.

"You busy tonight?"

No.

She wasn't.

"Let's do something."

"What?"

"I don't care. Whatever you want—"

"—as long as it ends in sex," she said.

He laughed.

"You know me too well," he said.

"Actually, I know myself too well."

She fired up the Gateway and did some quick research before heading over to Michael's. The death of Potter's daughter was totally unsuspicious, the result of a faulty landing gear. Even though she looked like Madison Blake, there was no connection. Madison was born to different parents.

Enough thinking.

Time to get laid.

Chapter Seventy-Eight

Day Ten—June 20
Wednesday Morning

BRYSON COVENTRY WOKE BEFORE SUNRISE and jogged three miles up and down the streets of Green Mountain before kissing Ja'Von as she slept and heading out the door. He stopped at the 7-Eleven on Simms for a thermos full of coffee and headed straight to Alan Ewing's house, intent on finding the man's secret compartment.

The one that held the bondage CDs.

With a Beatles disc spinning, and coffee in hand, Coventry checked every room for wall compartments.

Nothing.

He looked under carpeting for floor compartments.

More nothing.

He checked every dresser, table, drawer, cabinet and piece of furniture for false bottoms or hidden compartments.

Twice as much nothing.

Come on.

Where are you?

Maybe the CDs weren't here anymore. Maybe the killer took

them because they were incriminating.

THE TEMPERATURE OUTSIDE WAS NICE. Across the street, a middle-aged woman pulled weeds from an artsy flowerbed. Coventry wandered over to see if she was the one who had seen a car stalking Ewing's house.

She was.

Her name was Bunny Britt.

"So tell me what you saw," Coventry said.

"Well, like I told the detective—"

"—Shalifa Netherwood—"

"—right, her, a man drove by in a car a couple of times, always slowing down right in front of my house. I knew the car didn't come from this street. I've lived here for ten years and know what people drive."

"Would you recognize the man if you saw him?"

She laughed.

"Heavens no," she said. "This was always at night."

"So how do you know it was a man?"

She retreated in thought, as if not quite sure.

"I guess by the outline of his face," she said. "He had a moustache."

"A moustache?"

"Right, a moustache."

"Anything else?"

"Black glasses."

"Anything else?"

"A hat."

"What kind of hat?"

"A baseball hat."

Coventry took a sip of coffee. A robin flew by with another one on its tail. It wasn't clear if they were playing or fighting.

"Go back to the moustache for a minute," Coventry said. "Was it big or small?"

"I'm thinking big," she said. "Otherwise it wouldn't have made such an impression."

"How big was this guy?"

She chuckled.

"I don't know, he was driving the car."

"Right," Coventry said. "I appreciate that. But did he seem to sit up high in the seat, like a tall man, or down lower?"

She shrugged.

"I'm thinking lower, but I can't tell you why."

He nodded.

The robins flew by again, this time clearly fighting.

"One last question," Coventry said. "Could the man have been a woman disguised to look like a man?"

She paused and screwed an expression on her face as if she was trying to recreate the image.

"I suppose so," she said. "Like I said, it was dark and I didn't get that good of a look. Basically what I saw was the blurry silhouette of a head."

Coventry took a sip of coffee and said, "I like your flowers. We don't have any up where I live because they're just deer candy."

BACK IN THE TUNDRA, Coventry called Ja'Von, ostensibly to say hello. Then he headed back to his house after learning that she was out for the morning with her assistant, Hannah Trent. He hated to do what he was about to do but had no choice. After confirming that she wasn't in the house, he went through her suitcases.

Four of them.

Being careful to put everything back exactly as it was.

The red suitcase turned out to be something in the nature of a P.I. spy kit—binoculars, listening devices, bugs, transmitters, a GPS, a 9mm Glock, lock pickers, a small tool kit, hair dye, colored contact lenses and other assorted and sundry items. He also found what he hoped he wouldn't.

—A number of hats, including a baseball hat.

—Several false moustaches, beards and eyebrows.

—Three pairs of glasses with flat glass.

Damn it, Ja'Von.

HE CALLED SHALIFA AS HE DROVE TO HEADQUARTERS and said, "Meet me out front of the building in twenty minutes."

"Why?"

"You'll see."

They ended up taking a walk over by the Art Museum as Coventry explained what he found out this morning. "I think I'm at that point where I need to get out of the case and hand it over to you," he said.

She studied him.

And disagreed.

"You're reading too much into nothing," she said. "Ewing went to Bangkok, sure, but even after you spent hours tearing his house apart, and I spent hours interviewing his passengers, we have absolutely no proof that he ever frequented the place where Ja'Von was taken. So we really don't have a motive for her to kill him. She was in Denver when Ewing got killed, and presumably had opportunity, but so did a million other people, including you and me. The neighbor saw a man staking out Ewing's house, a man who could possibly have been a woman in disguise, but could also have been a man. And most importantly, you don't have a single shred of tangible evidence connecting her to the scene—not a fiber or a print or anything else."

He said nothing.

"All you have is a theory and a fear," she added. "That's not enough."

He disagreed.

"True it's just a theory, but it's the best one I have," he said. "If she didn't kill Ewing, then who did?"

Shalifa shrugged.

"I don't know—the guy staking him out, I assume—but I'll tell you one thing," she said. "If you dump the case on me, I'm not going to follow up on Ja'Von. There's not enough there to justify wasting my time. Not to mention that the last thing I need is to get in the middle of your love life."

He shook his head.

Beaten.

"You're too stubborn," he said. "I pity the guy who eventually marries you."

She chuckled.

"Well, no one's asking, so they're all safe."

Chapter Seventy-Nine

Day Ten—June 20
Wednesday Morning

JOOP WANTED MADISON BLAKE DEAD SO BAD that he thought about walking her into the mountains this morning, two or three miles from the boxcars, and getting it over with. But he worried about dogs tracing her scent to the boxcars if she ever got found. Plus, he couldn't exactly set out on a walk with her carrying a shovel. Meaning he would have to walk her into the mountain, kill her, leave her exposed while he came back for a shovel, then return and bury her.

Too many steps.

Too many complications.

Too much risk.

Too much work.

Too many eyes in the sky.

Plus it probably wouldn't save much time. The helicopter should be gone by tonight at the latest.

MID-MORNING, HE STUFFED HIS CAPTIVE back in the boxcar

and hoofed it up the road to see how things were coming with the helicopter. On the way, his contact called.

"Got a job for you," the man said.

Joop smiled.

A job meant money.

"Go on," he said.

"The mark's a woman named Ja'Von Deveraux," the man said. "It needs to look like an accident. You should know in advance that there's a complication."

"What kind of complication?"

"She's living with a cop," he said.

"Cops have guns," Joop said.

"We appreciate that and we're going to double your fee to compensate," the man said.

Double.

Good.

That was fair.

"Actually it's a detective," the man said.

"Who?"

"Bryson Coventry."

"Did you say Bryson Coventry?"

Yes.

He did.

"Then we need to go triple," Joop said.

The man paused and then said, "Done."

Joop smiled.

Oh yeah, baby.

"What's the timeline?"

"Tonight," the man said.

Joop laughed and said, "You're kidding, right?"

No.

He wasn't.

Not in the least.

WHEN JOOP GOT TO THE HELICOPTER—a Bell JetRanger—
it looked just as weird as it did yesterday sitting out there in the
middle of the road. Four guys with a crane were just starting to
harness the aircraft.

"What's the timeline?" Joop asked.

A rough looking man in an oily shirt didn't appreciate the
interruption.

"As soon as the flatbed shows up," he said.

Joop headed for the Audi and said, "Thanks. Have a good
day."

Then he headed to Coventry's house to scope things out.

If things went as planned, he should be able to kill both
Madison Blake and this new target, Ja'Von Deveraux, by midnight.

Then start tomorrow as a new man.

A rich new man.

He punched the radio buttons, got "Tainted Love," and
cranked it up.

Chapter Eighty

Day Ten—June 20
Wednesday Evening

PAIGE ALEXANDER AND THE ROCK STAR ended up walking down railroad tracks on the edge of the city. Fifteen miles to the west, the sun dropped further and further towards the mountains and would disappear in another hour. No one was around and no trains were in sight. Several seagulls rested on the tracks ahead.

"Recently a lawyer in your firm took the deposition of a man named Porter Potter," Paige said. "The man died not too long after that."

"From the deposition?"

She laughed.

"No, you guys aren't that tough. He slipped and hit his head in the bathroom," Paige said.

"Who took the deposition?"

"Someone named Emily Hand."

He nodded.

"She's one of our litigators, a nice gal." Then he got excited. "Is this on that drug case?"

"Yes."

"I wonder if Emily knows the guy's dead," he said.

Paige shrugged.

She didn't know.

"I hope she got finished," he said.

"I find it sort of weird that V&B keeps getting linked to dead people," Paige said. "First Mark Remington and now this guy."

The rock star wasn't impressed.

It was a big firm.

It did lots of stuff.

Lots of people die.

There's going to be overlap.

Plus this wasn't a "link."

It was just two normal things that happened to occur close in time to one another.

"I WILL ADMIT THOUGH," he said, "when it comes to the death factor, our firm has really been fortunate."

Paige looked at him.

"How so?"

"Well, for example, our Paris office had a huge case last year," he said. "It was a trial to the court. The trial judge wasn't seeing things our way. It was crystal clear that he was going to rip our client a new one. The evidence ran for three weeks and ended late on a Friday. The judge said he'd issue his ruling from the bench on Monday morning. Then something weird happened. He died on Sunday. The case got retried to another judge six months later. That judge saw the whole thing differently and ruled in favor of our client."

"How did the first judge die?"

He shook his head.

"I don't recall."

Paige picked up a stick and broke it in two.

"It seems suspicious to me," she said.

He laughed.

"Meaning what? That our client killed the judge to avoid a bad ruling?"

She shrugged.

"Whatever."

He shook his head.

Ridiculous.

"That kind of thing only happens in movies."

She spotted another stick by the tracks and snapped it in two.

"Maybe."

"Maybe?"

"Right, maybe."

"Meaning maybe not, too?"

She nodded.

"Right, maybe not, too."

"Trust me," he said. "Our clients aren't killing people."

Paige knew she should let it rest but couldn't.

"We're people, but deep down we're still animals," she said. "We do animal things."

He chuckled.

"I see your point," he said. "But if you're insinuating that a large law firm can be a killing machine, you're way off base."

"Why?"

"Because when people get together in a large organized group, like a law firm, the animal factor disappears—especially when that group has to exist in an organized and structured environment. That happens as a natural course of events because everyone's animal instincts will never kick in at the same time. If someone's instincts do kick in for whatever reason, they'll be subordinate to the group."

Paige cocked her head.

"This is getting too philosophical," she said. "All I can say is that I find it suspicious that the judge died right before he ruled."

Michael put his arm around her shoulder.

"I'm never going to win an argument with you, am I?"

THEY TURNED AROUND and headed back up the tracks. The sun sank lower over the mountains and filled the clouds with color, subdued at first, but then intense.

They sat on the tracks and watched.

Then when it was almost dark, Michael stretched out on a track timber.

On his back.

"Get on," he said.

She chuckled.

And looked at him as if he was crazy.

"You're kidding, right?"

No.

He wasn't.

She bit her lower lip and looked around.

Saw no one.

Then slipped out of her pants and got on.

Chapter Eighty-One

Day Ten—June 20
Wednesday Night

BRYSON COVENTRY HAD A REDWOOD DECK behind his house, nestled on the side of Green Mountain, that looked over the roof and onto the world. To the west, an incredible sunset unfolded. To the east, the lights of Denver began to twinkle.

The temperature was perfect.

The air was quiet.

Sparrows darted on silent wings and snatched insects out of the sky.

A streetlight kicked on.

Then another.

Ja'Von sat next to Coventry, wearing white shorts, sipping a glass of wine and looking out at the world. Headlights snaked up the street and drove past Coventry's house. They did a one-eighty in the turnaround at the end of the street and then headed back down the hill.

No problem.

They didn't belong to a black sedan.

Coventry took a long swallow of Bud Light, his second. Ordinarily right about now he would be feeling pretty good. But he couldn't get his mind away from the thought that the woman next to him might actually be a killer.

If that was true, he'd find out sooner or later.

And it would all tumble down.

How could he continue to build a relationship with someone who might get yanked from his life? But then again, how could he *not* when the woman was Ja'Von?

Without warning a stray thought entered his head.

ALAN EWING GOT KILLED before he even brought his luggage into the house. It had still been in the back of his vehicle. Shalifa went through it quickly, found nothing of interest, and left it in Ewing's car.

Including a digital camera.

No one had ever looked at the pictures.

Maybe Ewing visited the place where Ja'Von was taken.

And took pictures.

Which were still in the camera.

Coventry leaned forward in his chair and twisted the beer can in his fingers. Ja'Von must have sensed a change in his equilibrium because she asked, "What's wrong?"

Should he go to Ewing's now?

Or wait until morning?

SUDDENLY HIS CELL PHONE RANG and the voice of Dr. Leanne Sanders came through. "You never called me back with the name of Mark Remington's hotel in Bangkok," she said.

Coventry flopped back in his chair.

"God, I knew there was something—"

"Don't worry about it," she said. "I ran it down myself and had a few conversations with the Bangkok police as well as the hotel people. From the scraps of information I've managed to gather, I'm getting more and more convinced that Remington's suicide wasn't self-inflicted."

Coventry wasn't surprised.

"Meaning someone picked up where the Frenchman left off," he said. "What I don't get is why you care. I thought your assignment was limited to babysitting Boudiette."

"It was."

"But?"

"But now it's getting bigger. In fact, I may be coming back to Denver, so consider yourself warned."

He hung up and told Ja'Von, "That was my FBI friend. She thinks that Mark Remington's suicide was really murder. I'd feel a lot better if you weren't jabbing that law firm right now."

"They jabbed first," she said.

"Still, it's dangerous."

"They're all going down," she said. "Women are dying in that place even as we speak. That's not something I can turn my back on."

Coventry nodded.

"I wish I could, but I can't," Ja'Von added.

"I understand."

"I need you with me, not against me."

He squeezed her hand.

"I'm with you," he said.

She chuckled.

"What?" he asked, curious.

"You've never had a woman with so much drama," she said.

"I can tell."

He grinned.

"I just worry about you," he said.

She drank the rest of her wine in one long swallow and stood up, at this point not much more than a silhouette in the dark. Her ass wiggled and then her shorts and panties dropped down her legs and fell to her feet. She stepped out of them, kneeled in front of Coventry and unzipped his pants. "I want you to just sit back, relax and enjoy the hell out of this," she said.

He thought he heard a slight noise behind him.

But forgot about it just as fast.

Chapter Eighty-Two

Day Ten—June 20
Wednesday Night

_____

THE NEW MARK—JA'VON DEVERAUX—WAS TURNING out to be a major pain in the ass. Joop swung by Coventry's house a good ten times, only to find the place deserted. Precious time slipped away all day long and Joop had no idea where the woman was. Then she and Coventry showed up at eight o'clock in separate cars. They milled around inside, probably eating, and then headed up to the deck behind the house to watch the sunset and get drunk.

One thing was certain.

There was no way Joop would be able to kill the woman tonight and make it look like an accident. So which was more important?

Getting it done tonight?

Or waiting until it could be an accident?

He called his contact for guidance.

"Do it tonight if you can. Just don't get caught."

Perfect.

He parked on a side street around the bend of the mountain

and then snuck through the terrain on foot with an eight-inch serrated knife in hand, pondering the big question, namely whether he should kill Coventry too.

On the plus side, Coventry wouldn't be around to hunt him.

On the negative side, a hundred others would.

Relentlessly.

He scurried through the darkness as fast as he could, wanting more than anything to get to the deck before they went inside. A hundred feet away he spotted them.

Still there.

Oh yeah, baby.

He slowed and approached with a beating heart.

Then something beautiful happened.

The woman stood up and slipped out of her shorts.

Then dropped to her knees.

Joop didn't move until Coventry started moaning.

Then he approached on cat feet.

Quiet.

Not even there.

One silent step in front of the other.

HE TURNED THE KNIFE AROUND so that he'd be stabbing with the butt of the handle instead of the blade, put it in a white-knuckle death grip and then brought it down with all of his might on the back of Coventry's head.

A horrible sound escaped from the man's mouth.

Then he slumped over.

The woman looked at Joop.

Then screamed and ran.

JOOP CHASED HER DOWN THE STAIRS, through the backyard and down the side of the house. When he came around the corner of the garage a terrible thing happened.

He saw her.

Swinging a shovel violently at his head.

He tried to bring his hands up.

But didn't have time.

Then his face exploded with a terrible pain.

A pain like no other.

Bright colors flashed.

And he fell to the ground.

Then a pain exploded in his back.

Again.

And again.

And again.

Chapter Eighty-Three

Day Ten—June 20
Wednesday Night

HANNAH TRENT WAS WATCHING a Sex in the City rerun when Paige got back to the apartment shortly before ten. The woman wore black cotton shorts and a pink blouse. Her hair was tossed and disheveled—very sexy. They kissed, which is something they hadn't done before, but it was just a peck and didn't seem like anything to take notice of.

Paige fired up the Gateway.

Hannah poured boxed wine into plastic cups, handed one to Paige and said, "What are we doing?"

"Research on V&B," she said.

"What kind of research?"

"Research to find out if they're killing people to win lawsuits," she said.

Hannah shook her head.

As if Paige was messing with her.

"No, really," she said. "What are we doing?"

"Really, that's it," Paige said.

Hannah wrinkled her forehead.

"What does that have to do with Bangkok?"

"Nothing."

"Then why are we worried about it?"

"We're worried about it because we might be the only people in the world asking the question," she said.

Paige started with the dead judge in Paris that Michael Dexter told her about. It turned out to be quite the buzz at the time and there was no shortage of newspaper articles about it. The man got stabbed to death taking a walk after dark. His wallet and watch were taken. The police investigated for a long time but never found the killer. It didn't appear that V&B or its client, Singer Aerospace, were ever suspects.

Interesting.

THEN PAIGE FOUND SOMETHING ELSE INTERESTING.

It involved the Hong Kong branch of V&B.

In that case the opposing party was an individual. He died of a gunshot wound to the head a month before trial. The police weren't quite sure at first if it was a suicide or a homicide. In the end they felt it was a suicide and closed the file. The man's estate didn't bother to step in as the new party of interest, no doubt because the case was a loser without the man alive to testify. The court then dismissed the case for lack of prosecution.

Paige took a sip of wine and said, "V&B seems to have death on their side in their high-stakes litigation. Their Denver drug case fits that profile, but what I still don't get is why V&B would kill Porter Potter. His testimony *helped* V&B's case."

Hannah shrugged.

"Porter Potter's a good example of why your theory doesn't work," Hannah said. "I'll admit that you found a couple of suspicious things. But you have to focus on the big picture. V&B has *thousands* of attorneys worldwide. I can't even imagine how many cases they try in a year. You're going to find weird things happen simply because there are so many opportunities for weird things to happen."

"Maybe," Paige said.

She looked at her watch.

12:10 a.m.

"It's already tomorrow," she said.

They hit the sack.

Chapter Eighty-Four

Day Ten—June 20
Wednesday Night

A SWEET AROMA CUT THROUGH the antiseptic hospital smell. Bryson Coventry recognized it as Ja'Von's perfume and opened his eyes. She was sitting in a chair reading a magazine. He put his hand to his head and felt gauze. His thoughts were foggy but the pain had dissipated.

"I have one question," he said. "Was the *little fellow* in or out when the paramedics showed up?"

Ja'Von jumped.

Then smacked his arm and said, "Don't sneak up on me like that." She kissed him and added, "I put him away for you."

He grunted.

"Thanks."

"That doesn't mean I won't take him back out again later," she said. "By the way, Shalifa Netherwood wanted me to tell you that she's at your house working the scene, otherwise she'd be here." Then she told him everything that happened after he got knocked out.

Coventry stretched.

"How are you holding up?" he asked.

"Me? I'm fine."

"You sure?"

Yeah.

She was.

"I've been meaning to tell you something," she said. "I'm starting to fall for you."

"Starting?"

She grinned. "Okay, *have.*"

"How far?"

She squeezed his hand. "Too far. What I'm saying is, don't ever scare me like that again."

"I'll see what I can do," he said. "And ditto, about that falling stuff."

"So what are you saying?" she asked. "That you love me?"

He ran his fingers through her hair.

Then pulled her in and kissed her.

"Yeah," he said. "That's exactly what I'm saying."

HE KNEW HE SHOULDN'T DO what he was about to do. It was ethically wrong. And maybe legally wrong, he wasn't sure. But he also knew that he really did love this mysterious woman sitting on the edge of his bed. "I keep thinking about that pilot who got stabbed in the back, Alan Ewing. His death has something to do with Bangkok. My gut tells me he's been to that place you were taken."

Ja'Von looked nervous.

"Like I said before," she said, "I never saw him there."

"Right, I know that," Coventry said. "He's a bondage freak, but I couldn't find any fresh pictures at his house. Everything I found was just generic stuff that he pulled off the web three years ago. I've been back to his house three times looking for the new stuff, which is probably on CDs. But I can't find it."

"Too bad," Ja'Von said.

"I'm starting to think that the CDs existed but the killer took them because they were incriminating," he said.

"Incriminating how?"

Coventry shrugged.

"I don't know exactly," he said. "Maybe the killer is actually in the photos."

"I guess that's a theory," she said. "But if they're gone, you'll never know."

He nodded.

"Right," he said. "But I'm not sure that the killer got them all."

Ja'Von shifted her position.

"What do you mean?"

"Ewing got back from Bangkok right before he got killed," Coventry said. "His suitcases were still in the car. Shalifa did a quick inventory of them during our initial investigation, but didn't find anything of interest. There was a digital camera in one of the suitcases. We never looked at the pictures in it. It's possible that some of the bondage pictures that I've been trying to find are in that camera."

Ja'Von wrinkled her forehead.

"Why are you telling me this?"

Coventry shrugged.

"No reason," he said. "It's just shop talk. Anyway, tomorrow I'm going to head over to the man's house and check that camera."

Ja'Von retreated in thought.

Then she said, "There might not be any pictures in it at all."

Coventry shrugged.

"If not, then I guess I hit my final dead end," he said.

Chapter Eighty-Five

Day Eleven—June 21
Thursday Morning

DYLAN JOOP DRAGGED HIS ALCOHOL LADEN BODY out of bed and staggered to the mirror to survey the damage by the light of day. The right side of his face was a purple mess. His eye was swollen into a slit that he could hardly see through.

And his nose.

That was the worst.

Thoroughly broken.

Crooked.

Mangled so bad that he couldn't breathe through it.

It would have been worse if the woman had kept beating him with the shovel instead of running back up to the deck to check on Coventry.

Joop popped two more Tylenol and wished he hadn't drunk the JD last night to kill the pain.

What to do?

Before he could think, his contact called and Joop gave him the bad news.

"So your blood is at the scene," the man said.

"Unfortunately."

"That's not good," the man said.

"My DNA isn't on file anywhere," Joop said. "They can't use it to find me."

"But if they do find you then they can tie you to the scene," the man said.

"They won't find me."

"They will if you go anywhere with that face."

True.

"What's the status of Madison Blake?" the man asked.

"She was going to be the second order of business last night," Joop said. "Obviously I didn't get around to her."

"So what's the plan today?"

"I think you're right that I shouldn't be driving in the daylight," Joop said. "As soon as it gets dark I'll head out with the Blake woman. After that, I'm not sure. Ja'Von Deveraux will be impossible at this point. Maybe I'll get out of Denver for a while."

"Bad idea," the man said.

"Why?"

"You'll have to stop for food or gas or a hotel or something," the man said. "You can't do that with your face. It's safer just to stay where you are."

"We'll see," Joop said.

He could almost read the man's mind. The man wanted Joop where he could find him. Because Joop had screwed up too many times. And needed to be dead.

Joop headed back to bed. The man wouldn't try anything before Joop killed the Blake woman.

Meaning sometime tonight.

Chapter Eighty-Six

Day Eleven—June 21
Thursday Morning

SARAH WOODWARD CALLED EARLY Thursday and asked if Paige could meet this morning alone, without Ja'Von Deveraux.

"Why?"

"I'll tell you when you get here," the woman said.

An hour later they met.

This time, unlike before, Sarah Woodward appeared confident and sure of herself. She wore a wool-blend suit with a silk blouse that probably cost more than Paige's monthly rent. Paige sipped her coffee and tried to not be intimidated.

"The last time we met," Sarah said, "I told you that I would investigate the matter and get back to you. Since then, I've thrown a lot of time and energy at it and I've found out a few things that you'll probably find interesting."

"Good."

"Now, before we begin, I just want to be sure that I wrote things down correctly the last time we spoke." She referred to her notes and said, "From what I understand, your client arrived in Bangkok on or about April 11th. Is that correct?"

Paige searched her memory.

And recognized the date.

Yes.

That's what Ja'Von told her.

And what she told Sarah Woodward.

"That's correct," she said.

"And then that same night she got abducted," Sarah added.

"Right."

"Then, if I understand the story correctly, she was held in captivity for approximately one month, until about May 10th. At that time she was purchased for a snuff and escaped following a traffic accident."

"Right," Paige said. "I don't remember if May 10th is the day she escaped or the day she got back to the U.S., but it was sometime around then."

"Within two or three days, I would assume," Sarah said.

Right.

THE WOMAN PICKED UP a thin monogrammed leather brief-case from the floor, set it on the table, opened it and pulled out a stack of papers.

"Part of the investigation that I've been doing on this matter concerns your client," she said. "Here's what we found so far. Ms. Deveraux did in fact arrive in Bangkok on April 11th, as she claims. Here's a copy of her airplane ticket."

Paige accepted the document and studied it.

A copy of an airplane ticket.

Obviously genuine.

She set it on the table and asked, "How'd you get this?"

"We have resources," the woman said. "She then returned to

the U.S. on April 25th."

"No, we just talked about that," Paige said. "She returned on May 10th, give or take a few days."

The woman handed her another document and said, "This is a copy of her airplane ticket returning to the U.S. on April 25th."

Paige studied it.

It looked genuine.

Like the first one.

"No, this isn't right," she said.

"Your client then stayed in the United States for approximately two weeks, until May 5th," the lawyer said. "This is a copy of her bank statement for April and this is her statement for May."

Paige studied the additional documents.

"As you can see, your client made a number of credit card purchases here in the U.S. between April 25th and May 5th," Sarah said. "She gassed up the car a number of times and ate at Fisherman's Wharf twice, among other things. She also wrote a number of checks and paid a number of bills. Copies of the drafts are attached. You can see the signatures belong to her."

Paige found the woman's conclusions to be sound.

And said nothing.

"Then your client returned to Bangkok on May 5th," Sarah said. "Here's a copy of her airline ticket. While she was there she stayed at the Baiyoke Sky Hotel and made a number of credit card purchases. Those are also on her bank statements. Then she returned to the U.S. on May 10th. Here's a copy of her return ticket."

"Something's wrong," Paige said. "This can't be right."

Sarah Woodward leaned across the table.

"Here's what's wrong," she said. "Your client, Ja'Von Dever-aux, is a fraud and a liar. She claims she was in Bangkok in sexual slavery when in fact she was right here in the good old United States eating lobster at Fisherman's Wharf. She concocted the whole stupid story to try to extort money from this firm. Then she looked around for a lawyer inexperienced enough to believe her." She sipped coffee, looked Paige directly in the eyes and added, "And found you."

Paige's heart raced.

She felt faint.

The woman shuffled the papers and handed them to Paige. "Here," she said. "Take these with you and have a little heart-to-heart with your client."

Paige took the papers and headed for the door.

"One more thing," Sarah said. "There are lawyers in this firm who are convinced that you're in a conspiracy with this woman to try to extort money. That's a criminal offense, a *felony* criminal offense to be precise. They're hell-bent on taking the whole matter to the D.A. and pressing charges. So far, I've been able to talk them out of it. But if I see your face again, or hear anything more about this ridiculous matter—well, let's just say that wouldn't be a good thing. Have a nice day and a nice life."

Chapter Eighty-Seven

Day Eleven—June 21
Thursday Morning

BRYSON COVENTRY WOKE THURSDAY MORNING from a
deep, drug-enhanced sleep. He staggered to the bathroom, took
a long piss, splashed water on his face and headed back to bed.
Before he could get back to sleep, Kate Katona called and said,
"Guess where I am?"

He didn't know.

"Des Moines," she said.

"Des Moines, Iowa?"

"Right."

"What are you doing there?"

"I tracked our truck driver to here," she said.

"You mean the Vail Pass woman?"

"Right," she said. "She's on the road right now, but will be
back late this afternoon. I've got her scheduled to work with a
sketch artist. With any luck, sometime late today we're going to
have a composite of the man she picked up."

"I'm impressed," he said.

"I already talked to Jena Vernon," Kate said. "They're ready to put it on the air as soon as we fax it to them."

"I don't suppose the daughter has shown up yet."

"Not that I heard."

HE DIDN'T WAKE UP AGAIN UNTIL NOON. The doctors released him, reluctantly, and he headed directly to 7-Eleven for coffee and then to Alan Ewing's house to check the digital camera.

There were no pictures on it.

Not a one.

Maybe because there had never been any.

Maybe because Ja'Von Deveraux went there last night and erased them.

He didn't know.

And didn't want to know.

Chapter Eighty-Eight

Day Eleven—June 21
Thursday Afternoon

DYLAN JOOP SLIPPED IN AND OUT of a nasty dream where a hit man stuck a gun in the back of his head and pulled the trigger without emotion. He woke in a cold sweat mid-afternoon and took it as a premonition. Deep down he still had his doubts that the Frenchman had been a rogue as alleged by his contact. If the Frenchman had been engaged to kill Joop, then this latest fiasco at Coventry's house last night only made matters worse.

Fine.

Two can tango.

The pain in his head disappeared and his eye opened up enough now that he could see with no problem. He jogged all the way to the end of his driveway and up Highway 74 for a mile. The helicopter was gone as of sometime yesterday. The boulder still blocked the road in the opposite direction. The lack of traffic in the canyon created a nice silence that framed the sounds of the river.

An hour of exercise capped off the run.

He stashed the bow and quiver in the mountains.

In preparation of tonight.

Just in case.

Then he fetched Madison Blake from the boxcar and let her make supper.

In a couple of hours it would be dark.

Time for her to die.

Once and for all.

Chapter Eighty-Nine

Day Eleven—June 21
Thursday Afternoon

PAIGE ALEXANDER REPORTED TO SAM'S EATERY at noon, slipped on her apron and realized that she really was a waitress and not a lawyer. She had deluded herself for a while, but no longer. A real lawyer would have never fallen for Ja'Von's stupid story.

Not in a million years.

She reached into her back pocket to see if the letter was still there; the letter from the Colorado Supreme Court three months ago confirming her status as a duly licensed attorney in the State of Colorado.

It was.

She pulled it out, ripped it in pieces and threw it into the 30-gallon garbage can in the kitchen. Ten seconds later Amy walked over and scraped two used dishes on top of it.

So befitting.

Such an absolutely perfect statement.

JA'VON DIDN'T ANSWER HER PHONE ALL DAY.

Paige left ten messages asking her to come to the restaurant at Paige's 4:00 p.m. break to meet on an important matter. Miraculously, the woman actually showed up.

Smiling.

Looking lovely.

Paige grabbed her backpack, led her client outside to the sidewalk, and confronted her with the story that Sarah Woodward told this morning about Ja'Von being in the States and eating lobster when she claimed to be in sexual slavery in Bangkok. She handed the airline tickets and bank statements to Ja'Von and waited for an explanation.

Something.

Anything.

But Ja'Von said nothing.

"You lied to me," Paige said. "I can't believe that you actually lied to me about the whole thing and that I actually fell for it. How in the hell did you even think something like that up?"

Ja'Von looked vacant.

And then walked away.

"At least say you're sorry!" Paige shouted.

The woman didn't even turn around.

"Liar!" Paige shouted.

Ja'Von turned, looked over her shoulder and then kept walking.

Paige looked for a rock or something to throw at the woman.

But found nothing.

Then she slumped down on the sidewalk and cried.

Chapter Ninety

Day Eleven—June 21
Thursday Afternoon

———————————

WHEN JA'VON DIDN'T ANSWER her cell phone all day long, Bryson Coventry called Paige Alexander to see if she knew where the woman was.

"Ja'Von and I are through," Paige said.

"Why, what's going on?"

"That's a confidential attorney-client matter. She can tell you, but I can't."

"Wow. That doesn't sound good."

He almost hung up when he heard her talking.

"Are you still there?" she asked.

He was.

"As long as I have you on the phone, I may as well tell you something. This relates to Porter Potter," she said.

Coventry scratched his head.

The name was familiar, but he couldn't place it.

"He supposedly slipped and cracked his head while changing a light bulb," Paige added.

Bingo.

Right.

"What about him?"

"I don't think his death was an accident," Paige said.

"Why not?"

"I think that Vinson & Botts had him killed," she said.

"Why do you say that?"

"Because that's what they do in high-stakes cases."

"Based on what evidence?"

"Nothing concrete," Paige said. "Here's my theory about the man. Vinson & Botts took his deposition right before he died. That deposition actually helped V&B's client."

"So?"

"What I think happened is this," she said. "Somehow they got him to lie in his deposition. I don't know if they paid him or threatened him or what. But somehow they got to him. Then, after they got what they wanted, they had him killed. That way he couldn't recant his testimony later or contradict himself at trial. All they need to do now is sit back and read his deposition into the record. The story can't be changed."

"That's a wild theory," Coventry said.

"It's a wild world," she said.

Then the line went dead.

Chapter Ninety-One

Day Eleven—June 21
Thursday Evening

———————

THE WIND KICKED UP AND A DRIZZLE SET IN. Dylan Joop sat in the middle boxcar with the door open and the laptop booted up, pecking at the keyboard as he waited for darkness. The pain in his face subsided, but he still couldn't breathe through his nose. It would be better to get out of Denver for a while and deal with a hit man when he was in better condition.

He called Bethany and said, "I have a crazy idea."

"Like what?"

"I was thinking that maybe you and me could head out of town somewhere for a while," he said. "I've got money, so don't even worry about that."

"Somewhere where?" she asked.

"Wherever you want."

A pause.

"I've never seen the ocean," she said.

"Okay, California then."

"Are you serious?"

He was.

Very serious.

"I'll be your surfer girl," she said.

Nice.

Very nice.

"I have to tie up a few loose ends and then I'll come over to your place, probably sometime between eleven and twelve," he said. "We'll leave in the morning if that works for you."

It did.

"Oh," he added. "I took a fall rock-climbing. My face is a little messed up, so be warned."

Chapter Ninety-Two

Day Eleven—June 21
Thursday Evening

———————

BRYSON COVENTRY PACED next to the windows and called Ja'Von once again, for the Nth time, and got her voice mail again, for the Nth time.

Damn it.

Where was she?

Night approached.

And rain fell.

Everyone had gone home except Shalifa who was busy coordinating with the TV stations to get the composite sketch on the news tonight—the sketch of the man who dumped Brandy Zucker's car at Vail Pass; the sketch obtained by Kate Katona from the Des Moines truck driver who gave the man a ride.

Shalifa hung up the phone, walked over and said, "It's all set up."

Coventry frowned.

"I hope the weatherman can handle what's coming," he said.

Suddenly his cell phone rang.

He answered as fast as he could, hoping it was Ja'Von.

The voice of Jena Vernon, the TV 8 reporter, came through. "Bryson! I just saw the fax of that guy you're looking for. I know that guy!"

"You do?"

"Yes," she said. "I met him up on Highway 74 when our helicopter came down. He said he lived a mile down the road from there."

Coventry stopped walking.

"Are you sure it's him?"

"Positive."

"How positive—50 percent or 80 percent or what?"

"Ninety-five percent."

"Hold it," he said. "I'm trying to think. What's the best way up there?"

"There isn't one," she said. "The road's still blocked with the boulder. You'd have to swing all the way up I-70 and through Evergreen to get around the back way."

Not good.

That would take an hour.

"He drives an Audi," she added. "A brown Audi."

Coventry remembered that the ex-cheerleader across the street from the for-sale house saw a medium-colored foreign car.

COVENTRY STRAPPED HIMSELF IN tighter than tight, put his armrests into a death grip, and held his breath as Air One left earth and rumbled upward into a wet and ominous sky.

Shalifa said, "You should see your face."

He ignored her.

And concentrated on the jarring and shaking of the chopper.

399

He smacked the pilot on the side of the head to get his attention and said, "What's wrong with this thing?"

"Nothing."

"It doesn't feel like nothing."

"Relax."

"It feels like this thing is falling apart."

"For the last time, relax."

Streets appeared and disappeared below them.

Santa Fe.

Alameda.

C-470.

Then the twinkling city lights dropped behind as they entered Bear Creek Canyon, flying low, with the spotlight on.

"There's the boulder!" Shalifa said.

Coventry looked.

The back end of a squashed vehicle protruded from under a rock the size of a bus.

"Keep going," he said.

"What are we looking for exactly?" the pilot asked.

"A brown Audi."

"Nice of you to mention that."

"Sorry."

Five minutes later Coventry said, "Turn around. We went too far."

They doubled back.

Then Shalifa said, "There! A road—"

They followed it.

At the end they found three structures that looked like boxcars. A man and a woman were outside in the rain, looking up. Suddenly the woman ran. The man chased her and punched her in the back of the head. She went down. The man punched her again, picked her up, ran to a brown car and threw her in the back seat.

"We need to get down there!" Coventry said.

"Too many trees," the pilot said.

"Squeeze in somewhere!"

Suddenly bright flashes appeared from the ground.

And bullets hit them.

Bamm!

Bamm!

Bamm!

Bamm!

Then the chopper made a terrible noise.

The headlights of the car turned on and the vehicle sped down the road towards Highway 74.

"We're going down," the pilot said.

"Get in front of him!" Coventry said.

"I don't know if—"

"Block him in I said!"

The car reached Highway 74 and sped up the canyon.

The chopper followed.

Sputtering.

Losing altitude.

Smoke entered the cabin.

Then the engine seized and the aircraft dropped straight down.

Coventry's stomach shot into his mouth.

He braced himself.

Then they crashed.

Chapter Ninety-Three

Day Eleven—June 21
Thursday Night

DYLAN JOOP RACED UP HIGHWAY 74, barely in control, trying desperately to stay in front of the helicopter. If it blocked him in he was screwed.

Totally forever screwed.

It was right on his ass.

So close that he could hear the rumble of the blades.

Then suddenly the spotlight dropped out of the sky.

And hit the ground behind him.

Then exploded in a bright flash and went out.

It crashed!

So perfect!

So absolutely perfect!

He brought his foot off the accelerator and got the vehicle back to a safe speed.

He was free.

Free!

Yeah, baby.

The road curved to the right.

Then something bad happened.

Suddenly a hand appeared from the back seat.

Madison Blake's hand.

It grabbed the steering wheel and jerked it to the left.

The Audi almost rolled but didn't. Instead it left the road, shot over an embankment and splashed into the river.

The headlights went out.

And icy water entered the interior.

Chapter Ninety-Four

Day Eleven—June 21
Thursday Night

THE CHOPPER HIT THE GROUND with a spine-compressing thud. Coventry was hurt, but didn't know how bad and didn't have time to find out. He got his seatbelt off and frantically felt for the door handle.

He couldn't find it.

Then cold rain entered the cabin and someone grabbed his shirt.

"Come on!" Shalifa said.

Then they were out.

All three of them.

And ran.

Twenty seconds later the aircraft exploded in a fireball that lit the canyon like daylight for a full half mile.

Then something weird happened.

Up the road it looked like the car missed a turn and crashed into the river.

Shalifa ran that way.

"Come on!" she said.

Coventry pulled his gun and followed.

His legs didn't work right.

When they got there, the car was no more than a black silhouette jammed in the middle of the river.

A voice came from it.

A female's voice.

Screaming for help.

Stuck in the car.

Fifty feet from the bank.

Coventry stepped into the water.

It was stronger than he thought.

And ice cold.

"Just stay where you are!" he shouted.

Suddenly something cold and wet and strong had his head in a vice grip. Then incredible muscles twisted his neck and forced him under the surface. Water immediately filled his ears and nose and mouth. He shifted to break loose.

It did no good.

Instead he went ever farther under.

He kicked his legs but got no traction. His lungs would fill with water in seconds. He twisted, got his head above the surface and sucked precious air. Then he reached behind and got his hands to the back of the man's head. The other man lost his traction but got Coventry in the same position. They were back to back, locked together, each pulling as hard as they could, trying to snap the other's neck. Coventry tightened his neck to keep it from breaking.

His muscles screamed.

Then he pulled the man's head with every ounce of strength he had.

Chapter Ninety-Five

Day Eleven—June 21
Thursday Night

PAIGE ALEXANDER DRANK MARGARITAS at Jose O'Shea's on Union until her money ran out; then staggered home in the rain. The alcohol was supposed to erase the image of Sarah Woodward saying, "And found you," but it didn't work.

She got home to find Hannah Trent sleeping naked on top of the covers.

Ja'Von's little buddy.

What nerve, to still be here.

Hadn't Ja'Von told her that the charade was over?

Drunker.

That's what Paige needed to be.

Drunker.

She changed into dry clothes, poured a glass of wine and then sat on the couch in the dark as the storm battered the building. When the wine was gone she walked into the bedroom and slapped Hannah Trent on the ass as hard as she could.

"Get out of my apartment and out of my life!"

"What the—?"

"Now!"

She swung again.

This time getting the woman's leg instead of her ass.

"Stop that!" Hannah said.

But Paige couldn't stop.

She swung again.

And again.

Then the woman grabbed her hands and said, "Stop it!"

But as soon as she let go, Paige hit her again.

That was a mistake. The woman wrestled her to the carpet. She fought back but was no match. The woman twisted Paige onto her back, then straddled her and pinned her arms above her head. Paige tried to muscle loose but the woman just gripped her wrists tighter and shifted her weight even higher on Paige's chest, until her crotch was almost on Paige's face.

"Get off me!"

"I will," Hannah said. "But first you have to listen to what I have to say."

"I said get off!"

"No."

Hannah kept Paige pinned on her back until she calmed down. Then she said, "Stay," and loosened her grip on Paige's wrists. Paige immediately brought her arms down. Hannah grabbed them and pulled them back up. "Stay, I said."

This time when Hannah released her grip, Paige left her arms above her head.

"That's better," Hannah said. "I'm now going to make you my lawyer. That means that whatever I tell you is privileged and confidential, right?"

"I'm not your lawyer," Paige said.

"You better be, otherwise I can't tell you what's going on,"

Hannah said.

A pause.

"Okay, I'm your lawyer."

"That means that whatever I tell you, you can't tell the police or anyone else, right?"

"Right."

"Good."

"FIRST OF ALL, I KNOW YOU'RE MAD AT JA'VON," Hannah said. "Don't be and I'll tell you why."

"There's nothing you could possibly say."

"Hear me out," Hannah said. "Ja'Von was hired by a mystery law firm to follow someone named Bob Copeland to Bangkok and get dirt on him, exactly like she said. What she didn't tell you is that she took me with her. We both went to Bangkok."

"You went too?"

"Yes, I went too," Hannah said. "I was her assistant and she felt too intimidated to go there alone. At that time my hair was a lot longer and it was blond. That night we followed Bob Copeland to a blowjob bar in the Soi Cowboy district. I was the one who went inside while Ja'Von waited outside. Someone spiked my drink. I woke up in sexual slavery. It was me, not Ja'Von, who got abducted."

"You? Then why did Ja'Von say it was her?"

Lightning flashed outside.

Followed by the loud crack of thunder.

"I'm getting there," Hannah said. "Ja'Von was frantic to find me. She stayed in Bangkok for two weeks looking for me. Eventually, she heard about the place and learned that women could be purchased for snuffs. But she had no idea where the place was and couldn't go there even if she knew, because she'd be taken herself. So she went back to the United States."

"Okay."

"Are you following me?"

"Yes."

"She took a loan out against her house for $300,000," Hannah said. "Then she came back to Bangkok with a friend of hers—a man named Ernest Poindexter. He started to spread money around and asked about a dungeon where he could have some serious fun. It took a while but he eventually ended up at the place. He purchased me for a snuff at a cost of $250,000. Then we all came back to the United States."

"So Ja'Von bought your freedom," Paige said.

"Exactly."

"And there was no traffic accident."

"No. We had to make that part up."

Silence.

"All of the things that she told you that happened to her were all true, except that they happened to me," Hannah said. "One man was particularly brutal. He told me he was a pilot and lived in Denver but never told me his name. Ja'Von and I came to Denver to find him. Ja'Von did most of the work because I was an emotional mess. She dressed up like a man and stalked him. Then we confirmed he was the right person."

"Alan Ewing," Paige said.

"Right, Alan Ewing," Hannah said. "After we found him, I knew that I had to kill him. Ja'Von tried to talk me out of it a hundred times, but I was hell-bent on revenge. And then I took it. I stabbed him to death in his bedroom." She paused and then said, "I don't regret it. He got what he deserved. We made sure that Ja'Von was in a public place at the time so she had an alibi if she ever needed it."

"So you killed Alan Ewing," Paige said.

"Yes—but remember that's privileged and confidential," Hannah said. "You're my attorney. You can't ever tell anyone."

"I won't."

Paige was still lying on her back with her arms above her head.

"Can I get up now?" she asked.

Hannah let her up.

They poured wine and sat on the couch in the dark.

"Anyway, Ja'Von was worried about me getting caught," Hannah said. "She knew that there would be a murder investigation and had sniffed around enough to determine that the main guy in charge of the homicide department—a man named Bryson Coventry—would get involved at least to some extent. Ja'Von decided to buddy up to him to keep track of where they were. That way she could tell me if they were getting too close, at which point I would disappear to Mexico or whatever."

"So she wasn't serious about him," Paige said.

"Not at first," Hannah said. "She followed him around and looked for a way to meet him and make it look like an accident. He spotted her one night—actually, it was the same day I killed Alan Ewing—and lured her into a bar. They met. Then she fell in love with him."

"So she really does like him?"

"She's crazy for the man," Hannah said. "I've never seen her like this before. Anyway, with Alan Ewing dead, Ja'Von and I next set our focus on trying to find out who hired Ja'Von in the first place. That's when Ja'Von bumped into you."

Paige remembered.

"The problem was, though, that we were both scared to death that if my name came into the picture and got associated with Bangkok, the police might trace me to the murder of Alan Ewing. So we decided to keep me totally out of the picture and just pretend that everything had happened to Ja'Von instead of me. That was wrong, I know, but we had no choice. We both knew that there was a law firm that needed to be brought down. But because of Alan Ewing, Ja'Von needed to be the plaintiff instead of me. She had an alibi, so even if she got associated with Ewing it wouldn't make a difference."

"I see."

"So everything Ja'Von told you was true," Hannah said. "The only difference is that it happened to me instead of her."

"And she left out the fact that you killed Alan Ewing."

Hannah took a sip of wine.

And shook her head.

"Technically she didn't leave it out. It really doesn't have anything to do with the case against V&B. And you never asked her about it."

The rain pounded even harder against the window.

Paige scratched her head.

"Then how did Ja'Von recognize Remington as being in the dungeon?"

"Easy," Hannah said. "When you came up with the idea to have Ja'Von look at the V&B profiles to see if anyone in the firm had gone to the dungeon, Ja'Von made sure that I was there at the time. If I saw someone, I was supposed to kick her and then she would tell you. It turned out to be easier than that, though, because you went grocery shopping. I recognized Remington, told Ja'Von about Remington including his tattoo and the size of his dick, and then she called you as if she knew it all

411

firsthand."

Paige pondered it.

Then she said, "But you weren't there when Ja'Von identi-fied Kiet from the BJ bar, sitting in a booth with three or four women."

"True," Hannah said. "But what happened is this. Ja'Von came into the bar to look for me after I never came back out. That's when she saw him." Hannah sipped wine. "So I guess the question is—what do we do now? We still have a law firm to bring to justice."

Paige nodded.

True.

Very true.

"You're our lawyer," Hannah said. "Right?"

Yes.

She was.

"So what do we do now?"

Chapter Ninety-Six

July 21
Thursday Morning
(One month later)

PAIGE ALEXANDER WALKED through the heart of Denver's financial district under a bright Colorado sky. She wore a conservative pinstriped suit and carried a leather briefcase. The city bustled around her and felt like home.

She felt like a lawyer.

She *was* a lawyer.

A lawyer with a good man named Michael Dexter in her life.

Most of the picture had come into focus for her during the last month.

The information came from a variety of sources.

Dylan Joop, for example, left behind a wonderful laptop filled with places, dates and names. Apparently it was his way of getting back at V&B from the grave if the firm killed him. The firm didn't, of course. Instead, Joop died at the hands of Bryson Coventry during a horrible fight in the icy waters of Bear Creek. Still, the computer was found in Joop's middle boxcar and served its purpose well.

Some of the information came from Porter Potter's house.

413

Some came from the extensive interviews of V&B's attorneys conducted by the D.A.'s office, as well as interviews of V&B's clients. Some came from documents such as phone statements, financial records, day timers, personal notes, and the like. And some came from other sources—often unlikely sources.

Most of the information went to Coventry.

Then to Ja'Von.

And then to Paige.

In the end, a clear picture of a deadly, high-stakes international conspiracy of terrible proportions emerged.

THE LAW FIRM OF VINSON & BOTTS had two or three high-ranking partners in each of its offices throughout the world who functioned as part of a highly-solidified and clandestine group.

They called themselves rainmakers.

The rainmakers from Denver consisted of three people.

Mark Remington.

Thomas Fog.

And Sarah Woodward.

The rainmakers used carefully selected persons to *enhance* the law firm's advantage in high-stakes litigation. The enhancement might include, for example, the elimination, intimidation or coercion of a judge, witness or party.

In the United States, the enhancer was Dylan Joop.

Thomas Fog was his contact—the person who assigned the projects and arranged for payment.

In Europe, the enhancer was Jean-Paul Boudiette—a man who had become a person of interest to INTERPOL following the suspicious death of a Paris judge.

PORTER POTTER WAS AN IMPORTANT WITNESS who needed to be *enhanced*. But V&B didn't need him dead. What it needed was false deposition testimony from the man.

Potter's daughter had died in an airplane crash earlier this year.

The law firm located another woman who bore a striking resemblance to Potter's daughter, a woman named Madison Blake. The firm had Dylan Joop kidnap the woman. After the woman's abduction got reported in the media, the firm contacted Potter and made him an offer. If he lied in his upcoming deposition, the woman would be released alive and unharmed. If he didn't, the woman would die. The firm hoped that Potter would think of the woman as his daughter and be sympathetic towards her. They even let him talk to Madison Blake by telephone to confirm that they actually had her and that she was still alive and well.

The gamble paid off.

Potter chose to cooperate.

And lied in his deposition.

That swung a billion dollar case from a probable loser to a probable winner; a case that V&B had on a 25 percent contingency fee in the event of success, in addition to being paid on an hourly basis, meaning an extra $250 million or more.

At that point it was incumbent upon the firm to follow through with its end of the bargain and release the woman; otherwise Potter would undoubtedly go to the police and recant his testimony. Unfortunately, the woman had seen Joop's face and couldn't be released without risk. So rather than releasing the woman, the firm had Joop kill Potter and make it look like an accident.

Now they had the man's deposition to use as evidence at trial.

With no associated risk.

VINSON & BOTTS WAS NOT ENGAGED in human trafficking or an international conspiracy to lure women to Bangkok for sexual slavery.

However, Mark Remington was.

And had been doing it for years in exchange for money and unbridled privileges with any woman in the stable anytime he wanted. Tall, athletic blonds brought a high premium in that part of the world, both as a daily rental and as an outright purchase for a snuff. Remington came up with a wonderful idea to find female investigators who fit the physical profile and lure them to Bangkok.

Ja'Von Deveraux from San Francisco.

Rebecca Vampire from Miami.

Susan Wagner from Cleveland.

Shirley Jones from New York.

Ja'Von came to Denver to pursue a theory that her assignment had not been legitimate, but had instead been a charade to get her to travel to Bangkok of her own accord where her abduction was prearranged.

Ja'Von hired Paige.

Who rattled swords at V&B.

When the two other rainmakers—Thomas Fog and Sarah Woodward—found out what Remington had been up to, they decided that he needed to be removed. There was too great a risk that Ja'Von could actually file a public lawsuit alleging the firm's involvement in sexual slavery. That would result in tremendous media spotlighting, which might spill over to and uncover the whole rainmaker operation.

Since Joop was friends with Remington, they couldn't use Joop for the job. So they brought Jean-Paul Boudiette in from France. As long as he was going to be here, they decided to have him remove Joop too.

Joop had been getting too sloppy.

He let Madison Blake see his face.

He killed Samantha Rickenbacker.

He was a liability.

Remington then learned that he was being targeted. He learned that from the FBI profiler, Dr. Leanne Sanders, and from Bryson Coventry, when they came to Remington's office after Boudiette assaulted the profiler.

Remington fled to Bangkok.

Boudiette then went after his second target, Dylan Joop.

Unfortunately for Boudiette, Joop got the upper hand.

The law firm told Joop that Boudiette was either a rouge or else someone unknown was pulling his strings.

Joop fell for it and stayed in Denver.

The firm then flew its Hong Kong enforcer to Bangkok. That person hung Remington in his hotel room and made it look like a suicide.

VINSON & BOTTS PLANTED A BUG in Paige Alexander's apartment early on, almost immediately in fact. Paige actually remembered coming home one night and feeling as if someone had been there.

But the bug wasn't found until long after the fact.

In the meantime, Sarah Woodward and Thomas Fog learned that Paige and Ja'Von had suspicious thoughts about another law firm, one that had ties to Bangkok, namely Thung, Manap and Deringer.

They then fed Paige false information.

They told her that their Bangkok P.I. had uncovered information to suggest that the Thung firm and associated family members were rumored to operate the dungeon where Ja'Von had been taken.

All that was a big lie.

No one in the Thung firm had been involved at all.

The sedan that swung through Paige's apartment parking lot late one night was merely there to figure out why the three women had followed Kiet to Shotgun Willies.

THE DAMAGES TO JA'VON DEVERAUX came from Mark Remington, acting on his own, outside the scope of his employment, without the knowledge or consent of Vinson & Botts. Therefore the law firm wasn't liable for his actions.

That is, until the law firm got stupid.

Everything changed when the law firm, acting through Sarah Woodward and Thomas Fog, engaged in a variety of acts designed to aid and abet Mark Remington and to protect the law firm.

They bugged Paige's apartment.

They ran Paige off the road on her bike.

They gave Paige false information in an attempt to implicate the Thung firm.

They had Remington murdered.

And, most importantly, they hired Joop to kill Ja'Von.

That made the law firm liable under a number of legal theories including RICO and civil conspiracy.

OF COURSE, THERE WERE A COUPLE of additional facts that were known only to Paige, Ja'Von and Hannah, which they never shared with Coventry, V&B or anyone else.

Namely, Hannah went to Bangkok too.

Hannah was the one who got abducted, not Ja'Von.

And, most importantly, Hannah killed Alan Ewing.

PAIGE ALEXANDER PUSHED THROUGH the revolving doors of the Cash Register Building, walked across the lobby and took the elevator up to Vinson & Botts.

There she met with the new manager of the Denver office.

A man named Charles Meyer.

They met in the same conference room where Paige had once brought the Trek.

Meyer handed her two certified checks.

The first check was in the amount of $30,000,000 made payable to the order of Ja'Von Deveraux and Paige Alexander, Esq. Ja'Von and Hannah had made an agreement to spit their cut of the money fifty-fifty on the side, and keep Hannah's name out of it.

The second check was in the amount of $10,000,000 made payable to the order of Paige Alexander, Esq. and her new client, Madison Blake.

Meyer also handed her two settlement agreements.

"As soon as your clients sign the settlements and you get them back to me, you're free to cash the checks," he said.

Jim Michael Hansen

She stuffed everything in her briefcase and shook his hand.

"That will be later today," she said.

He nodded and said, "And please give them my apologies, on behalf of the firm."

"I'll do that."

Paige left.

She had the cases on a one-third contingency fee.

Meaning thirteen million and change went to her.

Pre-tax of course.

But still, not bad for her first two cases.

420

Chapter Ninety-Seven

July 21
Thursday Morning
(One month later)

BRYSON COVENTRY SIPPED COFFEE as he walked around the corner of the for-sale house and into the backyard. He put a rose on the ground where Samantha Rickenbacker died, looked at it for a few seconds, and then sat down on the patio in the sun.

The sky didn't have a cloud.

Robins flew.

Somewhere a block or two away a dog barked.

A ceremony was scheduled this afternoon for Brandy Zucker, the weatherman's daughter. Her body hadn't been found yet, but it was clear that she died at the hands of Dylan Joop, given the story of Madison Blake about how a female showed up at the boxcar one day and tried to set her free.

Thomas Fog and Sarah Woodward were in jail, without parole, facing the death penalty for hiring Joop to abduct Madison Blake, which proximately resulted in the murders of Samantha Rickenbacker and Brandy Zucker. Additional counts charged them with the murder of Porter Potter; hiring Joop to kill Ja'Von Deveraux which proximately resulted in the attack on Bryson Coventry; and hiring Jean-Paul Boudiette to kill Mark Remington which proximately resulted in the attack on Dr. Leanne Sanders.

COVENTRY LOOKED UP AS A FIGURE APPEARED.

Madison Blake.

She set a rose on the ground, next to Coventry's, then sat down next to him and stretched her legs out.

"Sorry I'm late," she said.

Coventry smiled.

"You look good," he said. "How's the baby-growing business?"

She patted her stomach and said, "Good. Paige Alexander called me a few minutes ago and said she had my settlement check in hand. I can pick it up this afternoon."

Coventry raised an eyebrow and asked, "How much did she get for you?"

"Ten million," she said. "I almost feel sorry for the law firm to be paying so much. It was only those three who were the really bad ones." She referred to Mark Remington, Thomas Fog and Sarah Woodward, the ones who had hired Joop to abduct her.

"Don't be too sorry," Coventry said. "The firm got rich over the years because of those three. This is just payback."

"Paige is letting me keep the whole amount even though she's entitled to one-third," Madison said.

"She is?"

"Yeah," Madison said. "She said I did all the hard work."

She paused and added, "I was thinking that since Paige doesn't want her one-third, I would give it to you."

He patted her knee.

"Thanks, but you keep it," he said.

IN THE AFTERNOON THE CLOUDS ROLLED IN. Ja'Von called, excited as hell about something, and talked him into breaking away from work for a half hour to meet her on the 16th Street Mall.

She wore white shorts, a baby-blue tank top and tennis shoes. But what really grabbed his attention was her hair—raven black instead of blond.

"You dyed your hair," he said.

"You noticed."

He laughed and said, "I like it. You could be on the cover of a book." He meant it too. He couldn't remember ever seeing a woman as sexy as she was at that moment. He had no more qualms about falling in love with her after finding out she had a solid alibi for when Alan Ewing got murdered.

She kissed him, grabbed his hand and said, "Follow me."

They entered a stone building near the Paramount Café and walked up to the second floor. Ja'Von opened a wooden door with a key and they stepped into an empty three-room suite that looked down on the 16th Street Mall.

The oak floors were scuffed.

The walls needed painting and repair.

The windows were dirty.

"What do you think?" she asked.

"I'd call it a unique fixer-upper," he said. "Are you looking to rent this, or what?"

She nodded.

"I've been thinking a lot about where my life goes from this point, now that I have more money than I could ever spend." She grabbed his hand and led him to the window. Outside, downtown Denver bustled. She put her arm around his waist and said, "Here's what I think I'd like to do. Rather than buy a big fancy house somewhere, I'd just like to keep staying at your place."

Coventry exhaled.

Perfect.

"Then, me and Hannah are going to rent this space and run our two businesses," she said.

"And what might those be?"

"Well, the first one is our P.I. business," she said.

"You're going to keep doing that?"

"Of course," she said. "And the second business is to wipe that Bangkok dungeon off the face of the earth."

"Are you serious?"

She nodded.

"I promised Mackenzie Vampire that I'd find out if her sister Rebecca is alive," she said. "Now I have the money to start."

"That'll be hard to do from here," Coventry said.

"Impossible is more like it," Ja'Von said. "That's why I'm going back."

"To Bangkok?"

"Yeah, but don't worry about me."

"You've got to be kidding."

"Really," she said. "I'll be totally safe."

"And what makes you think that?"

"Because you're coming with me," she said.

THAT NIGHT IT RAINED.

Stormed is more like it.

Thunderstormed is even more like it.

They drove to the trailhead at the base of Green Mountain and pulled into the back corner of a dark, empty gravel parking lot. Coventry killed the engine and the sound of the weather immediately intensified.

Perfect.

They got in the back seat and talked for an hour.

Then she slipped out of her shorts and straddled him. Just as she started to rock, he said, "By the way, just for the record, I'm not going to start being nice to you just because you're rich."

"Trust me, Coventry, I never worried about that for a second."

Photo by Yvonne Melissa Hansen

ABOUT THE AUTHOR

Jim Michael Hansen, Esq., is a Colorado attorney. With over twenty years of high quality legal experience, he represents a wide variety of entities and individuals in civil matters, with an emphasis on civil litigation, employment law and OSHA.

JimHansenLawFirm.com

For information on the author and the other *Laws* thrillers, including upcoming titles, please visit Jim's website. Jim loves to hear from readers. Please send him an email and let him know what you thought of this book.

JimHansenBooks.com
Email: Jim@JimHansenBooks.com